FORBIDDEN PLEASURES

BERTRICE SMALL

FORBIDDEN PLEASURES

NEW AMERICAN LIBRARY

New American Library
Published by New American Library, a division of
Penguin Group (USA) Inc., 375 Hudson Street,
New York, New York 10014, USA
Penguin Group (Canada), 90 Eglinton Avenue East, Suite 700, Toronto, Ontario, Canada
M4P 2Y3 (a division of Pearson Penguin Canada Inc.)
Penguin Books Ltd., 80 Strand, London WC2R 0RL, England
Penguin Ireland, 25 St. Stephen's Green, Dublin 2,
Ireland (a division of Penguin Books Ltd.)
Penguin Group (Australia), 250 Camberwell Road, Camberwell, Victoria 3124,
Australia (a division of Pearson Australia Group Pty. Ltd.)
Penguin Books India Pvt. Ltd., 11 Community Centre, Panchsheel Park,
New Delhi - 110 017, India
Penguin Group (NZ), cnr Airborne and Rosedale Roads, Albany,
Auckland 1310, New Zealand (a division of Pearson New Zealand Ltd.)
Penguin Books (South Africa) (Pty.) Ltd., 24 Sturdee Avenue,
Rosebank, Johannesburg 2196, South Africa

Penguin Books Ltd., Registered Offices:
80 Strand, London WC2R 0RL, England

First published by New American Library,
a division of Penguin Group (USA) Inc.

REGISTERED TRADEMARK—MARCA REGISTRADA

ISBN-13: 978-0-7394-7152-4
ISBN-10: 0-7394-7152-X

Set in Sabon

Printed in the United States of America

PUBLISHER'S NOTE
This is a work of fiction. Names, characters, places, and incidents either are the product of the author's imagination or are used fictitiously, and any resemblance to actual persons, living or dead, business establishments, events, or locales is entirely coincidental.

The publisher does not have any control over and does not assume any responsibility for author or third-party Web sites or their content.

The scanning, uploading, and distribution of this book via the Internet or via any other means without the permission of the publisher is illegal and punishable by law. Please purchase only authorized electronic editions, and do not participate in or encourage electronic piracy of copyrighted materials. Your support of the author's rights is appreciated.

For E. G., Paid in full.

FOREWORD

ॐ

The woman in the billing department looked at the record she was typing into the computer, and giggled. "Don't you ever wonder what Emily Shanski uses the Channel for, Gail?" she said to her fellow worker at Suburban Cable.

"Hey, like all the rest of us," Gail answered. "Long, unhurried, incredible sex. I don't know who invented this network or whatever it is, but I'm sure as hell glad they did." She looked at her companion. "What do you think it really is, Doreen? I mean there isn't another channel on the television that actually lets you dream up your personal fantasy, and then lets you physically enjoy it. Do you think it's magic? Or something worse? Ah hell! Who cares? Well, maybe my old man might if he knew what I was doing when he's on the night shift," she cackled.

Doreen laughed. "Yeah, I guess it's better we don't know," she said. "And I sure as hell wouldn't want my husband to find out about it. The men would either try to close the Channel down, or they'd want it for themselves. It's a woman thing." She hit the print button, and when the bill had rolled out of the printer already folded she put it in the preaddressed stamped envelope. "Lot of women in Egret Pointe using the Channel these days," she noted. "Hey, it's noon. Let's break for lunch, Gail. Too bad the Channel isn't available now."

"Nah," Gail replied. "It's better the way it is. If we could get it all the time instead of just between eight p.m. and four a.m. no one would get anything done. Where do you want to eat? How about the Chinese buffet down the street?"

"Yeah, Doreen agreed. "I like that place. Get your coat, and let's go."

CHAPTER ONE

"I've got bad news and bad news. Whadaya want first?" Aaron Fischer looked across the large mahogany desk at Emily Shanski, a.k.a. Emilie Shann. He was a stocky man in his sixties who wore impeccably tailored Armani suits, and had beautifully manicured hands. His gray hair, what was left of it, was nicely barbered around his balding pink pate. On the third finger of his left hand he wore a gold band engraved with a Celtic knot. The gold tie pin in his silk tie echoed the same design.

"You dragged me in from Egret Pointe for bad news?" Emily grumbled. She didn't like the look in Aaron's usually warm brown eyes. Those eyes were serious today. It did not bode well. "Okay," she sighed dramatically. "Gimme the worst of it first. Then the not so worst."

"I'm not sure which you'll consider the worst," he said slowly. "Kirk!" he called to his business and life partner. "Come in here a moment, will you?"

Kirkland Browne appeared like a genie from a bottle. Actually his office was directly next to Aaron's, and they had connecting doors that were usually left open. He was a tall, slender man who seemed to be all angles. He was as well dressed as his partner, and wore both the same ring on his left hand and tie pin in his cravat. "What?" he demanded impatiently, his light blue eyes peering myopically over his gold-rimmed reading glasses. "I'm working on the Scofield contracts, and they're a bitch."

"Emily wants to know which news is worse," Aaron said with a little shrug.

"Stratford won't renew your contract after this last book unless you write sexier," Kirkland Browne said bluntly. "Now, Aaron, you tell her the rest." He turned and was gone back into his office before Emily's surprised gasp died.

"What? What does he mean, they won't re-up? I've written for them for eleven years, Aaron. My books don't lose money. My returns are modest, and I have a very large and loyal fan base," Emily protested.

"They want sexier. Sexy is in. Kick-ass heroines are in. What can I tell you, Em? It's the nature of the business now. You've got to go with the flow, or retire," he told her with a little shrug. "You've made a lot of money these last years."

"I'm thirty-one years old," Emily said. "I'm too young to retire, damn it!"

"Then you gotta write sexier," he replied implacably.

Emily's brow furrowed, and she wrinkled her straight little nose. Write sexier? Impossible! Maybe not for some writers, but for her. "Aaron, I have written for Stratford my whole career. I get great reviews. The readers love me. I have a reputation to uphold. Shit! I'm called the American Barbara Cartland. I fill a niche."

"Cartland's dead, and so are her sales," he said sanguinely. "Besides you're a much, much better writer than Cartland ever was, Emily. And you write bigger books with better plots, more textured prose, and interesting characters. But you gotta write sexier on this book you're starting or I can't guarantee another contract. I wish it weren't so, and I don't disagree with anything you've said, but there it is, sweetheart. You write first for Stratford, and Stratford wants sexier."

"So much for loyalty," Emily muttered darkly. Then she remembered: bad news, and bad news. "What else?" she asked him nervously. Could there possibly be anything worse than what he had just told her?

"Rachel Wainwright has retired," he said, bracing for the outburst that was going to come with this news, and wondering if he should get out the smelling salts in his desk.

"I talked to Rachel late on Friday morning, Aaron. This is Tuesday. She said nothing about retiring. I think my editor would have mentioned that little fact," Emily responded in measured tones. "They pushed her out, didn't they? J. P. Woods pushed her out. She's never liked Rachel, the bitch."

"She retired," Aaron answered stubbornly. "There is no plot here. For God's sake, Emily, Rachel's seventy-five. It was time she enjoyed that house up in Connecticut, and her longtime friend is going to be your new editor. You'll like him."

"Him?" Emily's voice rose several octaves. "Him? I can't work with a man!"

"Michael Devlin is one of the good guys," Aaron attempted to reassure her.

"You want me to write sexier, and work with a man while doing it?" Emily's heart was pounding now. Her perfect, orderly little world was being destroyed, and she couldn't see any way to stop it. Of course, she could write her book, hand it in, and be finished with publishing forever. She didn't lack for money. But what would she do with the rest of her life if she didn't write novels? It was all she knew. Her passion. Her raison d'être. She sighed. She didn't want to stop writing, and she wasn't going to, damn it! There had to be a way around this edict from Stratford.

"I've arranged for us to have lunch with Michael Devlin at that little English tea shop you like over on Madison. Then you can catch the train out to Egret Pointe."

"Today? I have to meet this guy today? And I didn't take the train," Emily said. "I came into town with your sister. She wanted a day at Georgette Klinger. Then she'll do some shopping until I call her cell." *God!* If she had known she was having lunch with a new editor she would have dressed a bit more appropriately, worn one of her best-selling-author power suits. She felt tougher in a suit.

"Rina's in town?" He was surprised. His sister rarely came into town. "She didn't tell me she was coming." He loved Rina, but she made him nervous.

"She didn't want to go to lunch with us," Emily said with a small smile. "Sam says she's getting too plump and needs to take off a few pounds for her health. She's eating spa nibbles at Klinger's. You know how she gets on rabbit food."

"If she'd lay off the doughnuts she could drop her avoirdupois easily," Aaron replied, "but don't tell her I said so."

Emily laughed. "I won't, but jelly sticks are her downfall, I'll admit." Then she grew serious again. "I want to talk to Rachel before we go to lunch, Aaron."

He got up from his desk and, walking around it, said, "Use my phone. Don't waste your cell minutes, sweetheart. Rachel's Connecticut house is seven on my speed dial." At her surprised look he added, "Kirk and I go up for weekends." Then he left the room.

Emily stood up, walked around the desk, and settled herself in Aaron's comfortable big black leather chair. She heard a small click, and turned to see that the connecting door between his office and Kirk's had been discreetly closed. Picking up the telephone she hit seven, and listened to the electronic beeps as the number dialed itself. One ring. Two rings. Three rings. *Please be there, Rachel,* she thought desperately.

"Hello?" Rachel's warm voice came through the wire.

"Rachel, it's Emily. What happened? And why am I getting a male editor?"

Rachel Wainwright's grandmotherly chuckle greeted her query. "Have you met him yet? He's quite a hunk, Emily," she said. "If I were forty years younger I'd jump his bones. Honey, it was time I retired. Actually past time. Getting up and going to work at Stratford every day was just a habit. A bad habit."

"Will you stay in Connecticut?" Emily asked her.

"Yep. I'm putting the co-op on the market shortly, and retiring to the country for good and all," Rachel Wainwright said in a no-nonsense voice.

"Rachel . . ." Emily hesitated. "Will you be all right?"

"Oh, you sweet child! Yes, I will be all right. Martin has seen to it that I have a rather outrageous pension. Loyalty to Stratford paid off in the long run for me. Not like a lot of old editors in chief. I bought the co-op almost fifty years back. My father always said real estate was the best investment. It was paid off aeons ago, and in this market it is going to bring me a fortune. And with no one but myself to look after I won't suffer financially, my dear. And I've done pretty well in the investment market. I'm going to England in June, and I've rented a villa in Tuscany for August. Want to come visit?"

"They want me to write sexier, Rachel. I don't think I can," Emily said. "Aaron and Kirk said they won't renew my contract if I don't. I don't think a trip to Tuscany is in the cards for me this year, but it sounds heavenly."

"Aaron and Kirk are right," Rachel replied quietly, "but not to panic, Emily. You are a wonderful writer, and you can do this. I know you can. And you will have a marvelous editor in Michael Devlin. I've worked with him myself, and he knows how to bring out the best in his writers, my dear."

"His name is familiar," Emily said, "but I can't quite place him."

Rachel chuckled. "Okay, I'm going to tell you the story, but you have to promise me that you won't repeat it. Oh, Aaron and Kirk know it, but it's pretty hot stuff."

"Ohh, tell, tell!" Emily replied. "You know I love good gossip."

"Seven years ago Michael Devlin came to Stratford from Random House. He was already becoming well-known as an excellent editor, and Martin Stratford lured him over with the promise of his own imprint eventually. J.P. noticed him almost immediately. She had just become company president. I know you've heard the rumors about her, and they are all true." Rachel laughed. "She's Stratford's resident man-eater. She uses 'em and abuses 'em, and then moves on to her next victim. And because the lovers she chose were below her on the corporate scale, no one who valued his job ever caused a scandal or complained about her.

"Her mouth practically watered at the sight of Michael Devlin. She began to stalk him, but he ignored her and dodged all her attempts at seduction. J.P. was pretty surprised initially. No one had ever avoided her or said no. At first she thought he was playing hard to get. It tickled her because usually her lovers came meekly when chosen. She was intrigued that he appeared to be fighting his fate. This went on for well over a year, and then it all came to a head at the Christmas party six years ago.

"J.P. was wearing her usual winter-white outfit. I remember it well: a thigh-high light wool wrap dress with a deep vee neckline. It was around the time when she got that short cut and dyed her hair red. Flaming Mame, I remember Martin calling her. Well lubricated with a couple of margaritas, she managed to corner Michael Devlin, and I do mean corner." Rachel chuckled. "She started putting her hands all over him, and those hands of hers were everywhere. He tried to politely fend her off, but her inhibitions were long gone, and she was listening to her cunt and not her brain."

"Rachel!" Emily squealed at the use of the word.

"Sorry, dear, but there just isn't any other way to put it. J.P. wouldn't have minded if he stuck it to her right there in front of everyone, she was so hot for him. But of course he didn't. He took her by her upper arms and set her back from him, holding her there. Then he said in the coldest voice I have ever heard him use, 'I choose my own women, J.P., and I don't choose you.'

Releasing her, he turned away, walked over to Martin, and after wishing him a Merry Christmas, left the party."

"My God, how embarrassing for J.P. although I never thought I'd feel sorry for the bitch," Emily said. "How did he end up in London?"

"Well, Michael had no sooner departed the party than J.P. was buttonholing Martin, and demanding he be fired. She claimed he had come on to her and it was all she could do to fight him off. She couldn't work with someone like that, she told Martin. Martin, of course, had been privy to the whole incident, as had a number of other people. He had no intention of losing Michael Devlin, but he also wanted to have his cake and eat it too. J.P. is a very good president for Stratford Publishing. So he transferred Michael Devlin to our London office, which suited Michael fine. He was born and raised in Dublin. You'll love his Anglo-Irish accent."

"Why is he back now?" Emily wanted to know. "J.P. isn't a woman to forget an insult. She holds grudges, Rachel. You know she does."

Rachel paused a long moment, and then she said, "You might as well know, but this is also something that can't be bruited about, Emily. Martin is going to semiretire within the year. He and Anita want to travel. Neither of his daughters is interested in the publishing business. Both are married to doctors. But Martin isn't of a mind to sell. At least not yet. J.P. may be the company president, and Michael Devlin now the editor in chief, but Stratford is going to need a new CEO. J.P. thought she had it all sewn up, but she didn't. Martin is undecided, which is why he called Devlin back from the London office to take my job. Now J.P. is using you to get that CEO position while at the same time trying to get rid of Michael Devlin for good. You're right: She holds grudges, and she hasn't forgotten he publicly refused her. The tension between them is palpable."

"I don't understand, Rachel," Emily said, shifting nervously in Aaron's big leather chair. "What have I got to do with it?"

"Look," she said, "no one I know really likes J.P., including me. But she's damned good at what she does, and what she does is run Stratford. Martin has been easing himself out for the last two years, and the responsibility has fallen on J.P.'s shoulders. She wants the title of CEO of Stratford, and all that goes with it. The truth is that she deserves it, Emily. But Martin wants the company to remain strong, and that means he needs a first-rate editor in chief, so he's brought in Michael Devlin from London to take my place. J.P. and Devlin are going to have to learn to get along for the good of the company. And I've heard Martin himself hint that the position of CEO is up for grabs. He will play his little games, and J.P., for all her swagger, is just insecure."

Rachel sighed deeply. "J.P. has never been a fan of your books, but you know that. The company makes a tidy little profit off of you, but it's a sure bet that with your name and track record they can make an even bigger profit if you write sexier. But J.P. doesn't think you can do it. She thinks you're a prude and won't be able to make the transition from sweet to sensual. She also believes she can fill the hole you leave in Stratford's bottom line with half a dozen newbies who do write sexy. And one of them might well turn out to be very successful. You know publishing's a crapshoot.

"So she told Martin that it was up to Michael Devlin to edit you, as you were an editor in chief's writer, and to give you to just a senior editor would be a demotion for you. Martin agreed. He likes you, but you know that too. And he has great faith in Devlin. He knows how ruthless J.P. can be, but he's the type of man who wouldn't believe she'd ruin your career and endanger his company just to get back at a man who refused her lustful overtures years ago. You're a pawn on the chessboard, Emily. If Devlin can get you to write sexier novels, he wins. Right now, that is a threat to J.P. After all, the editor with the big-name writer has a certain amount of power. He could leave and take you with him. But if he can't get you to write that sexier novel, you both lose. Your career could tank, at least temporarily, and you know it's tough to get going again in this business. Devlin's reputation would certainly suffer, and since Martin will appoint J.P. to succeed him, she will make life so difficult for him that he'll leave. He's a proud guy. So both of you have to succeed."

"No pressure, huh?" Emily said dryly.

Rachel laughed. "You can do this, my dear," she repeated. "You are such a talented author, Emily. I know it's going to be difficult, but you will find your way. And Devlin will be there to help you. What have you titled the new book?"

"*The Defiant Duchess,*" Emily said. "It's set in the Terror during the French Revolution. It's a *Scarlet Pimpernel*–in reverse-story."

"Clever," Rachel said. "And rife with possibilities for a couple of hot love scenes," she noted. "Well, I've got to go, my dear. I have an appointment with a garden designer, and she seems to actually be on time. Call me if you need me. But, Emily, you can depend on Michael Devlin. Trust me."

"I always have," Emily responded. "But a male editor . . . I just don't know."

"Don't judge him until you've met him and worked a bit with him," Rachel said. "We'll talk. Bye."

The phone line clicked off, and Emily set the handset back in its cradle. She sat for several long moments in Aaron's chair, and then with a sigh stood up as her longtime agent stepped back into the room.

"Finished? How is Rachel?" he asked.

"Talking with a garden designer as we speak," Emily said. "She's going to stay up in Connecticut and sell the apartment here in town. She says she's well fixed. I hope she wasn't just saying that to soothe me."

"She wasn't. And not only that, she already has half a dozen manuscripts to edit freelance for a couple of publishers. When word got out yesterday, she said her phone started ringing off the hook. Are you ready? Our reservation is for one p.m."

"Let me use your loo to freshen up," Emily said. "I wasn't expecting lunch with a new editor. You might have warned me, and I would have dressed better."

"You look fine," he told her, chuckling at the dark look she threw him as she disappeared from his office.

In the ladies' room Emily peered into the mirror at herself. Well, it could have been worse, she thought. Her short, fluffy strawberry-blond hair was having a good day in the dry spring weather. But oh, how she longed for the pale blue suit she had just bought to add to her author clothes. Still, the cream-colored silk slacks and the pale pink silk shirt she was wearing weren't bad. The whole look was rich-bitch, old-money, screw-you casual, she thought. She washed her hands, fluffed her hair, and renewed her lipstick.

"Ready or not, here I come, Michael Devlin," she said low. "And just remember it's my work you're buying, so who cares what I look like." She went to join Aaron Fischer. "Let's walk," she said to him.

"Why not," he agreed. "It's only five blocks, and we'll get there faster."

"If you're going to Felicity's bring me back one of those divine little lemon curd tarts," Kirk called from his office. "I've ordered a salad in with these damned contracts. And one for Sandra too," he said, remembering their shared secretary, who sat at a large desk in the gracious and elegantly decorated reception foyer of their office, which took up the entire top floor of the small old Park Avenue office building where Fischer and Browne, Literary Agents, was located.

"Make mine fruit," Sandra said as the elevator doors opened up. She was an older, motherly-looking woman who had been with the partners for years, coming to them fresh from the Katharine Gibbs Secretarial School. "I'm not into lemon curd, and Kirk knows it. Better bring him two." She waved them off as the doors closed smoothly with a faint hiss, and they descended swiftly without a single stop.

They walked from Park and up Madison Avenue until they arrived at Felicity's Tea Company, which served both luncheon and high tea six days a week. It was Emily's favorite place to eat in the city despite the plethora of elegant restaurants available. She could hear herself think in Felicity's, and the food was delicious. Felicity herself came forward smiling as they entered, holding out her hands to Emily.

She was a pretty woman with premature silver hair and dark eyes. She and her waitresses always wore the flowered, low-necked panniered satin gowns of the eighteenth century, and adorable little snow-white caps.

"When Sandra called to book I was hoping it was you," she said, kissing Emily on both cheeks. "Your guest is already at the table. Wow! Who is he?"

"New editor," Emily replied glumly. "Rachel retired."

"Ohh," Felicity murmured. "I'd love to write with him. He is very hot."

Great, Emily thought. Every woman who saw him thought Michael Devlin was hot. Just what she needed: a hot man who was going to help her write sexier. And how was he going to do that? And then she saw him, and stumbled over her own feet like some fool of a schoolgirl. She caught herself up quickly, feeling her cheeks grow warm.

Michael Devlin stood up as they reached the table. "Aaron, good to see you again," he said, a small smile touching his lips. He was very tall.

There it was: the soft, poetic hint of Ireland in his voice. Emily felt her knees weaken. This was worse than she had anticipated. She barely registered that Aaron was introducing them, but managed to stick out her hand nonetheless. Looking at him she had the distinct feeling that she knew him—really knew him—and yet he was a stranger.

"Ms. Shann, I am delighted to finally meet you," Michael Devlin murmured, looking down at her. "Rachel has nothing but praise for you." He drew her chair out and seated her before sitting down again himself. "You have a wonderful feel for eighteenth- and nineteenth-century England. Your research is quite excellent." *Jaysus,* he thought. *She's utterly adorable. That fluff of hair, and those big cornflower-blue eyes. I'd like to eat her with a spoon. How the hell am I going to work with something so delicious when what I really want to do is take her to bed?* He was astounded by his own thoughts. He'd never had such a strong reaction to a woman before. It was bloody unprofessional.

"You've read my books?" she inquired softly. Her own voice seemed to be coming from a very long way away. He really was gorgeous. He had to stand at least six-foot-three, and he had a lean, elegant body. His face was one of those long, sculpted faces, more angles than planes. His hair was jet-black, and his eyes were deep green. He looked like one of her heroes, for God's sake. She couldn't look at him too much, because every time she did, her heart raced. She had never had such a strong reaction to someone like this before.

"Not all of them," he admitted, "but I will by the time you finish this next book for us. Would you like to tell me what it's going to be about? I haven't seen an outline yet, but I'll look forward to it."

"Emily doesn't do outlines," Aaron quickly said. "Well, not exactly. She can tell you what the book is going to be about, but not in detail. She doesn't like to be held down to an exact story line. The sales department is used to her."

"I always know roughly what I'm going to write," Emily told Michael Devlin, now recovering from the initial shock that her new editor really was hot. "But the story seems to write itself as I go along. I suppose that sounds silly, but that's how I do it."

"I am not a man to argue with success, Ms. Shann," he told her. He was getting a hard-on. What the hell perfume was she wearing? It smelled like lilacs.

"Shall we order?" Aaron said as their waitress came up to the table. "Em, the usual for you, or do you want something different today?"

She shook her head. "No. The usual, Aaron, please."

Aaron ordered the quiche lorraine and salad for Emily, and a mini chicken pot pie for himself. "And a nice large pot of Keemun," he finished the order, looking to his companion questioningly.

Michael Devlin ordered the sirloin and cheddar with Dijon mustard in a tomato wrap. "How big is it?" he asked the waitress.

She looked him up and down, and then said, "You'll need two."

He grinned disarmingly at her. "Make it two then."

"Three cups?" the waitress wanted to know.

"Three cups," Devlin replied. "And make certain it's good and hot, my lass."

"As hot as you, milord." The waitress chuckled, and bustled off.

There was a long, awkward silence. Emily didn't dare look at her new editor. Her thoughts bordered on lascivious, much to her surprise. Had she ever before this moment had such libidinous thoughts? Writers—at least, smart writers—didn't get involved with their handsome male editors. But then, she had never met such a good-looking man. Michael Devlin was really unique. And she sensed intelligence as well as the movie-star looks. She sneaked a quick peek from under her lashes. Yeah. He was that handsome. And that hot. And where the hell was all this overcharged libido of hers coming from all of a sudden? The lesson of her parents forever with her, Emily Shanski had always been careful where men were concerned. She was relieved to see that Aaron and Michael Devlin were now in serious conversation.

Their lunch came, and they ate quickly.

"Dessert?" the waitress asked with a twinkle in her eye. She had served Emily many times before. "The usual, Miss Shann?"

Emily nodded, grinning. "No visit to Felicity's Tea Company would be complete without it. I'm afraid I'm a creature of bad habits. At least where dessert is concerned."

"Mr. Fischer? Sir?" the waitress said.

"Bread pudding," Aaron replied. "And give me two lemon curds, and a fruit tart to go. And I'll take half a pound of gunpowder tea also."

"I'll have the caramel egg custard," Michael Devlin said.

The waitress bustled away.

"What's the usual?" Michael asked Emily.

"You'll see," she said with a small grin. "It's difficult to explain."

"Now I am intrigued, Ms. Shann," he told her.

"Please, I think if we're going to work together you should call me Emily," she replied. "May I call you by your first name?"

"My friends call me Mick," he responded. "And I suspect we're going to be friends, Emily." Reaching across the table, he took her small hand in his big one and smiled into her blue eyes. Then he released her fingers as quickly as he had taken them.

God in his heaven! She blushed. She was behaving like one of her heroines. No. She was behaving like one of their friends. Her heroines weren't this sappy. To her relief the desserts came, along with another pot of hot tea.

"What is that?" he wanted to know, staring at the plate the waitress set before her.

"It's a very thin slice of Felicity's Death by Chocolate cake, and a thin slice of her boysenberry pie," Emily said. "I love them both, but I could never make up my mind which to have. So Felicity came up with this solution. Pretty cool, huh?"

He laughed. "It's obvious you don't have a problem with your weight." Then he spooned up some custard. "This is good. She really does use eggs, doesn't she? My gran back in Ballyfergus made custard like this. She's gone now, of course."

"I thought you came from Dublin," Emily said.

"I went to school and university in Dublin," he explained. "My parents were killed in an auto accident when I was twelve. Gran Devlin took responsibility for me, but she wasn't up to having a growing lad in her house year-round. I went back to Ballyfergus during my school holidays to stay with her. We only had each other, you see. Very odd for an Irish family, of course. Most of them are big."

"We have something in common then, Mick," she said. She liked the way he spoke of his grandmother. There was warmth and genuine affection in his voice.

"Emily was raised by her two grandmothers," Aaron spoke up. "Right from her birth. I knew them both. Wonderful women!"

"Were your parents deceased too?" Mick asked solicitously.

"No. They were both too young for a baby, and they had other plans," Emily replied. Then she laughed at his look, which was half-shocked, half-curious. "It's a long story for another time."

Mick Devlin shook his head. "Sounds like your life is worthy of a novel, Emily." Having finished his custard he put his spoon down. He was charmed by her. She was a practical woman with a sense of humor, and an obviously very romantic nature, he thought, smiling.

"No, it isn't," she said. "It's my life, and nothing more." She licked a crumb of the chocolate cake from the edge of her mouth. He was a good listener, Emily considered.

"So," Aaron said before another silence set in, "you two need to get together to discuss how we're going to make this slight directional change in your work, Em."

"It isn't slight," she replied. "I'm known for writing sweet, not sexy. I'm not certain you can teach this old dog new tricks."

"You're a good writer, Emily, and we'll start easy," Mick told her. "It would be too much of a shock to some of your readers if we went too quickly. But not all of them will be shocked, judging by what's selling today. Your core readers will buy the book because you've written it, and you will gain new readers based on the reviews," Michael finished.

"You're presuming that the reviews will be good," Emily said.

"They will be," he assured her. "You're good, and readers love you."

"You'll have your editor out to Egret Pointe for a weekend," Aaron suggested. "That way the pair of you can get to know each other, and you'll work better."

Emily looked slightly surprised. The thought of being alone in her house with this man was rather intriguing. But of course it would be all business, she reminded herself.

"I wouldn't want to intrude on Emily's privacy," Mick quickly said. He used the British pronunciation of the word: *priv-ah-see*. God, a weekend alone with this fascinating woman would be heaven. But of course it would be all business, he reminded himself.

"No, no, of course you must come out," Emily told him. "Actually, it's perfect. I haven't started the book yet, and your input will be invaluable. Best to get started immediately, I suppose." She didn't sound wildly enthusiastic.

"Before you get frightened, write your usual story, and retire into anonymity," Mick murmured candidly. His eyes met hers briefly.

"Yes," she admitted, wondering how he could know her so well already.

"So let's set a date now," Aaron said. What was going on? He sensed something between Emily and her new editor. But how could that be? They hadn't known each other two hours yet. And Emily didn't have a boyfriend. He wondered if she ever had. Yet he also knew she wasn't gay. Something was happening here, but what?

A cell phone rang, and Emily reached into the thin purse she had hung over the back of her chair. "Sorry, I have to take this. Rina? Where are you? Oh. All right. We're at Felicity's. I'll be ready." She snapped the phone shut. "It's Rina. She's ready to go home. She'll pick me up here in ten minutes, depending on the traffic. She said you are not to go anywhere, Aaron."

"Oy vay!" the agent exclaimed. Then he looked to Michael Devlin. "My sister," he explained. Then he turned back to Emily. "I thought she was having a day at Klinger's. This is a day?"

"She said there were too many anorexic matrons with tight faces and expensive boob jobs for her taste. She did a manicure, pedicure, and facial. You know Rina isn't good in the city anymore, Aaron. She's become a real country girl. She and Sam love Egret Pointe."

Aaron shrugged. "Who would have thought a girl from Riverside Drive and Eighty-first Street would grow up to be happy in a place called Egret Pointe?"

"Hey, we've got a Krispy Kreme now," Emily teased him.

He chuckled, then got back to business. "So when should Mick come?" he asked her. "This weekend? Next?"

"Either is all right with me," Emily said. "I'll go with Mick's schedule."

He'd planned to look for a small summer rental at Montauk this weekend, but small rentals could always be found, especially if he didn't quibble over price. And besides, he wanted to know more about Emily Shanski, a.k.a. Emilie Shann. "This weekend will be fine," he said in his deep, lilting voice. "I've been back almost six weeks, and haven't had a weekend in the country yet. I like the country. Where would you recommend I stay?"

"Aaron has my number. Call me and I'll give you directions. Of course you will stay with me," Emily said almost breathlessly. A tall, handsome man with an Irish lilt in his voice wandering about the town would certainly attract attention in Egret Pointe. If she kept him bottled up in her house and garden for the weekend no one was likely to see him, and there would be no gossip about the good-looking guy with Emily Shanski.

"Good, good," Aaron said, relieved that it was all now settled. He let Michael Devlin pay the bill, and took the box with the tarts and the bag of green gunpowder tea from the waitress. They bade Felicity good-bye, introducing Michael Devlin before they went. Rina was just pulling up in her Lexus as they stepped out onto Madison Avenue.

She honked and waved.

"I will bid you good-bye, Emily," Mick Devlin said, smiling at her. "For now. I'll look forward to the weekend. I think we'll get some good work done. Aaron, I'll call you." Then he was off, striding down the street.

Rina had pulled over into a fire lane to allow Emily to get into the car. "Hey, big brother," she said. "When are you and Kirk coming out to open the cottage?"

"I'll ask him," Aaron said. "You look mah-vel-ous, Rina. Have you lost weight?"

"Go screw yourself, sweetie. Call me," Rina said as Emily climbed into the car and belted herself up. "Ta!" She gunned the car out of the fire lane, and back into the midafternoon traffic.

"Bye, Aaron," Emily called to him before Rina's window rolled up tightly.

"Who was the hottie with you?" Rina Seligmann wanted to know. "My God! Tall, dark, and handsome. You don't see too many of them today. Is he straight? Or is he one of Aaron and Kirk's friends? And why were you all having lunch together?"

"He's my new editor," Emily said. "Rachel's retired. It's a long story."

"It's a long ride home," Rina said. "Get talking, sweetie."

Rina Seligmann, née Rina Fischer, and Aaron's younger sister, was the wife of Egret Pointe's beloved doctor. Her husband had cared for both Katya Shanski and Emily O'Malley until their deaths. Rina had known their granddaughter, Emily, most of her life. Actually, the young woman sitting next to her was the same age as her oldest child. She listened as Emily outlined her morning with Aaron, and her luncheon with her new editor.

"Aaron doesn't want to move you to another publisher?" Rina asked.

"I suppose that will be the court of last resort," Emily said slowly, "but it really wouldn't make a whole lot of sense, if we can avoid it. All my backlist is with Stratford, Rina. Even with my name and sales record, it would be starting over again."

"It makes me so damned mad that none of this is your fault," Rina said.

"It's like Rachel said: I'm a pawn on a chessboard. If I'm going to check the bitch queen, I have to pull this off. J. P. Woods doesn't give a shit for me. She just wants Martin to make her Stratford's new CEO so she can get back at Mick Devlin."

"Do you think you can work with him?" Rina asked. "I mean, without trying to jump his bones. He really is outrageously attractive. I'm glad he's not gay. That would really be a waste. Still, if he were gay we could all be friends, and cause gossip in town."

"He seems very nice," Emily said. *Nice* wasn't quite the word she wanted, but it would have to do. How could she tell Rina that this man she had just met had her thinking about being on a beach naked with him?

"Nice? Nice? The guy is gorgeous, sweetie," Rina exclaimed. The Lexus swerved just slightly. "Hell, I wish I were your age."

Emily laughed. "You haven't looked at another man since you met Sam," she said. "Why, you've even made him your hero when you watch the Channel."

"Now, who told you that?" Rina demanded to know.

"You did, when you first introduced me to the Channel," Emily answered her. "You said you thought of the two of you in your younger days."

"I talk too much," Rina muttered. "So what have you been using the Channel for, sweetie? Isn't it fun?" She chuckled.

"I'm just an observer," Emily said. "I imagine my books, and have the characters act it all out. It gives me a chance to see if it's realistic and not just silly."

"You don't put yourself in the heroine's role?" Rina was surprised.

"Good grief, no!" Emily exclaimed. "Why would I do that?"

"Well, I thought you might, since you don't have a

boyfriend," Rina replied. "Did you ever have a boyfriend, Emily? I didn't think Katya and Emily O were that strict."

Emily thought a long moment, and then she said, "You know, Rina, I don't think I ever have had a real boyfriend. I mean, I like guys, and I was social in college, but no one ever really touched me emotionally. There was never any time, and the story of my parents' little misstep never really went away. I got the feeling the second I hit high school here that everyone was watching to see if I'd screw up like Katy and Joe. You know, some of my teachers taught them. That's why I took all those AP courses, so I could graduate early and get the hell out of Egret Pointe. But then I came back."

"But you were very popular at Egret Pointe High," Rina said. "And you were the class president for four years running."

"No one else wanted the job." Emily laughed. "Katy and Joe were king and queen popular. I was the likable nerd. Oh, I went to pep rallies, and games, and even a couple of dances. But I never let a boy get too close. And then I did college in three years too. Wellesley, like my mother. No boys at Wellesley." She chuckled. "And then just before I graduated Aaron sold my first book to Stratford, and the rest is history. I was a writer. I had a career, and no time for men. Actually, when I see some of the girls I went to school with I don't think I've missed a whole lot."

"You can't miss what you don't know, sweetie," Rina said as she swung off the parkway onto the Egret Pointe exit. "Or maybe you do know?" she probed.

Emily laughed. "I'll take the Fifth," she said. "Besides it makes me more mysterious to guard my privacy. People wonder just what I am guarding. And I don't want you selling my story to the *Star*."

"As if," Rina answered her. "Want to eat supper with Sam and me?"

"Thanks, but I'll take a rain check," Emily said. "I always get so keyed up when I have to make these city trips, and today was a shocker. I've got to sit quietly with some wine, and think about what happened. And my new editor is coming up this weekend, but don't you dare tell a soul, Rina!"

"What's he coming for?" the older woman wanted to know.

"He wants to work with me, and help me to direct the new story into a sexier mode," Emily said.

"And just how is he going to do that?" Rina queried, waggling her newly plucked eyebrows suggestively.

"I don't know," Emily said. "Writing sexy is a whole new ball game for me."

"Where is he staying? The Inn or the Motel 6?" Rina asked.

"He's staying with me," Emily said.

"Aha!" Rina exclaimed, pulling to a stop before Emily's house.

"Aha, what?" Emily wanted to know. "My reasons are based in practicality, Rina. Do I want a handsome hunk wandering about the town connected to me? I do not! The biddies would never rest until they had us involved in an affair. Mick Devlin is a nice man, and from what Rachel says a good editor. We're both in danger of losing our livelihoods because of that bitch Jane Patricia Woods. I don't know what Martin sees in her, but he sees something. So Mick will help me write sexy and keep my career, and by doing it I'll help him save his job. It's nothing more than that." She reached for the car door handle. "Thanks for the transportation. I'd still be on the train if it weren't for you." Leaning over, she gave the older woman a kiss on the cheek. "That's for Sam," she said.

"Hussy!" Rina shot back.

Emily chuckled and, stepping from the Lexus, closed the car door behind her.

With a beep of her horn Rina shot off down Founders Way, and turned the corner onto Colonial Avenue headed for her own home on Ansley Court. Emily watched her go, and then walked up the brick pathway to her house. It was a beautiful old home built in the 1860s. Her mother had been raised in this house. It stood next door to an identical structure in which she and her father had been brought up. Both homes had been built by Barnabas Dunham, a descendant of an early settler to Egret Pointe, as wedding gifts for his twin daughters. Mary Anne Dunham Smith and her husband had gone down on the *Titanic* in 1912. Their only daughter had sold her house to Jarek Shanski in 1922, and Emily's grandfather had been born in 1923. Mary Anne's twin, Elizabeth, also had a daughter, who had married Patrick O'Malley. Their grandson, Michael, had been born in this home in 1925.

Emily had inherited both homes upon the deaths of her grandmothers. She rented the Shanski house for income because she couldn't bear to sell it. She had been brought up in that house, as had her father and her grandfather. But she lived in the O'Malley house now. Her maternal grandmother, known as Emily O, had exquisite taste, and the house was furnished to suit her granddaughter. Besides, she held Emily O partly responsible for her becoming a writer. Emily O told marvelous stories, and could have been a writer herself.

And it had been Emily O who had opened up the world for her namesake. The summer Emily Shanski turned seven she went off on her first trip to England with Emily O. The highlights for her had been a pony trek in Wales, and visiting the city of Bath. And every summer after that new wonders were revealed to her. Europe. Turkey. India. Even China. And Emily O had not forgotten her granddaughter was an American. One summer they spent touring the continental United States in a lavishly furnished trailer with a driver so they might both enjoy the trip. There was a June cruise to Alaska, followed by a flight to the Hawaiian Islands, and a visit to Tahiti for several weeks.

She had loved it all, but Emily Shanski had returned to England as often as she could. The land, the people, the history all fascinated her. She spent days exploring Bath, and the sites of Regency London. She loved the museums and bookstores. Despite the lack of her parents Emily Shanski had had a wonderful childhood. She had been loved dearly by her two grandmothers, never missed Katy or Joe, and she knew how lucky she was in her life and in Katya Shanski and Emily O'Malley.

When she had been eight her mother had married Carter Phelps IV. Emily had gone to the wedding with her grandmothers, and Carter had insisted on having pictures taken of them all together. It was only when she was older and wiser that Emily understood that the now Senator Carter Phelps IV wanted no skeletons in his wife's closet when he one day ran for public office. Still and all, Carter was a decent guy, Emily thought, and on the rare occasions she saw her half sister and brother she was always made to feel welcome by the Phelps clan.

And then when she was almost fourteen her father had married, and his bighearted Irish-American wife wanted Emily to come and live with them. Her grandmothers had put a stop to that, and Joe's wife had gone on to have three sons in five years. There wasn't a holiday or family occasion that her stepmother hadn't included her and her grandmothers, or tried to. Emily actually felt far more comfortable with her father's down-to-earth family than with her mother's elegant political one.

Stepping inside her house she heaved a sigh of relief. There was no way she would ever be a city girl, Emily thought. It was good to be home. She had a lot to think about, and a guest room to air out and prepare. Walking into the kitchen she found a note from her housekeeper, Essie: *Meat loaf, mashed potatoes, and corn in the microwave. Do two minutes on high. See you tomorrow.* Emily smiled and, kicking off the elegant little shoes she had worn into town, pressed the appropriate buttons and waited for her dinner to get hot as she set herself a place at the kitchen table and poured a glass of wine. It had been an interesting day. And it looked like the days ahead were going to continue to be interesting. But she was going to survive this sea change in her life. She was!

CHAPTER TWO

"**M**y dear girl, I care not a fig what you think. I look like I look," Justin Trahern, the Duke of Malincourt, said to his creator, romance novelist Emilie Shann.

"You cannot look like Michael Devlin," Emily said stubbornly.

"You have imagined me this way," he told her, and, whirling about, he gazed at himself in the mirror. "Read what you have written. I am quite handsome, and most satisfied with myself. Your last hero wasn't half the man I am." He brushed an imaginary speck of dust from the silken sleeve of his plum-colored coat.

"Oh, go to the devil!" Emily said irritably. "If you insist on looking like him then do so. And what was wrong with the Earl of Throttlesby?"

"Much too fair for a man, I fear. And his chin was just a trifle weak, dear girl," the duke replied. Then, looking directly at her, he said, "I want my defiant duchess to look like you, dear girl. I do have a weakness for fair women, especially those with a touch of red in their hair, like yours." He grinned wickedly at her as he leaned casually against the mantel of his library fireplace.

"Oh, be quiet," Emily said, "and let me think, Trahern." She looked closely at him, considering that he appeared far different from her other heroes. He was more masculine, a bit rougher, and definitely more dangerous, if that look in his green eyes was to be believed—and she suspected it was. He looked like a man who had wild sex. She shifted herself in the big wingback chair. Her heroines had never looked anything like Emily Shanski, but somehow the idea of being the defiant duchess to Justin Trahern's duke was extremely tempting. "I have to write a more sexually explicit book," she said.

"Huzzah! Huzzah!" he answered her with a chuckle. And then he grew serious. "How experienced are you, dear girl? I want to delight you, but not shock you. A lady's sensibilities must be taken into consideration, y'know."

"What does my experience have to do with anything, Trahern?" she demanded to know. She had used the Channel for several years now to create her books so that she might see what she was writing before she wrote it. It allowed her to work more quickly, but until tonight she had always been an invisible and silent observer of her creations. This was the first time she had ever actually interacted with one of them.

"My dear girl, surely you understand that while the Channel may allow you to live your fantasies, it cannot substitute for, um, certain realities in your life," the duke said.

"Such as?" Emily asked him.

"Your novels of Georgian and Regency England have always been warm family dramas, dear girl. Your heroines have been chaste, your heroes manly, and when they are finally wedded the door has always closed on the nuptial chamber. There have been kisses and caresses, but never have you permitted a hero to put his hand below the waist of one of your maidens. And never before have you begun a book with the hero and heroine a married couple. You have observed marriage enough to write about it, but have you experienced passion or bald-faced lust enough to write about it? I think not."

"I have quite a few books on the subject, thank you," Emily replied sharply.

He laughed aloud. "Not good enough, dear girl," the duke told her. "If you have not rolled amid the tangled sheets, sweaty and naked with a man you at least liked, the pictures in one of those books you have will not suffice. What experience will you draw upon to write of such an emotional encounter, dear girl? What knowledge? No, no, your virginity will not do. It simply will not do."

"I did not say I was a virgin," Emily snapped, but she was blushing.

"But you are, aren't you?" he responded. "There is no shame in it, dear girl. Actually it's quite charming."

Emily sighed. "But if you make love to me then I will be able to write what they want of me, Trahern," she told him. *God!* She never thought she would use the Channel for sexual gratification, like some of the women she knew. It was embarrassing.

"I can't," he said quietly. "Oh, I could go through the motions, dear girl, but you would feel nothing at all, because in reality you would remain exactly as you are. You will have to lose that tiresome virginity of yours in your own reality before we may begin to enjoy each other here within the Channel, I'm afraid," Trahern told her.

"And how the hell am I supposed to do that?" Emily demanded of him. "Perhaps I should put an advertisement in the *Egret Pointe Times*. 'Wanted: Studly gentleman to relieve me of my virginity so I may write sexier books.' " She stood up, reaching for the nearest objet d'art to throw. This whole situation was infuriating.

The duke stayed her hand. "No, no, dear girl, that vase is one of Josiah Wedgwood's newest creations. I'd prefer if you didn't destroy it in your pique. The answer to your dilemma is really quite simple. You have imagined me as someone you know. *Obviously you are attracted to him.* Seduce him, dear girl, and your problem is solved. I do not know why you didn't think of it yourself. And afterward when the deed is done, you and I will embark upon a delicious and—I promise you—a most wickedly delightful adventure."

"I don't know how to seduce a man," Emily said almost sadly.

"Within each woman, my lovely duchess, is the knowledge and the skill to seduce any man she desires," the Duke of Malincourt said. "Just this once, dear girl, wouldn't you like to enjoy the Channel as a visitor, and not an observer? Entice this man who attracts you, and you will gain everything you have ever wanted."

"But I just want to write good books and earn my living." Emily sighed, sinking back into the big wing chair.

"Unless you write more sexually detailed novels, dear girl, it seems you will not be able to do that. Have you any idea how that sad and woebegone little face of yours cries out to me to kiss you?" he asked her. "You have been kissed, haven't you?"

Emily nodded, and when she had the duke touched his lips to hers gently.

"You are very sweet, dear girl, and I will admit to longing for more than just the touch of your lips. Seduce the gentleman in question so we may begin our adventure."

"You say nothing of love," Emily noted.

"Nor do you," he replied with a small smile. "Is there such a thing?"

"I don't know," Emily answered honestly. She closed her eyes. "Farewell for now, Trahern." She sank away, and when she opened her eyes again she was in her own bed. Reaching for the channel changer Emily turned off the television. But she could not sleep. It was close to four a.m., and the sky outside her window was already beginning to grow light. A mourning dove cooed softly in the large pine by the corner of the house nearest her bedroom.

Seduce the man, Trahern had said. All well and good for him, but how the hell was she going to entice Mick Devlin into making a woman of her? To begin with, it had to be totally inappropriate for an author to sexually harass her editor. Still Devlin was, if the gossip was to be believed, a man who could be tempted. She had called her old friend Savannah Banning yesterday afternoon. Savannah also published with Stratford, and lived outside of London with her husband. Savannah knew everything of interest there was to know about in the world. Her curiosity, like her libido, was insatiable. If Mick Devlin had a reputation, she would give Emily the whole story, chapter and verse.

"Em!" Savannah had squealed when she answered the phone in her plummy British accent, flavored with South Carolina. "How are you? What's the news from New York?"

And Emily had told her.

"So old Rachel has been put out to pasture. Well, high time, darling. Nice as she is, she really is quite past it."

"Rachel is a wonderful editor," Emily defended Rachel.

"But Mick Devlin! Darling, you are just the luckiest girl. He's been editing me for several years. If I didn't love being old Reggie's wife so damned much I would have tried for Mick myself. Damn! If he's back in New York who is going to take care of me? I'll probably get stuck with old Prunella Baines-Harrington. She's a decent enough sort, but darling, she is the most booor-ing woman."

"Tell me about Devlin, Savannah," Emily said softly.

"What's to tell?" Savannah replied slyly, and then she giggled. "The women flock to him like flies to jam, darling, but he is very particular about his women. And no one has ever gotten close enough to slip a bridle on him. There was one little Sloan's Ranger who thought she had the inside track until he showed up at her birthday party with a really smashing model. Lady Something-or-other-hyphenated. The birthday girl proceeded to get very drunk, picked a fight with Lady whoever, and got shoved into her own birthday cake for her trouble." Savannah chortled. "Why do you ask?"

"I have to work with the man, Savannah, and Aaron told me a story about J.P. and Devlin. I've never worked with a man. Rachel and I got on so well."

"The story about J.P. and Devlin is true," Savannah said. "What else?"

"Stratford won't renew my contract after this book unless I write sexier," Emily wailed. "The rumor is that Martin wants to semiretire, but he can't decide into whose hands to put the company, J.P. or Michael Devlin. That's why he was brought back." She sighed. "I'm screwed, Savannah. I can't write sexy. And especially for a male editor. I worked perfectly with Rachel. What am I going to do?"

"Darling, I should only be in your slippers," Savannah said, sighing dramatically. "What should you do? Throw yourself on his mercy, is what you should do. You're really just his type, you know, Em. You're intelligent, funny, and quite lovely. And I expect he's at that vulnerable age when he might even be considering settling down."

"What are you saying?" Emily asked her friend, surprised.

"Look, darling, if Mick has to turn you into a sensuous instead of a sweet author, and he fails, the evil J.P. gets Martin's nod. But if he succeeds, Mick will get the company, and you'll both live happily ever after. His future is every bit as much on the line as yours is, Em. Use that to your advantage," Savannah advised.

"What exactly are you saying, Savannah?" Emily repeated.

Savannah laughed her low, husky laugh. "You know exactly what I'm saying, Em. Have a love affair with the guy. Seduce him! You might even win a gold ring."

"Seduce my editor? I wouldn't know where to begin, Sava."

Savannah laughed harder. "Sure you do," she said.

"It's inappropriate!" Emily protested.

"Oh, pooh! If you do it's going to make it all the more fun, especially when you run into J.P. You'll have that glow that a well-fucked woman gets, and she'll know Mick is going at you like a mastiff in heat. But you aren't a girl to kiss and tell. And J.P. won't ask, but it'll kill her anyway." Savannah choked on her laughter. "Revenge is so sweet."

"You are really quite dreadful," Emily told her, but she was smiling.

"He's a lovely man, darling. Enjoy yourself. Come to think of it, I don't think I've ever known a time when you did enjoy yourself with a man. Any man. Either you are the most discreet woman in the world, or . . ." And then Savannah gasped.

"I have to go, Sava," Emily said quickly. She did not want to get into a discussion about her virginity with Savannah Banning, whose novels, it was rumored, were printed on fireproof paper. "Say hi to Sir Reginald for me. Toodles!" And she rang off.

Emily turned restlessly in her bed, and asked herself for the third time just how she, inexperienced as she was, was going to seduce a sophisticated and urbane man like Michael Devlin. And he would be coming to Egret Pointe, to her house, for the weekend in just a few days. And suddenly she heard her grandmother O'Malley's voice as plain as day, saying, "The way to a good man's heart is through his stomach, Emily." She almost laughed aloud, remembering how he had gobbled down those two beef-and-cheddar wraps at Felicity's. The man had a good appetite on him.

"I'll bet no woman ever cooked for you, Mick Devlin," Emily said aloud.

Outside her window a cardinal started calling, and the sparrows in the pine tree were chattering noisily. The clock on her fireplace mantel struck five a.m. She was not going to go back to sleep. Emily sat up and swung her legs over the side of the bed. She had menus to plan for the weekend. And shopping to do. And she would ask Rina and Dr. Sam to dinner Friday night to help her get over any shyness with Devlin. She had a man coming for the weekend whom she had only met once. And she was going to seduce him. Well, she was going to try. With his reputation it would probably be easy. A prime rib, a good red wine. Chocolate mousse or trifle. He would be putty in her hands. If there was one thing Emily Shanski could do as well as write, it was cook.

Michael Devlin swung off the parkway onto the Egret Pointe exit. Turn right at the bottom of the ramp, Emily had told him. He did. When he'd heard her voice on the phone, his cock had tingled, and he was again surprised by the effect this woman was having on him. He was forty years of age come August, not some kid in heat for the first time. Two miles down County Road 3 he saw the sign: WELCOME TO EGRET POINT. FOUNDED 1723. He was enchanted, for it had the air of a New England village, yet it wasn't New England. He was just seventy-five miles from the city.

The main street was lined in ancient maples just now greening up. There was a village green with a gazebo; a duck pond, on the far side of which were pink Kwanzan cherry trees in full bloom. The shops were deliberately small, and charming. Some had offices above them, for he saw a sign that read, JOHNSON AND PIETRO D'ANGELO, ATTORNEYS-AT-LAW. And the streetlights were real antique gas lamps, not those faux modern ones you saw in so many places now. Devlin almost missed his turn onto Colonial Avenue at the far end of the village. He paid closer attention to his driving so that he was prepared for the turn onto Founders Way.

"It has just five houses on it," Emily had told him. "The first two are genuine Colonials. The next two are Empire, but one is modern. I'm the big Empire at the bottom of the street. It's not really a cul de sac, but similar to one. You can park your car at the very end of the driveway. I'll be watching for you."

He made the turn and drove to the end of the little street,

pulling all the way up into her driveway, and catching his breath as she came out from the house to greet him. Damn, she was lovely! She was wearing khaki slacks that hugged a very round little butt, and a cream-colored silk shirt. She wore no lipstick, and it tickled him. Emily Shanski was obviously not a girl who doted on her appearance. It told him she had enough confidence in herself not to worry about such things. All the women he knew did.

"You drive a Healy!" were the first words out of her mouth, and she hurried by him to admire his car. "It's a 'sixty?" Emily ran her hand over the cream-colored fender.

"'Sixty-one," he said. "I brought it with me from Ireland to New York to England, and back to New York again. They are very rare now, I'm told."

"I have a 'sixty-three in the garage," she told him. "I just found it about five years ago, and had it restored. Mine is Racing Green, but I've got the roll-up windows."

"A distinct advantage when it's about to rain," he admitted.

"Oh, I'm being so rude," she exclaimed, blushing. "Welcome to Egret Pointe, Mr. Devlin. Grab your bag, and I'll show you to your room. I hope you don't mind coming in the kitchen door, but it seems silly to drag you around to the front at this point."

"Mick," he said. "My friends call me Mick. And I prefer the kitchen door. Back in Ireland when I grew up only the priest came in the front door." He pulled the elegant bag from the back of the car and followed her up two small steps into the house. His nose twitched. "Is that roast beef I smell cooking?" he wanted to know.

"I took the chance you didn't keep a meatless Friday," Emily admitted. "But if you do, I have some salmon in the freezer I can cook."

The look on his face was beatific. "No, I do not keep a meatless Friday, Emily, and rare beef is my favorite meal. There would not, by chance, be some potatoes roasting around that meat, would there?" The hopeful look on his face made him appear boyish.

"Now, sir, what kind of an Irish girl would I be if I didn't have the potatoes roasting about the beef?" she teased him.

"It's O'Shanski then, is it?" Devlin teased back.

Emily laughed. "My mother was an O'Malley," she explained, "and this was my Grandma O'Malley's house once upon a time. Both she and Granny Katya taught me to cook. I do a mean kielbasa and pierogies too."

"I think you may be the perfect woman, Emily," he flattered her. "You write wonderful novels, and cook as well." *And I'll bet you fuck like a dream, too,* he thought to himself, his eyes briefly sliding over the twin mounds beneath the silk blouse. He had never been more tempted in his life, and he was going to have a difficult time keeping his hands off of her, which surprised him. He had always managed a strong reserve where women were concerned. *Enjoy what they offer, but don't get emotionally involved* was his longtime motto.

"Reserve your judgment until you've tasted my dinner," Emily advised him. "Come on. I promised to show you to your room." She hurried from the kitchen, and he fell into step behind her.

The home had a gracious center hallway with a graceful staircase. As they reached it the doorbell chimed, and then the door opened to admit an older couple.

"Rina, Dr. Sam," Emily greeted them, turning. Then, looking back at Michael Devlin, she said, "Upstairs to the left, second door. And come back down to meet my friends." She gave him a smile before she moved away to welcome her other guests.

He mounted the staircase, and as he went he heard the newly arrived woman say, "My God, Emily, he's even more gorgeous close up! Are you sure you want us to stay for dinner? If I were in your shoes I'd want him all to myself." Devlin grinned to himself.

"Rina, he'll hear you," Emily said, and felt her cheeks growing warm.

Dr. Sam Seligmann chuckled. "I'm not going anywhere, Rina. I smell roast beef."

"Like I never cook?" Rina Seligmann said as they entered the gracious parlor of the house. She plunked herself into a comfortable club chair.

"You cook fine, but not like our Emily," Dr. Sam answered his spouse. "Shall I make everyone a drink?"

"For you and Rina, and Mick when he comes back down," Emily said. "We're having wine with dinner, and you know me—two glasses of anything is my limit."

Dr. Sam stirred up a pitcher of martinis, and had just poured one for his wife and for himself when Michael Devlin entered the room. Catching his eye, Dr. Sam held up the pitcher and tilted his head to one side quizzically.

"Martinis?" Devlin asked.

"Yep," Dr. Sam said.

"We're having wine with dinner," Emily put in quickly.

"Then I shall satisfy myself with a sherry, if you have it," Devlin replied.

"One sherry coming up," Dr. Sam answered, putting the martini pitcher down. "I'm Sam Seligmann, town doctor. My wife, Rina."

"You were the driver for Emily the other day in the city, weren't you?" Devlin asked, now remembering the brief glimpse he had had of Rina Seligmann. "You're Aaron Fischer's sister. Am I right?"

"His little sister," Rina responded with a grin. "He was almost eight when I came into the world. The prince of the family until my arrival." She chuckled.

"And he's terrified of her," Emily said, laughing.

"As well it should be," Rina Seligmann answered smugly.

Devlin laughed too. "I'm an only child," he told them. "I envy you a sibling."

The small talk continued back and forth, with Emily running

in and out of the kitchen overseeing her meal. Finally she announced it was ready, and they all trooped to the table. Taking her place at the head of the table, she asked Devlin to sit at the other end, and the Seligmanns took their place on either side, as was their custom.

"Will you carve the roast beast?" she asked him, and he saw she had placed the platter with the meat before him. Before it was a carving knife and fork with bone handles. They were obviously very old.

The meat had been done perfectly. As he carved, he saw the medium-rare pieces fall from his knife from the outside, and the very rare bit of the meat was farther inside. He asked for preferences, and placed the appropriate slices upon the plates. The platter was then taken from him by Emily to be set upon the sideboard. A bowl of exquisitely roasted potatoes was passed. Then a smaller platter of fresh asparagus. There were two gravy boats: one with the au jus, and the other with a flawless Hollandaise sauce for the vegetable. There were dainty hot rolls, a silver dish of sweet butter, and tomato aspic salad on separate plates to each diner's left.

As they ate he learned that Dr. Sam's family had been early settlers of Egret Pointe. He was surprised until Dr. Sam explained that his ancestors had come to the Americas in 1709. It wasn't, Dr. Sam said, a well-known fact of American history, but there had been a number of Jewish families who had emigrated then. "We fought in the Revolution," he said proudly. "On the winning side, of course."

"And then he went and married a girl from the Upper West Side whose family was chased out of Russia by a troop of Cossacks," Rina said.

"But that's what makes our country so great," Emily spoke up. "We're such a wonderful mixture of peoples and cultures." She was glad she had asked the Seligmanns to help her defuse what might have been an awkward evening.

When they had finished almost everything Emily had prepared, she and Rina cleared the table for the dessert while the two men sat talking.

"God, he has such charm," Rina said, scraping the plates for the dishwasher. "He looks like a Celtic prince, and that delicious hint of Ireland in his voice." She sighed.

"He's very nice," Emily murmured.

"Huh?" Rina replied, looking closely at her younger companion. "Oh, my! You're attracted to him, aren't you, Emily Shanski? Well, why not, says I?"

"I don't even know him," Emily protested. "We just met on Tuesday. We've spoken once on the phone, and today is Friday."

"You've got an itch for him," Rina accused her with a grin. "I've known you most of your life, Em, and I've never known you to be attracted to any man. There have been times I've wondered if you weren't gay, like Aaron."

"I haven't got an itch, Rina, and I'm not a lesbian," Emily responded. "I just haven't had time for men, and I sure as hell didn't want to be like Katy and Joe. Have you any idea how hard it was for me in high school, with most of the same teachers they had had always watching, always waiting for me to fall from grace?"

"They never knew your mother had fallen from grace, as you so dramatically put it, until she was graduated, and at Wellesley," Rina said. "Thanks to your grandmothers your impending arrival was quite the surprise to everyone in Egret Pointe."

"That's what made it so hard for me," Emily replied. "Katy fooled them. Was I fooling them? Why do you think I worked so hard to get out of here, and into college?"

"Water under the bridge," Rina said. "You're a best-selling author now with a hot new editor. He isn't married. You're both fancy-free. Hell, if I were you I'd lay him!"

"Why does everyone keep saying that to me?" Emily wanted to know.

"Who else said it?" Rina asked.

"Savannah. I talked to her the other day. He was her editor in London, and I wanted to know more about him," Emily answered.

"And?" Rina's look of curiosity was so blatant that Emily had to laugh.

"To quote Savannah, the women flock to him like flies to jam, but he likes to pick his own friends," Emily said. "I doubt I'm his type."

"I think you're just his type. He's Irish, for heaven's sake. They like their women intelligent, good cooks, and just a little helpless at the right moments. You can play helpless, can't you, sweetie? Where's the dessert?"

"Fridge," Emily said. "I am not helpless, Rina."

Rina Seligmann opened the refrigerator door and pulled out a large glass bowl. "Don't tell me you haven't thought of having him between your legs, because I won't believe you. A woman would have to be made of stone to look at that man and not want him. What is this?" She looked suspiciously at the bowl she was holding.

"Chocolate trifle," Emily answered. "I couldn't make up my mind between mousse and trifle. So I made chocolate lady fingers, and mousse for filling with the sliced strawberries."

Rina began to laugh. "Yep, you're hot for him."

"How can you say that?" Emily wanted to know. It was embarrassing to be so damned transparent. Did Michael Devlin see what Rina saw?

"The double chocolate is a dead giveaway," Rina replied.

Emily blushed furiously. "Do you think he'll notice?" she asked nervously.

"Nah," Rina reassured her. "But you do know he likes you, don't you?"

"Rina, we've just met," Emily said exasperated.

"Look, sweetie, if there is one thing I understand, it's men. I know, I know. I've been married to Sam since I turned twenty, but I still know human nature. It isn't how long you've known someone. If there's chemistry it's there from the start. And there is definitely chemistry between you two. Enjoy it! You've worked hard all your life trying to make up for what you consider Katy and Joe's mistake. You weren't a mistake, Emily. Oh, I know. Your parents weren't lovers, and their coming together was a onetime thing. But they were best friends from the time they were in diapers. You were created from that loving friendship. You don't have to be a saint to make up for them. They created you, had you, and moved on with their lives. Time for you to move on, sweetie. Is there any whipped cream to go with this devilish creation?"

Emily didn't know whether to laugh or to cry. "I don't know what I'd do without you, Rina Seligmann," she said. "Since the grans died, you have been my rock."

"Of course I have," Rina replied calmly, brushing away the single tear that had slipped down Emily's cheek. "You could be my daughter, sweetie. And I could never have enough daughters. Sam will tell you that. 'A son's a son till he takes a wife. But a daughter's a daughter all of her life.' My mother always said that, but if truth be known my brother was a better daughter to our mother than I ever was." She chuckled.

"I'll make the whipped cream," Emily said. "It won't take long. Check to see if the men want coffee or tea. And would you take that bottle of ice wine in? The glasses are here on the tray." She pulled out the dark, slender bottle of the sweet dessert wine and handed it to Rina. Then she set about whipping the heavy cream, transferring the finished product into a cut-glass bowl with a scalloped silver spoon to serve it.

They had all decided upon tea, and Rina brewed a large pot of American black-leaf tea from the only tea plantation in the United States that was located outside of Charleston, South Carolina. Emily's friend Savannah Banning had introduced them to it. Emily spooned out the dark-chocolate trifle, adding a lavish dollop of the freshly whipped cream to each serving, and passing the plates around. There was virtual silence as the diners devoured it. Rina was in charge of the teapot and the ice wine.

Finally Michael Devlin pushed back his chair and sighed deeply. "I do not know when I last ate such a grand meal," he said, his green eyes on Emily.

"I'm glad you enjoyed it," she said almost shyly.

Rina saw Devlin's eyes soften. *Hoo, boy,* she thought. *He wants her, all right. I wonder how long it will take for them both to realize it.* She looked at her husband and saw that Sam was finally noticing the attraction between Emily and Michael Devlin too. Rina's eyes met her husband's in silent understanding, and Dr. Sam stood up.

"I hate to eat and run," he said, "but I've got rounds at the hospital early. Rina, come! Emily, as always, a wonderful dinner. Thank you, darling, for asking us. Mick, delighted to meet a fellow rare-roast-beef lover. I hope we'll see you again."

"I hope so too, Dr. Sam," Devlin replied.

"I'll see you to the door," Emily said, and she did, waving her two friends off as their car pulled away from in front of her house.

"Where do they live?" Devlin asked. He was standing next to her, she realized.

"A subdivision nearby. It's called Ansley at Egret Pointe," Emily said. "It's the only one in town, and has been there for years."

"When I came through the village I didn't see any serious shopping facilities," he replied, "and that wonderful beef had to have come from a real butcher. Let's sit. It's lovely out here on your big porch."

"The dishes," she protested.

"I'll bet you and Rina have everything in the dishwasher but for the dessert things," he said softly. "It's twilight, and I hear a robin singing. They have the sweetest song, and you hear them only at dusk and at dawn in the spring. Spring is already half-gone, Emily. You won't hear the robins until next year if you miss them now." He sat in a large wicker rocker, motioning her into a nearby chair.

She sat. "I never knew a man who recognized a robin's song, or knew when they sang," she told him quietly.

"I grew up in the country," he said. "Actually, I prefer it to the city."

"I couldn't live in the city," Emily admitted. "My father does, and my mother lives just outside of D.C. But I'm not a city girl at all. I have lived in Egret Pointe my whole life, and I never want to live anywhere else. I suppose that makes me a world class stick-in-the-mud." She laughed. "Did you like living in London? It's a wonderful city."

"I was very fortunate," he said. "I lived in an elegant little row house directly across from a lovely park. Actually, I own it. I've let it out for a year to a wealthy American widow, complete with my butler, Mr. Harrington, until I see how things go now that I'm back. I'm not certain I want to stay here."

"Oh." She sounded disappointed. "Why not?" she asked him. Then, "It's J.P., isn't it? She really is a dreadful creature, but she has made Stratford exceedingly profitable, and in publishing today profit is the name of the game. Martin couldn't do without her."

"You know what's happening then?" he said quietly.

"Yes, I know," Emily answered him candidly. Then she stood up. "I really want to get the table cleared and those dishes started, Mick."

"I'll help," he said, escorting her into the house.

They hardly spoke another word as together they cleared the rest of the dishes and glasses from the table. When everything was in the dishwasher and Emily had started it, she told him to take off the lovely Irish linen cloth that had covered her Duncan Phyfe dining table, and gather up the napkins.

"Essie, my housekeeper, will do them on Monday," she said, putting them in a basket in the laundry room off the big kitchen.

"Is that a laundry tub?" he asked her.

"One of the benefits of living in an old house," she replied as she set up the coffeemaker for the morning. "First one down turns it on," she told him.

"I'm not usually an early riser on Saturdays," he admitted with a grin.

"I thought we were going to work tomorrow," Emily said. "I have so much to tell you, and I've already fleshed out the story, Mick."

"It's still early," he responded. "I thought we might work a little tonight."

"Oh," she replied.

"Or we could sit out on your porch for a while longer, and get to know each other better," he quickly suggested, seeing her dismay. "You aren't a night person, are you, Emily?"

"Not really. My brain functions better when the sun's up," she confessed.

It was almost dark when they came out again to sit on the porch. They watched the night envelop everything about them, and they couldn't even see each other's faces, just their silhouettes. The stars came out to twinkle brightly in the blackness of the firmament. They talked about themselves, learning to become more comfortable with each other as the time slipped by.

"What's that?" he said, suddenly hearing a chiming coming from the village.

"The Episcopal church, St. Luke's, has a clock tower. Didn't you notice it before?" Emily wondered. She had gotten so used to it she rarely ever heard it.

"No, I was too interested in listening to you," he told her. "God, it's eleven o'clock, isn't it? I hadn't realized it was so late."

"Do you turn into a pumpkin at midnight?" she asked mischievously.

He laughed. "Did you leave any lights on in the house?" he asked her.

"I'll go put some on so you don't break your neck coming in," she replied, getting up to do exactly that.

Able to see his way in he thanked her for a lovely evening.

"You have your own bathroom," she told him as he made his way upstairs. "The house may be an antique, but I've modernized all the electric and wiring. And I am the proud possessor of three and a half bathrooms. Get up whenever you want, Mick. Good night," she called to him as he reached the landing.

He looked back, but she was gone. Gone to do what? Lock up? Put away the clean dishes in the dishwasher? Prepare a pan of sweet rolls for the morning? He had enjoyed this evening. Enjoyed the food, the Seligmanns, Emily. Closing the door of his bedroom he looked about him. The furniture was American Empire, large and mahogany. The dresser had carved feet. The big bed was a sleigh bed. He turned on the bedside lamp and, taking down the simple heavy white cotton coverlet, he folded it neatly and placed it on the spread rack at the foot of the bed. He stripped off his clothing and hung it up and, after walking into the bathroom, showered. Dried off, he opened one of the bedroom windows and climbed into the bed naked. He always slept naked. The bed was made European style, with just a bottom sheet and a down coverlet. It all smelled of lavender, and was surprisingly comfortable. He turned off the bedside lamp.

He wasn't yet sleepy. He heard Emily come upstairs, and listened to hear where she would go. He heard a bath running, and imagined her naked amid a tub of bubbles. She had little round breasts. He could tell that from the way her blouse clung. Were her nipples small or large? Dusky or a perky, pinker flesh? Her slacks had revealed by their fit a deliciously round little bottom. He imagined smacking that tempting little butt until she was wet with her desire, and ready to be mounted. He groaned softly and reached down to rub his dick, which was distended and hard with his lascivious thoughts. What the hell was the matter with him? He barely knew the girl, and if she was thirty-one, with no husband or visible male friend, it might be that men weren't her preference. Which, of course, didn't stop him from desiring her. She couldn't be gay. But there was an innocence, an untouched quality about her that just begged to be explored. And that was so damned unprofessional.

Martin Stratford had brought him back to the States for a reason. He couldn't disappoint him by losing his reason and fucking the ears off of Martin's prize writer. He had to get Emily to write a more sexually involved novel. The days of Georgette Heyer and Barbara Cartland were long over. Oh, there was a small, loyal market for those books, but it wasn't enough to generate the kind of profit a publishing house had to generate these days. Every book had to be an instant hit. A moneymaker.

Stratford did have the benefit of being a family-owned company—one of two left in the business. It allowed them the advantage of patience that the big conglomerate-owned publishing houses no longer had. Michael Devlin knew he could bring out more in Emily Shanski than she ever imagined she had in her. Make her books more profitable, which, of course, was a double-edged sword. If *The Defiant Duchess* turned out to be a really big hit among the readers—so much so that they bought it new rather than secondhand—one of the bigger companies might try to snap Emily up. She had a good track record. Her agent was no fool. He would want the best deal for his client.

Rachel had let Emily continue to write basically the same books. Maybe she hadn't seen it. Maybe her age finally caught up with her, and she was glad to get a clean, well-written manuscript that she didn't have to fuss with a whole lot, or request rewrites with all those deadlines looming. Emily's reputation was one of a writer who turned her work in on time and did her few rewrites, her line and copy editing, her galleys when requested, if not a bit before. She was reliable. There was no temperament involved with Emily Shanski, according to everything he had managed to learn about his new author. He was growing sleepy at last. His hard-on was fading with more sensible thoughts, but he wondered what she was doing as he finally fell asleep.

There had been no light under his door when she came up,

Emily had noted. But she had heard the shower running when she was finishing up in the kitchen. He was a well-made man, and didn't appear to have any excess fat on him. No beer belly for Michael Devlin, although he certainly ate like he was starving, she remembered with a smile. She liked a man who enjoyed his food. And he hadn't sat back and let her do all the cleaning up. He had pitched right in to help her. His Irish grandma's influence, no doubt, Emily thought with another smile.

Then her thoughts turned, and she wondered what he looked like beneath those tailored slacks and that obviously custom-made shirt. One button had been open at the top of that shirt. She had seen no chest hair poking out. The bit of skin revealed had been smooth. She thought about what it would be like to run the palms of her hands over that skin. Was it soft? Was he hard beneath? He looked like he might be fit and hard.

The water in her tub was cooling. She quickly washed and stepped out, damp-drying herself with her washcloth, then using her towel to finish the job. Naked, Emily walked into her bedroom and looked critically at herself in the large mirror that stood on the floor. She certainly wasn't skinny, like his model friend must have been. She had inherited her Irish family's delicate bone structure, but she had meat on those bones like her Polish relations, and she wore a size twelve. Twelve was considered a larger size in this day and age. Would he think she was fat? Was she pretty enough to seduce a man who had been bedding English nobility?

She stared hard into the mirror. Her breasts were nice. Small, but perfectly rounded. Her hips were a little wide, but they were nicely curved, and her thighs, thanks to her regimen at the Awesome Woman gym, were slender. She peered over her shoulder at her butt. Fleshy, but firm and shapely. Okay, so she wasn't a model, but she had a nice body. He'd either like it or he wouldn't. But it didn't make any difference as long as she could get him to seduce her so she could then write about sexual encounters, and know what the hell she was really talking about.

She wondered how many times she would have to do it with him. Would once be enough? What if they had to do it more than once, and he didn't like the way she did it, and he wouldn't continue? Well, then she would simply go to her duke. Hadn't he implied that once she lost her virginity he was there to take over for Devlin? Maybe not exactly, but she had understood that once she had experienced passion in her own reality, it could also be there for her in the reality of the Channel.

But how was she ever going to seduce Michael Devlin? He was very sophisticated, and his reputation was that of a man who chose his own women, made his own decisions. All the books she had showing in copious and colorful detail the sexual encounter, the positions, and how they could be done offered nothing on how to get a man to do them. What had Savannah said? "Throw yourself on his mercy"? "You're just his type"? Emily wouldn't have thought an urbane guy like Devlin would look seriously at her twice. But then, maybe he was bored with his elegant and worldly women. Maybe. Just maybe a little country girl who needed his help would appeal to him. Could she pull it off without making a complete fool of herself? Well, she was going to find out soon enough. Picking up her sleep shirt from the chair where she had put it earlier, Emily slipped it on, wondering if she should maybe go down to Lacy Nothings in the village tomorrow and pick out something sexier in which to be seduced. Or would that be much too patent? A soft old cotton sleep shirt was hardly the garment in which to be seduced. She'd wager his women all wore elegant silk-and-lace lingerie when they bedded Mick Devlin. But wouldn't it look obvious if she did? As if she were expecting him to make love to her? Undecided, Emily climbed into her bed. She was in a dreamless sleep before she even knew it. It had been a long, hard day. And it was surely going to get harder before it got easier.

CHAPTER THREE

ᐸᕑ

H e wasn't sure if it was the smell of the coffee or the cinnamon rolls baking that had awakened him first. He had
been lying on his belly. Turning lazily over onto his back, he
sniffed appreciatively. The big tall clock in the upstairs hall
began to chime. Nine o'clock. He looked across the room
toward the window, and saw the day was fair. And for some
reason he found that, unlike most Saturdays, he wasn't the least
bit sleepy. He had slept like a damned log the entire night
through. Michael Devlin climbed out of bed, peed, brushed his
teeth, shaved, and got dressed. Then he headed directly downstairs toward the delicious smells coming from Emily Shanski's
kitchen.

"Damnation!" Emily dropped the pan she was taking from
the oven quickly onto the counter, and flung the towel in her
hand into the sink.

He was at her side before she even realized he was there, taking her hand and sticking it under cold running water. "It's not
bad. What happened?"

"I almost forgot the rolls, and instead of taking an oven mitt
I grabbed a towel," Emily replied. She turned her head to say

thank you, and found herself nose-to-nose with him. Her blue eyes widened with surprise, and then he kissed her.

Her lips were incredibly soft, and she smelled of sweet rolls and lilacs. He slid an arm about her waist, and his kiss deepened as he felt her yielding against him. What was happening? He groaned and let her go. "I'm sorry. I shouldn't have done that," he said, stepping back a pace.

"Why not?" she asked him, suddenly knowing she had to take the initiative. For all his reputation Devlin was a gentleman. His kiss had been wonderful! She had never before been kissed quite like that. It was fierce and tender all rolled into one.

"I think we both know the answer to that, Emily," he replied stiffly.

"Sit down, Devlin," she told him, already pouring him a mug of coffee, and gestured toward the kitchen table. "Have a sweet roll, and let's discuss the fact that we seem to be attracted to each other." *God in His heaven!* Had she really said that? The look of surprise on his face told her she had.

"I'm your editor," he replied.

"And Savannah Banning tells me you're a very good one," Emily answered him. "Why should the fact that we're being drawn to each other change that?"

"You know Lady Palmer?" he asked her.

"We go way back," Emily said. "I was her witness when she and Sir Reginald went to the registry office seven years ago. I'm the Honorable William's godmother."

He nodded, surprised. It had never occurred to him that Emily Shanski would know the beautiful and flamboyant Savannah Banning. And God knew what the gossipy Lady Palmer had said about him. "More than a business relationship between us would be inappropriate," he tried to explain, but he sensed she knew that.

"Oh, piffle!" Emily responded. She plunked a roll on his plate and pushed it and the butter toward him. "Do you want to sleep with me?" *In for a penny, in for a pound,* she decided.

She didn't have a whole lot of time, after all, and a sexy, hot *Defiant Duchess* was due to Stratford at the end of December.

He choked on the bit of roll in his mouth, his face growing red, coughing. "Water!" he gasped, jumping up. She got it for him. Swallowing it, he managed to regain what he hoped would pass for composure. "You're joking, of course," he said.

"Are you amused?" she countered dryly. Her blue eyes were actually dancing with merriment, and her lips twitched, as if she wanted to burst into laughter at him.

The little witch was enjoying his discomfiture quite thoroughly, he thought. What would happen if he called her bluff? he wondered. Would she fall into his arms, or run shrieking from her sunny kitchen? Michael Devlin didn't liked being played for a fool, and he always made it a point to be the one who initiated any sexual encounter. But this was just too good to resist. If he was ever going to have any credibility with his writer, he had to make damned certain from the start that Emily knew who was the boss.

"As a matter of fact," he told her, looking down into those big cornflower-blue eyes, "I don't want to sleep with you, Emily Shanski. Let's tell it like it really is. I want to fuck you. I've wanted to since I first saw you. It is totally inappropriate for us to get involved, but I've never been a man to play entirely by the rules. If you're game, so am I," Devlin said wickedly. He almost laughed aloud at the look of surprise on her face. He had shocked the adorable Miss Shanski with his rather blunt and crude language.

Emily swallowed hard, and worked to feign an imperturbability she was far from feeling. "All right," she finally said. "Then we'll do it tonight." Her pulse pounded.

"Oh, no, angel face," he responded, surprised, but not about to let her get the upper hand. "I don't play that way. No appointments for you and me. I like spontaneity. I think now is as good a time as any to begin our little adventure, don't you?"

Standing away from the table, he moved toward her, his mouth twitching with his amusement.

"It's morning!" Emily protested, taking a step back.

"Haven't you ever done it in the daylight, angel face? It's just as much fun. Sometimes even better, because there is always the chance someone will come in and discover you getting your ears fucked off on your well-scrubbed oak kitchen table." His green eyes glittered as he moved closer and closer to where she now stood.

Emily backed away again, eyes wide. People made love on kitchen tables? She didn't know whether she should be shocked or intrigued. She swallowed hard once more and said coolly, "I far prefer the comfort of a bed, Devlin, and I'm not interested in voyeurism. It's vulgar, and speaks badly of the couple in-volved." There! That should set him back on his heels—she hoped. What was she getting herself into? she suddenly won-dered. Was this a good idea? Maybe she should just rent some X-rated videos.

"Very well," he drawled. "Your room or mine? And yes, now!"

"Now is not the best time," Emily said, gasping as he sud-denly reached out and pulled her into his arms. God, he smelled so good!

"Are you a cock tease, Emily?" he asked her softly, taking her hand and pressing it against his groin. "That's not nice, you know."

Her fingers moved involuntarily against the hard ridge press-ing against his jeans. "Oh," she half whispered. His penis was very hard beneath her hand.

"If you want to stop, Emily, this is the time. Keep touching me like that and there will be no going back for either of us," he warned her. He nuzzled her hair. It was soft.

She didn't know what to say. Had she come too far to cut and run? *Coward,* the voice in her head said. *You want knowledge, and you have the chance to obtain it.*

Okay! Okay! I'll do it, damn it, she said to that irritating voice. She looked up at Devlin, her lips half parted, wondering what was going to come next.

His hand caressed then cupped her face. The green eyes searched her face. "Emily?" he asked, his voice rough. Devlin was shocked by the incredible reaction he was having to her. He wanted to bury himself deep inside her, make her scream and beg him for everything he could give her. And then he would give her more and more until they were both so weak and exhausted they couldn't move for another day. What was it about this woman that was making him feel this way? He barely knew her, but then, that had never been a hindrance to his lusts. And she seemed to feel the same way, yet there was a shyness, an innocence about her that made him want to be gentle. "Emily?" he repeated. "Yes or no?"

"Yes." She half whispered the word. This wasn't at all what she had expected, she thought as he led her upstairs and into his bedroom. Where were the candles flickering in the soft evening breezes? The roses to perfume the air? This wasn't romantic at all. It was raw and primal, but to her own surprise she knew it was what she wanted from him. They weren't in love. She needed a man to take her virginity, and then show her everything she needed to know if she was going to write that explicitly sexy novel Stratford wanted out of her. This was research. Research to ensure authenticity. Research so she could save her career. *Hell!* An editor was supposed to help a writer. The sound of the bedroom door closing snapped her back to reality.

"You aren't afraid of me, are you?" he asked her gently. "We both want this, don't we, Emily?" He was giving her an opportunity to stop this madness.

She nodded. She knew what was to come, because she had read enough in this past week about the sexual situation, but she was shaking inside, and afraid that if she spoke her voice would give her away. Then he might not do it. She had been wearing a yellow cotton tee. He pulled it up over her head and arms, laying it aside on the chair.

"I like your taste in scanties," he said with a small smile, fingering the top of the lacy little bra she was wearing. "Now let's see how this opens. Ah, the front." He unhooked the garment and slid it off over her shoulders, tossing it to where the tee lay. "Oh, Emily," he said softly, staring at her breasts. "How lovely these are." Reaching out he cupped a single breast in his palm. She had small, pointed pink nipples.

What was she supposed to do? Emily wondered frantically. Well, she was certainly beginning to understand the necessity of practical experience. Her books did not cover anything like this. It would seem she should begin undressing him. Her fingers fumbled with the small buttons on his sports shirt. Getting them all open, she pushed the shirt from his broad shoulders, letting it fall to the ground. Her fingers splayed out over his broad chest. His skin was soft, but he was hard beneath. In one of her books she had seen the woman kiss the man's nipples. Bending her head, she did so now.

His hands were now undoing her jeans, and he lifted her from the pile of denim. "For a proper miss you wear very sensuous panties," he told her, eyeing the silk bikini bottom, amused.

"They match the bra," she said low. "Pretty undergarments are my one vice," Emily told him. Her hands imitated his, and she undid his jeans, thrusting them down over his lean hips. "Oh!" she gasped, surprised. "You don't wear . . ." Her voice died.

"No, I don't," he said. "And from now on I don't want you to either. No bra. No panties when you are with me. I want you ready whenever I want you, Emily. And you will be a very good girl and do what I tell you, won't you?" He tipped her face up to his even as he ripped the lace-and-silk bikini from her body. Then his hand slipped quickly between her legs to cup her mons.

Emily caught her breath, surprised. "No underwear?" she managed to say.

"When I want to fuck you, angel face, I don't want to have to waste the time pulling off your clothes that I could spend making us both happy," he told her.

"Do you treat all your women this way, Devlin?" She could not lose control of this situation. Oh, God, his hand was so warm. He fingered the curls of her pubic area and she couldn't contain the shiver that ran up her spine.

"Are you a good girl or a bad girl?" he asked her. His tongue began to harry her small ear. "I think you might be a bad girl under all that propriety."

"I don't know what I am, but I'm sure you're going to tell me afterward," she said spiritedly. "I already know you're a bad boy, Devlin." She was naked in the arms of a naked man. And she still had the ability to carry on a conversation? What in the name of heaven would her grandmothers think of her? Well, at least she wasn't Katy.

"Like all writers, you talk too much," he said, and then he kissed her mouth hard. His tongue ran suggestively along her lips, and instinctively she opened them, allowing him entry. Their tongues curled about each other.

He had pulled her against him. Their naked bodies were touching, and the sensation was very exciting. Was this what was called a French kiss? she asked herself as their tongues began to caress each other. Not bad, and his breath tasted of mint and coffee. She let her tongue stroke his.

He pushed her back onto the bed. Her butt was on the mattress, but her legs were dangling over. Then he knelt and, lifting her legs up, rested them over his shoulders. What was he doing? He pulled her legs apart, and his dark head dove between them.

Emily squealed with surprise, almost fainting with shock when she felt him open her labia and begin to lick a part of her flesh she had never anticipated would be touched by another's tongue. Vaguely she recalled seeing pictures of a man between a woman's legs in her books, but she never knew exactly what was happening. Well, she did now! "Oh, God!" His tongue had touched her clitoris, and it was incredibly sensitive. The tongue flicked relentlessly back and forth over that rosebud of flesh. She was almost unconscious with the pleasure his tongue was giving her. She shivered once, twice. "Please," she said. "Please!" She wasn't quite sure what she wanted, but she wanted something.

He stopped, disentangling himself from her slender limbs.

"No!" she said, shocked by her own reaction. "No!"

Laughing, he pulled her up, giving her a kiss. "That's how you taste, Emily, and you are delicious." Then he sat quickly down on the bed, yanking her over his knee, and gave her bottom three quick, hard spanks. "I figured you for a bad girl, angel face. Let's be bad together now." He stood for a moment again, and then pushed her back onto the bed. "Those darling little tits of yours need some loving attention," he told her. Flinging himself next to her, he lowered his dark head and closed his mouth over one of her nipples. "Ummm," he said. "Almost, but not quite as tasty as your sweet cunny."

Oh, Lord, Emily thought. Her books had certainly not prepared her for all of this. What else didn't they show her? She had to do something herself to prove to him that she was enjoying their encounter. "Hey, give me a turn!" she said and, pulling away from him, began to kiss his nipples. Boldly she licked them and then let her tongue move down his torso as far as his belly button. His pubic hair was thickly curled, and the color of midnight. And his penis . . . For a moment she was frightened. The men in the picture books she had didn't have penises like that. He seemed far bigger. Thicker. Longer.

"Don't take me in your mouth." Devlin groaned. "I want to come inside you this first time, angel face. Do you have any condoms? I didn't quite expect this."

"No," Emily said, shaking her head.

"It's all right. I've been tested. I'm fine. How 'bout you? You're on the pill?"

"Uh-huh," she lied, suspecting he'd stop if she told him the truth: that she wasn't on the pill because she didn't need it. That she had never before had sex.

He pulled her up and on top of him, rubbing his penis between her thighs. Then suddenly he rolled Emily over, spreading her thighs wide, fitting himself between them. He took her face between his big hands. "I never wanted a woman so quickly before," he told her. "What is this magic about you, Emily Shanski?" Then he kissed her slowly.

It was the most sensual kiss she had ever imagined. His mouth was warm and seductive against hers. She felt as if her bones were melting as his lips worked against hers. Still, Emily was very, very aware he was positioning himself to enter her. She tensed, surprised when he immediately noticed.

"I'll go slow this first time," he told her. "I want to ram myself home, I'm so damned hot for you, angel face. But I want you to always remember the first time Mick Devlin fucked you." The head of his penis pushed gently into her vagina barely an inch. "Do you know how hard it is for me to be patient? You are so tight, angel face, and so ready for me." He kissed her again, moving himself another tiny distance.

Emily's eyes were closed tight. She was barely able to breathe. Her whole consciousness was focused on what was happening to her. His thick penis stretched the walls of her vagina. She could feel her body enclosing him, feel him moving inexorably forward. When did it end? And where was that mysterious thing called orgasm that was supposed to happen to her? Would she know it when it happened?

Michael Devlin struggled in the face of his own overwhelming lust to give his partner every bit of enjoyment that he could. He knew if he did, she would retaliate in kind. The orgasm building up in him was going to be enormous, he sensed. And then suddenly, to his great surprise his slow sweet progress was blocked. At first he thought he was imagining it, but no, he was not. "Jaysus!" he swore. "You're a virgin!" He looked down at

Emily with her tightly closed eyes. "Open your eyes, you con-
niving little witch, and tell me the truth. You're a virgin, right?"

Emily did not open her eyes. "Uh-huh," she whispered.

"Oh, Christ, I can't stop now, angel face," he told her. "I'm
sorry." And then without further ado, he pulled his raging penis
back and drove through her hymen.

Emily shrieked. "You're hurting me," she sobbed. Why
hadn't anyone warned her about pain? Would it always be like
that? All her books were useless.

"Lie still," he told her. "The pain will go away in a minute.
You damned little fool, you should have warned me." His hand
caressed her face tenderly.

"If I had you wouldn't have done it," she whimpered.

"Probably not," he agreed. "Why?"

"Is this the time to be discussing this?" she asked almost
ruefully.

"No, angel face, it isn't," he said. Then he was kissing her
gently, softly, and moving on her with tender care.

The pain was gone almost as quickly as it had come. Her eyes
closed again, and she let herself slide away into a world of sensation. Her body was accepting him far more easily now. He
whispered little prompts in her ear, and she followed them easily. Her legs wrapped about his torso, and she gasped with distinct pleasure as he moved deeper into her vagina. "Oh, yes!"
she heard her own voice say, and he laughed low. The rhythm
between them was like nothing she had ever experienced. This
was wonderful!

"I've got to come!" he groaned. "Sorry!"

And she felt his cum flooding her body. Emily sighed deeply
with the sheer pleasure of it. "Can I have more, sir?" she asked
him.

Michael Devlin rolled off of her and lay breathing heavily for
several long minutes. He had just fucked the first virgin he had
had since he was fifteen, and he had never been entirely sure
that Maureen Duffy was indeed a virgin, although she had

sworn she was. But Emily Shanski certainly had been a virgin. Her very tight little hymen had shattered beneath the persistent battering of his penis. He had felt the warm blood. Glancing down he saw it on his dick, on her thighs, on the bedsheet that had been beneath them. "This will not happen again," he told her in a stern voice. But he knew he didn't mean it. He didn't care what had convinced her to give him the gift of her virginity, but he was certainly not unhappy about it. And he wanted more.

Emily propped herself up on an elbow and looked down into his handsome face. "Devlin," she said, "let's get one thing straight right now. Unless you continue to instruct me in the arts of passion I will not be able to write that damned sexually explicit book Stratford wants of me. You see our problem, don't you? And you're my editor, aren't you? You're supposed to help me, right? It's your job, isn't it? I don't intend to let my career go down the toilet because J. P. Woods can't get over the fact that you wouldn't service her seven years ago."

"My God! You seduced me!" He started to laugh. "And here I thought it was the other way around, angel face, but you seduced me."

"Yep," Emily admitted, "and now that we have my virginity out of the way you are going to teach me everything I need to know to write an explicit and sexier novel. Hell, Devlin, your ass is as much on the line in this situation as mine is," she told him.

He grinned up at her. He couldn't help it. Here he had thought she was a prissy little miss, and that he was going to have a difficult time getting the results from her that Stratford wanted. Emily Shanski had sure as hell fooled him, and he had to admit he admired her for it. She was a survivor. "First off, woman, I need my breakfast to restore my strength," he told her. "And then you have to tell me where I can get condoms. Drugstore? Shopping center? And you had better get a prescription for the morning-after pill from Dr. Sam. And some birth control pills. You're not on the pill, are you, you bald-faced little liar."

"Why would I be on the pill? I never had sex before." She grinned back at him.

"I'd spank you except I suspect you like it," he told her.

"So we're going to be lovers, Devlin?" Emily asked softly.

"We are lovers, angel face. But we shouldn't be, and you know it," he said.

"You said you wanted to fuck me the moment you saw me," she reminded him.

"Wanted to didn't mean I would have," he replied. "Oh, I know the reputation I carry around: Devlin, the Irish Casanova, but I've never before banged one of my writers, Emily. You know the old saw about mixing business and pleasure."

"How about, 'All work and no play makes Devlin much too serious'?" she teased.

"I'm sending you to the showers," he responded.

"Only shower in the house is in your bathroom," she said sweetly. "Come with me?"

He shook his head in wonder. "Jaysus! What have I unleashed?"

"Owww," Emily said, getting up from the tangle of sheets on the bed. "Ohh, I hurt. You're the expert. How soon will it go away?"

"See how you feel after your shower," he suggested.

She nodded and went into the bathroom. He heard the water begin to run. What had he done? he asked himself once again. This was pure insanity. What if she fell in love with him? What a mess that would be. What if he fell in love with her? And then he admitted to himself that he was already in love with her. He hadn't known her a week, and yet the first time he had seen her he had known on some deep level that Emily Shanski was the woman he'd been waiting for his whole life.

And he had lusted for her. God, he had lusted for her. Every time this week he had thought of her for more than a minute or two he found himself getting a hard-on. How could something so magical have happened to Michael Devlin, the lady-killer, the love-'em-on-my-terms-and-then-leave-'em guy? He didn't deserve a girl like Emily Shanski, and he had damned well better keep these sixteen-year-old's feelings he had oozing out of his almost forty-year-old body to himself.

They would have a love affair that would be strictly business. Their private business. No one else had to know. He'd teach her enough to write the book the company wanted of her, and that would be that. When was the book due? End of December, he recalled. Well, they would have a wonderful summer and autumn together, Michael Devlin decided. And after that he'd tell Martin Stratford that he wanted to return to London. Random House wanted him back. They were even offering him his own new imprint, and a staff to implement it. Let J. P. Woods become CEO of Stratford. Aaron Fischer would see that Emily got a good new deal wherever she went.

She walked out of the bathroom with a towel wrapped about her. "Your turn," she told him. And when he had showered again and come out to dress, she was already in her jeans and yellow tee, her panties and bra in her hand. "I'll put these away and meet you down in the kitchen," she said with a smile as she walked out the door of his bedroom.

"Okay," he said, his naked body warming up as her eyes swept admiringly over him. Damn! He was getting another hard-on. *Get a grip, Devlin,* he told himself. First food, and then he was going to take her to bed for the rest of the day. He pulled his jeans back on, wincing slightly at the tightness in his crotch. He had gone down barefooted earlier, because that was how he behaved in his own house. She hadn't objected, and so he went downstairs without his shoes again.

Emily was already scrambling eggs. "From the look in your eye," she said mischievously, "we're going to need our strength. A little protein can't hurt."

He walked up behind her, one arm going about her waist, the

other hand reaching up to slip underneath her tee and cup a breast. "Eggs will be fine," he told her, nipping at her earlobe. His thumb rubbed against her nipple.

"I've got sausages in the other pan," she said, indicating with her head. Her breasts were getting tight, and she could suddenly feel a sticky wetness between her thighs. "Devlin, if you keep doing that we are going to end up on the kitchen table. Stop it! I'm going to burn everything if you don't. I don't want the whole town to know about us."

He removed the hand, but continued holding her against him. "Why are"—he corrected himself—"were you a virgin at thirty-one?" he asked, curious.

"You know I was raised by my two grandmothers. That my parents grew up next door to each other. This is Gran's house— Gran O'Malley. She was the last of her branch of the Dunhams, who were among the founders of Egret Pointe. She was Katy's mother. This house and the one to its right were built by a Dunham for his twin daughters when they married in 1860. Gran descends from one of the twins, Mary Anne Dunham. Her sister, Elizabeth Maude, had the other house, but her line ended in 1954, when her twin spinster granddaughters died. That was when Grandpa Shanski bought the house. Katy and Joe were born in 1957 and 1956 respectively. Actually, they're just six months apart, which was why they were in the same school grade together. My father was born on St. Joseph's Day in March, and my mother in September on the Feast of St. Michael and All Angels," Emily explained, spooning eggs onto a warm plate that had been in the oven, and then adding the sausages. "They grew up best friends. Sit down, Devlin, eat.

"Then in their senior year Joe led our local high school team to its first state football championship. He was that boy quarterback you see in those movies Hollywood made in the 1940s. Katy was the cute blue-eyed head cheerleader. Everyone knew Joe Shanski and Katy O'Malley. And everyone loved them. Even their peers. The whole town got drunk celebrating. Katy and Joe got a little drunker, and continued their celebration in the back of his car. In the morning both admitted it was a mistake. They decided they'd forget about it, and went back to their old best-friends routine. They were both a little embarrassed by the whole thing, Joe has said." She filled her plate with eggs and sausages and sat down at the table with him.

"But then you came along," Devlin said with a small smile.

"Yep," Emily agreed. "That I did. When Katy realized, she told Joe, and then they told the grans. Grandpa Shanski was already gone, leaving Grandma a widow with two sons to raise. By this time it was March. Katy had a scholarship to Wellesley, and Joe had one to Princeton. They couldn't have gone to such wonderful schools without those scholarships, and both had serious careers in mind. So Katy hid her condition in order to avoid getting kicked out of high school, and the grans sneaked them off to another town for a nice civil marriage ceremony so I'd be born on the proper side of the blanket. After their graduation Katy was supposed to go off to Europe on a grand tour before college. Actually she went into a nice church home for naughty girls until she had her baby. I was supposed to be put out for adoption to a good Catholic family, but once the grans saw me they agreed they couldn't let me go, and took me themselves to raise."

"Your parents divorced then?" he said.

"Actually the civil union was annulled on the grounds that Katy was under the age of consent when they had married. The fact that their parents had arranged the marriage in the first place was conveniently overlooked. And this allowed both Katy and Joe to be married in the church when they finally chose mates one day, which of course they did. Katy went to Yale Law after Wellesley, and eventually married Carter Phelps the Fourth. She has two kids, Phoebe and Carter the Fifth. Joe's a doctor, a pediatrician, actually. He married a nice Irish girl named Mary Shannon, and they have three sons, Joe, Frank, and Sean."

"You don't call your parents Mom and Dad," he noted.

"I never thought of them like that," Emily said. "My mother and I never saw each other at all except at Christmas, when she came home because my Grandmother O'Malley insisted she do so. I don't think she ever even thought of me except when she had no other choice. Please don't misunderstand, though. Katy's a nice lady, and a good mother to my half brother and sister, but for her I was a mistake to be forgotten. Of course, when she married Carter the Fourth she had to tell him about her little slip from grace before the engagement was announced. They both knew Carter the Fourth would be going into politics. I was displayed most prominently at their society wedding with Gran O'Malley. Carter the Fourth had wanted me to be a flower girl, but Katy drew the line at that." Emily chuckled. "I was referred to as her child from a brief high school union that had been annulled. I like Carter and his kids. My half sister is actually quite a fan of mine. Katy is quite astounded by my career and by my success. Now and again you'll see a media piece referring to me as Senator Phelps of Virginia's stepdaughter. But not often. I prefer to be my own woman."

"I've discovered that," he said, reaching for another of her sweet rolls and buttering it lavishly. She was a senator's step-daughter? Could he be deported for making wild love to a senator's virgin stepdaughter? "What about your father?"

"Oh, Joe's a good guy. I saw more of him as a kid than I did of Katy, but medical school takes up a lot of time. He always remembered my birthday, though. When he married Mary Shannon she wanted me with them, but the grans put their collective feet down. So she went and had three sons of her own. Joey and Frank are in high school now, and Sean's in middle school. I always get invited for the holidays, of course. Mary Shannon is a grand, bighearted Irish girl, and while Gran Shanski was a bit put off by her enthusiasm, she appreciated her loving nature. But you can understand why I never called them Mom and Dad. They gave me life, to be sure, but they weren't my parents at all." She stood up. "Are you through, Devlin? You're going to get sick if you eat another sweet roll," Emily told him, reaching for his plate. "You've had four already."

"We have work to do, Emily Shanski," he told her with a grin. "But first I need to get to a pharmacy for some condoms. Want to tell me where?"

She did, and then added, "Try not to attract too much attention to yourself, Devlin. I mean between the fact that you're a striking man, and that Healy." She sighed. "You don't want anyone at Stratford to know we're having a love affair. And I don't want anyone in Egret Pointe to know. It's a small town, Devlin."

"I grew up in one," he said as he headed out the back door for his car with a wave. He knew just what he wanted: the thinnest rubber on the market, lubricated. He hoped the store she was sending him to would have them. And she had to get on the pill. He didn't want to wear those damned rubbers any longer than he had to. He wanted nothing coming between him and Emily Shanski's wet, hot cunt. He backed slowly out of her driveway and headed down Founder's Way just as Rina Seligmann was turning her Lexus onto the little street. They waved at each other.

Where was he going? Rina wondered as she pulled up in front of Emily's house. She called out as she entered the front door, "Emily, it's Rina."

"I'm upstairs making the bed," Emily called down. "Be right with you."

"No, I'll come up and help you," Rina said, hurrying up the stairs. "Why are you changing the sheets in the guest room? This isn't the Grande Hotel, sweetie, and I'm sure Mr. Gorgeous has slept on the same bedsheets a couple of nights in a row." Then something caught Rina's eye. "Oh, my God," she said dramatically. "You screwed him! Was he wearing a condom? I'll tell Sam to give you a prescription. No, I'll have him give you a couple of months of samples. You don't want everyone in town knowing you're screwing your editor. I never asked before, but it was your first time, wasn't it?"

Emily was almost beet red in the face with Rina's blunt questions. "If it was my first time, Rina," she said, "how would I know if he was good?"

"You'd know," Rina replied. "It's instinct."

"Then he's good."

"Why now? And why him?" Rina wondered. "Oh, the sexy book." She started putting fresh pillow slips on the pillows.

"Hey, he's my editor, and he's supposed to help me," Emily responded with a little grin. "And his career is just as much on the line as mine. He's not married, and he's not involved with anyone else, so why not him?"

"Well," Rina said, "he looks like a great first-timer. Why didn't you use the Channel?"

"It seems their reality and this reality have to be in sync for it to work," Emily explained. She sighed. "And my new hero looks just like Devlin. Go figure."

Rina nodded. "Then you wanted him right from the get-go," she said as they tucked in the sheet and fluffed the down coverlet.

"It was the oddest thing, Rina. The second our eyes met I felt as though someone had hit me in the pit of my stomach. I felt like I knew Michael Devlin even though I had never before set eyes on him. Go figure that one out. Don't put the spread on."

Rina chuckled. "Okay," she said, grinning. "Then I had better get going. I'll go get you some birth control samples from Sam. Pills or the patch?"

"Devlin went to get condoms. It's okay for this weekend," Emily replied.

"Unless he gotcha the first time," Rina considered.

"Rina, you know women don't get pregnant the first time," Emily told her.

Rina Seligmann looked both astounded and appalled at the same time. "Who in the name of God ever told you that?" she wanted to know. "Not your grans."

"I guess I wasn't thinking too straight at that moment," Emily muttered.

"Oy vay!" Rina muttered. "When your editor goes home tomorrow you come right over and let Sam have a look at you, Emily Shanski. I promised both your grans on their deathbeds that I'd look after you, and I'm not about to break such a promise."

"You mean I could have gotten . . . could be pregnant from that one time? Oh, my God, Rina! Then why the hell did my friends in college say stuff like that if it wasn't so?" Emily looked distinctly unhappy. "God, I'm Katy O'Malley all over again, and I've tried so hard not to be." She looked like she was going to burst into tears.

Rina put comforting arms about Emily. "Sweetie, it's all right. More than likely you aren't pregnant, but you've got to be careful. Girls in school believe all kinds of silly things in order to justify behavior they know damned well they shouldn't be doing." She laughed lightly. "Come see Sam Monday after Hot Stuff has gone back to the city, but I'm sure you're okay." She set Emily back a pace, and wiped a tear from her cheek. "And you are nothing like Katy O'Malley. You are sweet and thoughtful and very dear. That woman who birthed you has none of those qualities."

"You never liked my mother, did you, Rina?" Emily said.

"No, I don't like her. But neither do I dislike her. She just isn't my cuppa, sweetie. I guess it's that too-cool, too-sure-of-herself attitude that gets me. I remember when your gran died. Her own mother, and she didn't show up until the morning of the funeral. Came in a limousine, as I recall. And left immediately afterward. Didn't even stay for the luncheon you had arranged for the mourners."

"She had to get back to D.C., she said," Emily remembered. "An important deposition, as I recall. Some big case she was working on."

"She could have rescheduled it. It was her mother, for God's sake," Rina said sharply. "But your gran always said Katy let nothing stand in the way of her success. Not even having a baby." She took up the sheets. "I'll stick these in your laundry on my way out. I don't want to run into himself on his way back from the drugger."

"Thanks," Emily said. "And Rina . . ."

The older woman turned. "Yeah?"

"I love you," Emily told her.

"Go on with yis," Rina Seligmann said, using what had been a favorite expression of Emily's grandmother O'Malley. Then with a smile she hurried down the stairs.

Emily looked about the room. It looked the same, and yet she would never look at this room again in the same way. It was in this room that she had lost her virginity. She still felt a little sore, but she would live. She heard the front door open and close as Rina left. Well, she had better go downstairs herself and decide what to do for dinner. There was beef left over from last night. And gravy. Lots of gravy. Open-faced hot roast-beef sandwiches and a salad sounded good. And a dessert. She'd do a simple yellow cake with raspberry jam between the three layers and powdered sugar on the top.

Michael Devlin found her in the kitchen when he returned from his shopping expedition. "Mission accomplished!" he told her, holding up a little bag. "But before I take you to bed again, Miss Shanski, I want to know something about this book you are going to write. And I want to know if there is a wonderful restaurant in Egret Pointe where we may have dinner tonight. I'll book a reservation now."

"I thought I'd do dinner for us. Just leftovers, and this cake I'm putting in the oven now," Emily told him. "But we could have it for tea."

"No, I want to take you out," he said firmly.

"Let me think," Emily said. Lord, Saturday night was the night that everyone who was anyone in Egret Pointe ate out. If they saw her with a strange man it was sure as hell bound to cause talk. And she did not want to answer any questions. At least, not yet. "I think the nicest restaurant around is the old inn up in East Harbor. It's a bit of a drive, but it's along the bay road, and quite pretty. Would you mind?"

"No," he said. "How long a drive?"

"About half an hour," she told him, closing the oven door on the three cake pans and setting her timer for thirty minutes. She drew open a cabinet drawer and pulled out the local Yellow book. "Here. Better call them now. Saturday night's a big night, especially at this time of year. Spring seems to bring everyone out again."

He took the directory from her, found the number, and, using his cell, called to make a reservation. "Eight o'clock all right for you?" he asked.

Emily nodded, then said, "I'll go get my notes. With cake in the oven I'd rather do our work here, if you don't mind." He didn't, and she was quickly back, carrying a wire basket and a pink file folder. "Sit," she told him, and took a chair for herself.

"You haven't written anything yet?" he asked.

"No," Emily answered him. "Only a couple of descriptions. I wanted to run some things by you first. I always did that with Rachel, and talking over the plotline usually makes everything clearer for me. Can we work that way too?"

"Of course," he agreed. "I'm not here to change your work habits. Just to help you to get back on track. Sex, as you've now discovered," he said with a mischievous grin, "does happen in real life, and so your plot should reflect real life too."

"I don't know enough about sex yet," she told him, "so why don't we just start with the main focus of the plot?"

"Go," he said with a nod.

"You know the story of the Scarlet Pimpernel?" Emily asked.

"I do. Great swashbuckling tales of Sir Percy Blakely by Baroness Orczy."

"Same sort of thing, but with my heroine in the Sir Percy role," she told him.

"Why?"

"Why what?"

"Why is she traveling into France to rescue people from the Terror?" he wanted to know. "There has to be a damned good reason."

"Her mother is a French noblewoman, her father an English earl. Caroline is seventeen, and has been in Normandy with her mother for almost a year. They had gone the previous summer to visit her mother's family. The earl learns that his wife and daughter have been caught up in the arrest of his wife's family. They have all been imprisoned in her grandparents' cellar. Her father is pulling every string he can to get them released. Meanwhile in France, his wife and daughter are struggling to survive. Caroline catches the eye of their jailer, but her mother saves her by submitting to the man, who afterward hands her over to several of his men because she hasn't given him the pleasure he anticipated from raping a hated aristo. Caroline's mother grows mortally ill from her harsh treatment just as the order comes through from Citizen Robespierre, who has accepted a large ransom from the English earl for the release of the two women. The mother swears her daughter to secrecy about what has transpired, and then dies as their ship is in sight of the English coast. I may make some changes, though, before I even begin to write it."

"Great opening!" he said. "Dramatic, poignant. I like it. Okay, so how does she end up rescuing others? I mean, if she's seventeen she's hardly in a position to do something like that in Georgian England."

"Her father is so distraught by his wife's death that he commits suicide. But before he does he makes certain provisions for his daughter. The earl's heir is his wastrel brother, and while he is going to inherit the title, the earl's estate isn't entailed upon an heir. The earl makes a will that gives his daughter the bulk of his fortune, leaving the rest in the form of a trust to care for the estate and provide his younger brother with a small income.

"Then he goes to a friend of his, the Duke of Malincourt, who is an elderly man with no children. He arranges with the duke to marry Caroline so her fortune will be kept safe from his brother. The marriage, of course, is in name only. The fortune will be hers when the duke dies, so she will, as a young, beautiful, and wealthy dowager duchess, be an excellent marriage prospect for the man she will eventually fall in love with. Without a husband for Caroline, her uncle would have had access to her monies, and probably would have gambled them away, leaving her impoverished. Caroline knows nothing of her father's plans, but as an obedient daughter, and still in shock over what has happened in France, she accepts his decision to marry her off to the duke. The day after the wedding the earl puts a pistol to his head.

"Grief-stricken, Caroline is horrified to learn the truth from her kindly old husband as to how her father has protected her before taking his own life. She vows then and there to get back at the revolutionaries in France for destroying her family. She seeks out others among her class who are like-minded, and begins her operations. She is known to her enemies as Lavender, for she always leaves a sprig of the flower behind when she has snatched someone from the clutches of Madame la Guillotine."

"Very nice," he said, "but where are we going to fit the sex in, m'dear?"

"The old duke dies when Caroline is twenty," Emily continued. "His heir is his nephew, and the nephew wants to make Caro his wife, a fact known to the old duke, who fully approved. He even suggested to Caroline that after a proper period of mourning she marry his heir. But of course, Caro fears a young and alert husband will discover what she has been doing, so she resists. But the new duke, Justin Trahern, seduces her. She tells him she will be his wife, but she will be answerable to no one but herself. He agrees because he is deeply in love with her.

"By accident—and don't ask me how because I haven't decided yet—he learns what she is doing. At first he is outraged that a woman would behave so. Then he becomes frightened for her. He tells her he knows, and in an effort to make him understand why she does what she does, Caro tells him the truth of what happened to her mother. Trahern realizes the only chance he has of stopping the woman he loves from putting herself in constant danger is to find the jailer and the men who raped her mother, and see them dead."

"I like it," Michael Devlin told her. "I like it very much. It's clever, and we should be able to make the love affair between Caro and Trahern sizzle. Women who have had tough times will identify nicely with the heroine. She's suffering survivor's guilt, of course, and that does make you do things you might not otherwise do."

The timer on the counter pinged, and Emily got up to check her cakes. They were perfect. Turning off the oven, she drew each pan from inside, carefully setting them on her counter to cool before turning them out onto her cake racks.

"Smells good. What kind of cake is it going to be?" he asked her.

"Just an old-fashioned kind my grans taught me. Raspberry jam between the layers, and powdered sugar on top," Emily explained.

"My gran in Ireland used to make that," he said. "It was always my favorite."

"I think everything is your favorite." She laughed. "There isn't anything I've cooked so far that you haven't scarfed up like a starving man, Devlin. I think you have a tapeworm," Emily teased him.

"Roast beef, chocolate trifle, cake with jam," he replied. "What isn't to like?"

She laughed again. "I like you, Devlin," she told him. "I was really upset when I learned Rachel had gone, but I'm not as upset now."

"I haven't edited your manuscript yet," he said with a small grin. Then he said, "I think turnabout is fair play, Emily Shanski. I'm going to make you lunch. I'll need bread, rat cheese, honey mustard, and olive oil or butter. And a cast-iron frying pan."

"Grilled cheese sandwiches!" she said. "Now, those are my favorites."

"Get going, woman, and fetch me my supplies." He chuckled, giving her bottom a small smack.

"Yes, sir!" Emily replied, and she bustled off to find what he needed. "And I want you to know I'm a connoisseur of grilled cheese. These had better be good."

"I'm good at everything I do, Emily, as you are about to discover," he said.

And she laughed. "I'll be the judge of that," she told him.

He grinned, suddenly realizing that he was happy. And Michael Devlin couldn't remember the last time he had been really happy.

CHAPTER FOUR

Emily hurried downstairs. Devlin was waiting for her in Gran's old-fashioned parlor, which was across from the more modern living room. It was filled with the furniture that had been in the house when Gran was a girl. "How do I look?" she asked as she came into the parlor. She was wearing a violet-sprigged cream-colored dress with a fitted bodice, and a flirty, floaty skirt with a scalloped hemline. She twirled to give him the full effect. He had made love to her a second time this afternoon, and then they had napped together in his bed. It had been even better the second time, and Emily was feeling more relaxed than she had ever felt in her life. Making love was quite a revelation, yet she couldn't help but wonder if it would have been different with another man. Better, or worse?

The green eyes looked her over admiringly. Then he said, "Are you wearing panties and a bra, Emily?"

"Of course. We're going out," she replied.

"No," he said, shaking his head. "I thought I made myself clear this morning. When you are with me you do not wear undergarments. Take them off."

"We're going to be in a public place, Devlin," she protested.

"What if I want to pull over on our way home to make love to you in the car?" he asked. "If you want to question me, Emily, then perhaps you should find another lover."

"Damn it, Devlin, I don't want another lover! Where would I find one in this town? And I most certainly don't want people gossiping about me and some local. You're the perfect lover. You live in the city. Besides, you understand my dilemma and the reason I've taken you for a lover. You're not going to go all postal on me when I say I've learned enough from you and tell you to go away," Emily said.

"Then trust me enough to do what I say," he told her. "If you want me for your teacher then you have to obey me. I will never harm you, angel face. In fact, I'm going to teach you something right now about passion. Take off the panties and bra, Emily."

Reaching up, she unhooked the bra through her dress, sliding one strap off under the fabric, then the other, and drawing it out through the short sleeve, laying it aside on a balloon-backed burgundy-colored velvet chair.

"You do that like you've done it before," he told her with a grin.

"Shut up," she said. "It's the quickest way to take a bra off when you get home, and every woman in the world knows that." She reached beneath her skirt and pulled her panties off, flipping them onto the chair next to the bra. "Satisfied? God, I hope no one can see through this dress," Emily muttered nervously. "Can you?"

"No," he said, but he lied. The faint shadow of her slender legs was very visible.

"Can we go now?" she asked him.

"Nope," he replied. "Pull up your skirt and let me see your pussy."

"Devlin!" Her tone was shocked.

"Pull up your skirt," he ordered her in a hard tone.

"It's vulgar," Emily said, and then she squealed as, gripping her wrist, he pulled her facedown over the high rolled arm of the settee, yanked up her dress, and began to spank her, his other hand now on the small of her back to hold her down.

"You are a very, very, very bad girl, Emily Shanski," he said, each word punctuated by his hand on her bared bottom.

She was more surprised than harmed by his actions, and if the truth were known it was rather exciting too. She felt a distinct tingle in her clitoris.

"Now tell me you're sorry, and you won't be such a bad girl again," Devlin said.

"Won't!" Emily replied, getting into the spirit of the game, and wanting him to spank her some more. "And you can't make me either!"

He grinned, delighted that she had caught on so quickly. "Yes, I can!" he told her, and his hand began to fall on her flesh again until her buttocks grew pink, and she finally begged him to cease. "Stay exactly as you are," Devlin ordered her.

"Yes, sir," she mocked him. Then she heard the faint sound of his zipper, and the tearing of a condom envelope. "Ohh," Emily whispered. "You're going to fuck me."

"Do you want to be fucked?" he asked, and, grasping her hips in his hands to steady them, he slid into her vagina in a single smooth stroke. She was very wet, and the spanking had obviously made her very lustful, he noted as she wiggled her buttocks against his groin. "Do you? Say it, Emily. Say, 'I want to be fucked.' " He remained perfectly still within her.

She felt him palpably. He was very big, thick, and long. He throbbed hungrily against the walls of her body. "I want to be fucked, Devlin!" she told him without hesitation. *Oh, yes!* She did indeed want to be fucked bent over the arm of Great-great-great-grandmother Mary Anne's velvet settee. "Do it to me!" Emily hissed, and then gasped. His penis began to move, and it had touched something inside her that sent shock waves of sensation rolling through her body. "Oh, my God! What's happening?" Nothing had ever felt so good! "Don't stop! Don't you dare stop, Devlin! Ohh, God!"

He had found her G-spot, and he worked it hard. She was bucking and sobbing with the passion that was beginning to roll over her. His penis flashed back and forth, back and forth, driving her along. Her cries of delight increased his own lust until he thought he would burst, but he held back, giving her time. And then it happened.

Emily felt herself close to losing consciousness. Her body seemed to explode from the inside out. Waves of tremors racked her body, filling her with the most incredible feelings, and she knew: So this was orgasm! Wonderful! Wonderful! "Come, damn you, Devlin!" she cried out. "I want us together this first time!"

"Ready?"

"Go!" she almost shrieked.

He did, and for a brief time it seemed as if it would go on forever for both of them. But at last he collapsed atop her. They were both gasping for breath. Then slowly he pulled himself off of her. "You all right?" he asked, his tone faintly concerned.

"I will never be all right again," Emily said. "That was incredible!" She pushed herself up. "God, what must my ancestors have thought of us?" And she laughed softly, gazing at three portraits on the parlor wall.

"I suspect the arm of this sofa has been used in the past for such sport, angel face," he told her. "Those Victorians were very lusty people, despite their protestations otherwise. Well, if I wasn't hungry before I sure as hell am now," he said.

"Me too," she admitted. "Give me a few minutes for a quick cleanup, and you might want to get rid of that," Emily said, pointing to the full condom on his penis.

"Agreed," he said with a faint smile. "You do bring out the best in me, angel face."

"You're just a horny fellow, Devlin," she told him, and then hurried off.

Fifteen minutes later they were tucked into his Healy and pulling out of her driveway. The porch light had been left on for their return. Following her directions he piloted them onto a lovely two-lane country road that ran along an expanse of blue water that was Egret Pointe Bay. The yellow-green May foliage was lush along one side of the road. He noted osprey platforms with nests already inhabited with tenants. It was lovely country, and he wondered if he could find a summer rental in Egret Pointe. It seemed a quieter place than Montauk was going to prove come summer.

They spoke very little as he drove. He wasn't sure what the protocol was for an editor who had spent the entire day fucking his author. And how quickly Emily was learning. She had understood his subtle prompts in that semibondage scene that they had just played out in the elegant little parlor of her house. He was intrigued with and fascinated by her. The thought of spending summer weekends working with her caused his cock to twitch. He forced his thoughts to something less volatile.

"Better start slowing down," she suggested. "East Harbor Inn is on our right just around the next bend, Devlin. Parking lot is on the edge of the road."

The Healy banked around the curve and swung into the parking area. He got out and hurried around the low-slung sports car to open the door for her. East Harbor Inn was charming, very Colonial, with touches of Laura Ashley. The dining room had beamed ceilings, and lots of candles, from those in the pewter chandeliers hanging from the beams to those on the tables. To Emily's relief it was not crowded, and she didn't recognize anyone from Egret Pointe. So far, so good.

"Not busy tonight?" she said to the waiter who came to take their order.

"Heavy bookings late," he said. "First performance of the spring musical at the Egret Pointe Playhouse. We'll be crowded after ten thirty. May I suggest the lobster? They just came off the trawler at our dock in midafternoon."

They ordered. Devlin wanted raw oysters as a starter, and then the lobster and the baby field greens. Emily ordered a fruit compote with a miniscoop of homemade strawberry sherbert, a spinach-and-cheese ravioli, and salad. The waiter suggested a Lenz Blanc de Noir, and Devlin ordered a bottle. The service was leisurely, but they were never left waiting long between courses. When the dessert menu came they both ordered the homemade crème brûlée and coffee.

"If it were July I'd get the plum cake," Emily said. "It's outrageous. They make it only when the plums are fresh from one of the local farms."

"I'll have to try it then," he said. "I've been wondering, Emily, if you know of a summer rental around here. I was planning to go to Montauk, but Egret Pointe is more my style. Quiet. No faux celebrities, and no bother of getting through the Hamptons just to get there."

"Won't you be coming to me on the weekends?" she asked him.

"I'm taking most of August off," he said. "You've been making a very concerted effort all weekend not to be seen with me, and you're not going to be able to keep that up for too long. An editor coming on the weekends to work with you is one thing, and we can probably get away with that reasonable explanation even when one of your neighbors finally notices the Healy in your drive every weekend. But if I spend several weeks with you, your reputation is going to be compromised, angel face."

"I'll ask Rina," Emily replied. "She knows everything."

And Rina did. She came up with the perfect solution as she and Emily sat talking over coffee on Monday morning. "Aaron and Kirk's cottage," she said, reaching for a jelly stick. "The boys are going to Italy in August. They've rented a place in Tuscany for a couple of weeks on a friend's recommendation. And Aaron wants to go to Capri for a few days. Kirk says it's a zoo in August, but you know how he indulges my brother's little whims. I'll call Aaron today, and then he can call Mr. Hot Stuff. They can make their own arrangements. And speaking of your editor, when is he coming again?"

"He's coming every weekend for the time being. Not next weekend, though. It's the long one, and he's flying to London to check up on his tenant. He has a house there, and he's let it out to an American for a year," Emily explained.

"Will you miss the sex?" Rina asked frankly. "Oh, Sam says you dodged the bullet this time, but to be careful, and start on the pill."

"I won't have time to miss anything," Emily told her friend. "I have to start writing. Today. And please thank Dr. Sam for me." She leaned over and hugged the older woman. "And thank you for not telling me what an idiot I am."

"The grans never said a thing to you?" Rina was surprised. Katya Shanski was, of course, a reserved woman, but Emily O hadn't seemed like that at all.

"Sex was definitely taboo in both houses. I think they were still trying to get past the fact that their kids had sex once, and I was the result. They were both pushing fifty when I was born, and the grandfathers were over fifty. It had been a bad year too. Joe's big brother had been killed in 'Nam, and Grandpa Frank went into a decline that killed him before I was three. I don't even remember him."

"Yeah, Frank Shanski really loved his older son. Nothing Joe did after that pleased him either. I remember Frank was always saying, 'Well, Frankie would have done it better, or faster,' or whatever. The truth was, Frankie was a big dumb jock, and it was Joe who had all the brains. Water under the bridge." Rina sighed. "So how did you learn what little you knew about sex?"

"We had to take a health ed class in high school," Emily said. "I found it embarrassing. I just learned what I needed to pass the course, and then forgot it."

"You weren't curious beyond that?" Rina was amazed. It had been all she could do to keep her kids from asking and reading about sex. And doing a little hands on investigation as well.

Emily shook her head. "I was afraid of being like Katy and Joe and disappointing the grans," she admitted.

"Well," Rina said with a sigh, "they did a wonderful job raising you, even if they weren't perfect. And Michael Devlin must be one hell of of a lover, sweetie. I've never seen you glow like you are right now."

"Rina," Emily said slowly, "what if I fall in love with him?" Rina shrugged. "Then you do," she said fatalistically. "What's the worst that could happen? You end up with a broken heart. Hearts mend. Trust me. I know."

"I don't think I could have sex with him if I didn't like him. And, Rina, I really do like him so much," Emily said softly.

"Don't let him know that, sweetie. The second you go all mushy on a guy like your Mr. Devlin, he'll panic, bolt and run. He's a wily bachelor, a ladies' man. Only if he tells you that he likes you first can you suggest that the feeling might—just might—possibly be mutual," Rina advised.

Emily went home. She climbed up into the widow's walk of the house, where she had her office and library. She used a computer as a word processor, but wasn't connected to the Internet. Now she sat in front of the large flat-paneled screen and stared. Finally, knowing that the only way to start a novel was to put her fingers on the keyboard of her PC and write, she did so. She centered the title: *The Defiant Duchess*. Then she scrolled down and typed out on the lower left side of her paper, *A novel by Emilie Shann, c/o Aaron Fischer, Browne and Fischer, 500A Park Avenue, New York City 10022. (212) 477-1548, AF@BrowneFischer.com.* She went to the next page. *Prologue.* And then she began the backstory of how Caroline, Duchess of Malincourt, became Lavender, a daring woman who rescued the oppressed from the Reign of Terror in Revolutionary France. It was dark before she had finished.

For the entire week and into the first official weekend of the summer, Emily worked. Essie, her housekeeper, saw that she was fed, and even left food in the freezer for the weekend. To her annoyance Devlin called only twice: on Monday morning to thank her for the weekend, and on Thursday to tell her he was off to England and would give her a ring on Tuesday when he was back in the office. He told her to thank Rina for her suggestion: He had rented Aaron and Kirk's cottage August through Labor Day, when they would be away in Italy.

"Don't you want to know what I'm doing?" she asked him Thursday.

"Working that cute little butt off on your book, I hope," he said.

"I'm in bikini panties, and a lace bra," she said teasingly. "The ones you made me take off last Saturday before we went out to eat. Remember?"

"Umm, I have a faint recollection," he admitted. "Pull the panties down, Emily." They were on his cell, and he felt safe speaking with her this way.

"Why?" she asked softly.

"Because I want you to play with that naughty little clit of yours, and tell me exactly what you are doing and how it feels," he said in a husky voice.

"I've got them off, Devlin," she murmured low. "I'm brushing my right hand over my pubic curls. It's almost, but not quite, as if you were here."

"Touch yourself," he told her. "Tell me which finger you're using."

"The middle finger. Ohh, I'm getting wet already, Devlin. I wish it were your tongue there. Ohh. Ohhh, that is so nice. Are you getting a hard-on?"

"Yes," he admitted.

"And I'm not there to soothe it away," she murmured. "Will you teach me to suck your cock next time, Devlin? Ohhhhh. Ummmm. That feels soooo good. Not quite as good as your tongue, but it will do for now."

He groaned. "When I get my hands on you, Emily, you will regret teasing me like this," he threatened.

"I've taken my bra off, Devlin. I'm totally naked up here in my office. I'm cupping my tits in my hands, and the nipples are all puckered because I'm imagining you sucking on them."

"Put your hands back on your cunt," he said. "Play with yourself again, Emily. I want you to come. I want you to think about my cock inside of you, thrusting and thrusting, hitting that little spot that sets you afire, making you scream. I'm going to bring you a present from England to help you relax when I'm away from you. There's a shop in London that carries some very wicked sex toys, and I'm going to find a special one just for you, Emily."

"Ummmmmm." She sighed into the telephone as she gave herself a delicious little clitoral orgasm. "Nice, Devlin, but not as nice as you," she told him. "Yes, bring me a toy. I've never had one."

"Good-bye, angel face," he said, and the line went dead.

Irritation had raced through her. She had wanted more dirty talk from him. She hoped his hard-on lasted for half an hour, Emily thought, piqued. And now it was two a.m. Sunday morning, and she missed Devlin. And she missed the unbridled sex that they had enjoyed last weekend. Getting up, she went downstairs to her bedroom and, finding the channel changer, picked it up. She had ordered the Channel for the entire weekend earlier in the day. Because she was a single woman she could get it like that. There was no danger of some young girl flicking it on and finding her fantasy in her face before she was ready for it. Emily hit the correct numbers and clicked enter. She was immediately within the candlelit bedroom.

Yes, it was perfect, she thought, but shouldn't the velvet curtains be green, and not red? And with the thought the curtains and bed hangings were a perfect forest green, with heavy tasseled gold ropes holding them back. She was wearing pants and riding boots, and her cape was wet with the rain outside the windows.

"Oh, m'lady!" The duchess's maid ran into the room. She was a young girl, as opposed to an older, more seasoned woman. "The duke arrived an hour ago. I told him I didn't know if you would be down to dinner, as you weren't feeling well."

"Well-done, Mary!" the duchess replied. "Help me out of these wet garments."

"Was the trip to France successful, m'lady?" Mary asked. She was in on the secret of what her mistress did to aid others, and admired her tremendously for it. Indeed, she helped her mistress with the refugees when they arrived in England, dealing with any servants who might have been rescued with them, comforting the children.

"Indeed it was," her mistress replied. "We rescued the Duchesse d'Almay, her sister, and their children right from under the nose of Madame la Guillotine. Monsieur Robespierre will have some explaining to do to his citizens committee." She laughed as she pulled off her boots and wet stockings.

"I have a hot bath ready for you, m'lady," Mary said. "You're always punctual, even when the roads are bad."

The duchess removed her garments and climbed into the tub that her maid had set up before the fire in her bedchamber. She was no sooner ensconced than the door to the room opened and the duke walked in, lifting his quizzing glass to gaze at her curiously.

"Mary said you were not feeling up to par, madam, yet I find you in your bath," Justin Trahern remarked, his green eyes flicking over her lazily.

"I have been quite fatigued most of the week, milord," the duchess answered him. "But it does not prevent me from keeping myself clean. Actually, I shall feel better for a bath, and may even join you for dinner. How are things in London?"

"Dull," he replied, and then he feigned a yawn. "We might have dinner here in your chambers, madam. I should not like to tax your strength. Is there a chance you might be breeding? Malincourt could use an heir, as I have none."

"That is not entirely so," the duchess replied. "There is your sister's son."

"He will not do," the duke told her. "Mary! That is your name, isn't it?"

"Yes, milord," Mary said, bobbing a curtsy.

"Go and tell Cook her ladyship and I shall dine here. But not for an hour. No one is to disturb us until then. Do you understand, Mary?"

"Yes, milord," Mary said, blushing to the roots of her yellow hair. Then she turned and ran out of the room.

"Really, Trahern, that was not particularly subtle," the duchess said.

"I am not of a mind to be subtle, madam. The most delicious women in London have been importuning me, yet I want no woman but my wife. I am forced to return home to Malincourt. A shocking state of affairs, madam, wouldn't you agree?" He removed his bottle-green linen tailcoat and laid it aside. He undid his wide white cravat and laid it atop the coat. Then he slowly undid his frilled shirt and set it with the coat and cravat. Sitting down, he pulled off his beautifully polished riding boots, then stood again.

"Trahern, what are you about?" the duchess demanded of her husband.

"I mean to fuck you, my dear," he answered pleasantly, undoing his tight riding breeches, pulling them down and off along with his drawers. "I am not ready to keep a mistress yet, and you have not given me an heir. Once you have produced two sons, Caro, I shall leave you to your own devices, if that is what you wish. Until then I will curtail my own social life, devoting myself to you and the production of our nursery.

"I know why your father married you to my late uncle. It was to protect you and your fortune from his own impecunious brother. And it was my uncle's wish that I take you for my own wife when he died and I inherited. As there was no other woman in my life I felt suited to be my duchess, I agreed. I waited through a year of mourning, Caro, and we wed. Your first marriage was a celibate one. But this union is not, nor is it meant to be such a marriage. In an effort to consider your sensibilities I have been patient. I do not mean to be patient any longer. Now, get out of that tub, madam!"

"I have not denied you your rights, milord," the duchess said coolly.

"But neither have you joined into our bed sport with any enthusiasm," he complained to her. "You lie beneath me like a board. Do you feel nothing of passion? Is your heart a stone? Do you even have a heart?"

The duchess arose from her porcelain tub. The water sluiced down her lush body. "I have a heart, milord," she told him. "I am just not ready to fill a nursery. The three years I was married to your uncle I spent nursing him. Then I spent another year mourning him. I was married to you but a month after my mourning ended. We have been wed but six months. You spend much of your time in London. I prefer the country. Am I not entitled to a few months of peace for myself, milord, before I must take on the great responsibility of our family? *And how,* she wondered silently, *can I allow myself to become enceinte when I spend my time traveling back and forth between England and France in order to rescue the innocent?*

"Damn it, Caro, I am in love with you," the duke said. "I always have been, since the day my uncle introduced you to me as his new wife. The old duke knew how I felt. And he also knew that neither of us would ever betray him. We never did. He realized that you would be safe with me after he was gone. That was why he gained our promise to wed then. He wanted you to have a normal life. The kind of life a woman should have. And he wanted me to have you." The duke lifted a large towel from the rack by the fire and, coming close to the duchess, wrapped her in it, lifting her from the water. "It has been almost two years since my uncle died. I want children, and I want them now!" He dried her roughly and then, picking her up, carried her to her bed.

"Trahern!" she protested. "You are behaving like a barbarian."

"I am behaving like a husband who desires his wife," he said through gritted teeth. "Do you dare to refuse me, madam?"

Do I want to write the scene like that? Emily wondered to herself, and then she awakened to find herself in her bed. Should he admit to being in love with her? She glanced at the clock on her bedside table. It was just four a.m. Well, so much for the Channel. She would have to clock in earlier tonight. Yes, the duke should admit to loving his wife. It had to be her passion to revenge herself that kept her from admitting that she was in love with him. Yes, that felt right. Turning over, she punched her pillow and attempted to sleep.

She had slipped out of the Channel just as Trahern was about to make love to his duchess. But for the first time she had not simply been an observer. She had been in the duchess's skin. She had been Caroline Trahern. It had been an interesting experience. It had been exciting, and yet she had not been ready to make love with the duke. It was ridiculous to think as she was, but she felt as if it would have been cheating on Devlin. But the duke looked just like Devlin. And the Channel was a fantasy, not reality, wasn't it? Or was it that she was just a little shy about making love within the confines of the Channel, and then transcribing the experience onto the pages of her book? Yet she certainly could write what she and Devlin had been doing.

He wasn't due back in New York until Tuesday. He wouldn't be in Egret Pointe until Friday night. She had plenty of time to write her first explicit love scene before he wanted to see what she was doing. But no! The story line wouldn't be to that point by Friday night. But perhaps she could show some of the early sexual tension between Caro and Trahern by then. Give Devlin an idea of where she was going with it. And make love with him. Emily hadn't realized that, once she had savored sex with a man she liked, how much more she would want to keep repeating that same experience. But she did.

She missed the feel of his bulk against her in the night. She missed his weight on her, the incredible sensation of his penis inside of her, his mouth exploring her sensitive flesh. Emily shivered. She needed to sleep. She needed to escape her thoughts of their naked bodies against each other. Did all women feel like this with their first affair? She climbed out of her bed and, going into the bathroom, opened the narrow floor-to-ceiling medicine closet to pull out the aspirin bottle. Dumping two of the extra-strength tablets into her hand, she gulped them down with some water. She was obviously too keyed up to sleep. The aspirin would soothe her jangled nerves. Taking two antacid tablets to buffer her stomach against the aspirin, Emily went back to bed, lying on her back, her palms open and flat so the tension in her would drain out.

When she awoke it was almost noon, and the rain was coming down in sheets outside of her bedroom window. It was obviously a day to hole up in bed. But first she needed sustenance. Climbing out of bed she went down to her kitchen. She opened a can of meat ravioli in sauce, dumped it into a grab-it, and nuked it. Essie kept the ravioli for when her grandchildren stopped by. However, comfort food was comfort food. If Emily couldn't have wild sex with Devlin, then ravioli and marshmallow cookies would have to suffice. Putting the bowl on a tray, she rifled through her pantry closet and found the greatest sin of all—something she always hid away for an emergency. She set the double box of Mallomars on the tray, and pulled two small bottles of Pellegrino from her fridge. Napkins. Fork. A little shaker of Parmesan. She carried the tray upstairs.

As she sat in bed consuming the contents of the tray, she wondered if Devlin liked eating in bed. She would serve them an outrageous meal to be eaten here in her bedroom when he came out next weekend. Raw oysters on the half shell, all briny with hot sauce. Lamb chops with asparagus vinaigrette. Fresh local strawberries dipped in dark chocolate, and a bowl of whipped cream for dipping. And they would drink a bottle of Pindar Long Island Spring Splendor, and then make love. *Oh, God!* She was off on that tangent again. How long until the Channel opened up again? Almost eight hours—worse luck. She'd sleep, and when she woke up again she'd consume the other box of Mallomars for supper, along with her other bottle of Pellegrino. It was a plan.

It was still raining hard when Emily awoke again. The light outside of her bedroom windows was gray. Rolling over, she looked at her clock. Just after seven. Less than an hour until the Channel kicked in. Was she brave enough to let the story flow tonight? She would set her mind to the month before Trahern and Caro married. No. That wouldn't do. She could write a scene like that with her eyes closed. She would set the scene for their wedding night. Caro's first sexual encounter with the so- phisticated Trahern. *Yes!* That would allow her a sexual experi- ence to take the edge off of her own lust for Michael Devlin. But would it? Well, she would soon find out, Emily decided.

Trahern looked like her editor. Emily's subconscious had made him so. But there was just the faintest sense of roughness about the duke that wasn't at all like the smooth and elegant Michael Devlin. The duke was very much a man of his own time period, which was as it should be. There was a hint of danger in the green eyes. He was a man who was very comfortable with who and what he was. And he was a man who would have his own way. Emily shivered. But that was as it should be too. She had made all of her previous heroes far more civilized and ur- bane than Trahern was. Trahern was almost a throwback to an- other century. But she liked him, and she knew her readers would fall in love with him to a woman. Bad boys were always far more interesting than good men. Michael Devlin certainly was, she thought with a little grin as she finished consuming the second narrow container of Mallomars. They were half the size

Mallomars used to be, she thought, annoyed. But then, she had to suffer only half the guilt because of it.

Emily got up and took the tray downstairs, rinsed the grab-it, and stuck it in the dishwasher. She dumped the evidence of her Mallomar consumption in the garbage, and recycled the two green bottles. Then, returning upstairs, she took a lavish bubble bath, pulled on a clean sleep shirt, and, grabbing the channel changer as the upstairs hall clock struck eight o'clock, she turned on the television. Almost at once she saw a gray stone country church. The scenery about the church proclaimed it full high autumn. The oak and the ash trees were gold and red. The ducal coach drew up before the church. A footman jumped from his perch and hurried to open the door on the right side of the vehicle and let down the steps. Then he handed out Caro Trahern.

She was dressed in a gown of pale blue watered silk. The full skirt had a pleated hemline that hung just off the ground. The fitted bodice and skirt formed a single garment. While the neckline was low, the bride wore a delicate lace fichu that was fastened in front with a beautiful brooch of pearls and gold. The sleeves of the dress were fitted to the elbow, and from them hung the same delicate lace as the fichu. Her shoes were flat-heeled and embroidered with rounded toes. On her head she wore a broad-brimmed hat trimmed in lace and ribbons. And in her hand she carried a posy of rosebuds and lavender tied with matching blue ribbons and lace.

Emily reached out and pressed the enter button on the channel changer as the duchess began to walk into the small church. Music swelled from the small organ that was being vigorously pumped by a rather beefy lad she recognized as the blacksmith's son. Once again she had put herself into the skin of her heroine. The duke awaited her inside the church vestibule. Their eyes met. She took his arm, and together they traversed the center aisle of the little church to where the Reverend Mr. Playfair awaited them. The congregation, Emily noted, was made up of villagers and servants. Caro's second marriage would not be a grand affair, given the fact that she had been widowed for only thirteen months. The ceremony was the simple Anglican one, and over quickly. The bridal couple traversed the aisle.

Outside the Duke and Duchess of Malincourt greeted their villagers, who cheered them off as the open coach awaiting them took them back to Malincourt Hall. The day was so beautiful that Emily felt her eyes fill with tears. Her new husband noticed, said nothing, but put his hand on hers. She looked at him and smiled a weak smile.

"What are you thinking?" he finally asked her.

"Of the day I wed your uncle at St. George's in London," the duchess answered him. "It was June, and the king and queen came. My father hadn't even given me a season, but he and your uncle insisted upon a grand society wedding. They were making a very strong public statement so that my uncle Richard would have no basis for a claim on my inheritance. Of course, I didn't know then that my father intended to kill himself. Your uncle Godric was very good to me, Trahern. But I think if I am to be honest with you, I must say I prefer this wedding day to the other. I am not a woman for show."

"I hope you also prefer this groom to the other," he replied. "And tonight you will have a true wedding night. Something you did not have with my uncle, I know."

The duchess blushed prettily. "Sir, you are too bold," she half whispered.

He leaned over and murmured in her ear, "Surely you know how much I want to make love to you, Caro, my darling. I know you are an innocent, and I shall be patient and gentle. But come tomorrow morning you will be a woman in every sense of the word. I am not my uncle Godric. I am a man in the full flush of his manhood. I desire you very much, Caro. I only hope you desire me too." He kissed her ear softly.

Her cheeks felt very warm. "I have no knowledge of what

you expect of me, sir. I would not have you disappointed, but in matters of the heart I am lacking in education."

"And it will be my supreme pleasure to educate you, my darling," he told her.

She could not stop blushing, and was quite relieved to reach the house. There a light repast had been set out for them in the magnificent dining room. They ate in silence, and when they had finished repaired to the family salon. It was late afternoon. The servants had seen to the fires, and the room was comfortable.

"Why do you not repair to your chamber and take a little nap?" the duke suggested. "I am going to read. I will join you later."

She stood up quickly and curtsied, saying, "The day has been fatiguing, milord. I shall take your good advice."

"It will probably be one of the few times you do, Caro," he replied, a twinkle in his eye. Then he chuckled at her expression of surprise. "Run along, my dear."

Well, Emily thought as the duchess hurried upstairs to her bedchamber, *you are turning out to be an interesting man. My duchess will have to be very clever to avoid her husband discovering what mischief she has been up to for almost three years.* Poor Godric had never known, but then he was old and sick, and only wanted his comforts. As long as he had them, and Caro visited him when home from London, which was where she always claimed she had been, Godric Trahern was contented. He had married her to protect her, and she certainly had never realized that he would see to her future when he was gone. But he had, arranging first with his nephew and heir, and then with her, that she would marry Justin Trahern after a single year of mourning.

"No longer, Caroline," he had said. "You are a very wealthy woman in your own right, and your father did not want you taken advantage of; nor do I. You know little of the world, my dear. You must be protected."

Yes, her first duke had been a good man.

Emily shifted her mind-set back to the duchess, who reaching her own chamber, had her maid, Nancy, help her to disrobe. Bathing in a basin of perfumed water, she let the young girl help her into a delicate pale peach silk negligee.

"I shall not need you again tonight, Nancy," she said as she lay down to rest. When the duchess was once again aware of herself, the sky outside of her bedchamber window was dark. She heard the door connecting her room with the duke's open, and she turned over to see him in the light from the fireplace.

"Do not get up," he said quietly. "I have come to join you, Caro."

The duchess swallowed hard. Of course, this husband would want to claim his connubial rights as soon as possible, and it was their wedding night. "You will have to lead me, sir. As I have previously told you, my experience is nil." She saw in the firelight that he was wearing a red paisley silk robe, but she suspected that beneath was naught.

"Under the circumstances of your first marriage I would not expect you to have had any experience, my dear. I know you are a virgin. My uncle assured me of it before he died." He slid beneath the coverlet next to her. "There are many men in my position who would take from you what they believed was their due without so much as a by-your-leave. But I have found a woman who enjoys the act of copulation is a far better partner in bed sport." He pressed her gently back among the pillows and touched her lips with his. "Tonight I will make love to you slowly and with great care, Caro. And tomorrow night I will begin to teach you how to respond in kind." He kissed her gently again, his tongue tracing the outline of her mouth.

"Oh!" the duchess murmured softly.

He raised himself up, balancing upon an elbow, and carefully undid the ribbons at the neckline of her negligee. The garments opened to reveal her snowy-white bosom. The duke's dark head bent, and he began to kiss the flawless flesh. His free hand pushed the fabric aside further, his mouth closing over a perfect little pink nipple. His tongue licked. His teeth carefully worried the sensitive nipple.

She could sense it all, Emily realized, delighted. She felt everything her duchess was supposed to be feeling: a tiny, almost imperceptible tingle between her legs, a longing she had not understood before. Her arms wrapped about the duke. "Oh, Trahern," she murmured in his ear. "What is this magic you are making with me?"

In answer he ripped the delicate silk of her negligee open so he might have total access to her lovely body. A hand cupped her breast. He nuzzled it, and kissed the sharply pointed nipple. "I adore you, Caro!" he murmured against her ear. "I only want to give you pleasure, and more pleasure."

She found her hands fumbling with the tie about his robe. "Take it off, Trahern," she begged him. "I find your kisses and caresses have made me curious for more. For everything! Hurry, milord!"

He untangled himself from her briefly in order to shrug the robe from his muscular body. And while he did Caro pulled the shreds of her negligee from her own body and threw them carelessly on the floor. Then, gathering her into his arms, he began to kiss her until her head was spinning. "Do you know what I am going to do to you, my adorable bride?" he asked her low.

"You are going to fuck me," she whispered back. "And I want you to, Trahern! Oh, how very much I want you to fuck me!"

But he was true to his intent. He began to kiss every inch of her body available to him. He turned her this way and the next, his lips caressing, his tongue licking her flesh until she was afire. She gasped when his finger invaded her body, a tiny bit of fear touching her nerves, but he sensed her anxiety, and soothed her even as a second finger joined the first, and he began to move them back and forth.

She was burning with a desire she had never known existed.

"Oh!" she cried. "Oh!" as the fingers slipped from her, and the tip of one of them touched the rosebud hidden between the folds of her nether lips. The fingertip worried the sensitive little nub until she was almost weeping with the burning hunger she felt.

He mounted her naked body, his big hands first pushing her milky thighs open, then guiding his lover's lance into her body. Her virginity quickly gave way, and he rode her fiercely. His big cock flashed back and forth within her, and her low moans grew in intensity until she was almost screaming with the pleasure he was giving her. Then, just as the world exploded around her, the duke bent low and whispered in her ear, "I promised you, Emily, that we would begin a grand adventure, and we now assuredly have, my darling."

Her orgasm came in hard, hot bursts even as her eyes flew open and widened at his words. "Trahern!" she cried, and then fell into unconsciousness as his own lust spurted forth in the great jets of his love juices. And when she opened her eyes again she was in her own bed. The dawn was beginning to break outside of her windows, and the screen of the television was blank with snow.

Emily Shanski lay quietly on her back. Her sleep shirt was up to her waist, and she was sticky and wet between her thighs. *My God!* What had happened to her? She had slipped into the duchess Caro's skin, or so she thought. But the duke had known that she was there. And in that moment of perfect pleasure he had told her so by addressing her by name. Briefly she was frightened. Perhaps it was not such a good idea to interact with her characters. But she had to admit that she felt more relaxed now than she had when she had turned on the Channel eight hours previously. Her sexual tension had completely vanished.

Emily climbed out of her bed and, barefooted, hurried out into the hall and up the stairs into her office. She had to get the scene she had just played out with the duke down on paper before it faded. With luck she could have the story line right up to that scene before Devlin arrived Friday night. Would he be pleased with her? God, she hoped so! Her career was the one thing in the world now that meant everything to her. If she had to write explicitly sexy love scenes to save it, then she was going to learn how to do it. And now, Emily realized, she had two lovers to learn her craft from.

She turned on her PC, and sat down. Two lovers. Of course, Devlin was going to take full credit for her metamorphosis, she chuckled to herself. Well, let him. The Channel was something special that belonged only to women. Men didn't have to know about it. At least, that was what Rina had told her when she had introduced Emily to it. It was a delicious and dirty little secret, and while Emily had enjoyed being an observer as she imagined her novels in order to make certain they were believable, she had to admit that being an active part of the fantasy was even more fun. And for the first time in her life Emily decided that she wanted to have fun. She began to write, and it wasn't until four hours later that she came down from her aerie.

The day was as clear and warm as the previous had been rainy and chill. She was hungry, and decided to fix herself a Sunday style breakfast even if it was Monday. Rina and Sam were coming by to take her to the Memorial Day parade, and then they were all going out to the club for lunch. French toast! That was what she wanted. French toast with lots of butter and syrup and sausages. She had begun to pull the ingredients together when the phone rang. Answering it, Emily heard Devlin's voice, and her heart beat just a little faster.

"I took the red-eye home. London was lonely. I think I needed you with me," he told her. "How about if I take Friday off and come out Thursday night, angel face?"

"Only if you'll eat lamb chops and asparagus in bed with me," she said with a happy smile. "And local strawberries. I dip them in dark chocolate laced with Grand Marnier. And we'll have a bowl of whipped cream."

"I won't promise to confine the whipped cream to the strawberries," he told her.

"Where do you want to put it?" she asked. She could almost hear his grin.

"All over you, and then I'll slowly lick it off," he said.

"Come early," she told him.

"I will." He chuckled, and then he rang off.

Reality was better, Emily decided happily as she turned her sausages in the frying pan. He had missed her. Well, she had sure as hell missed him too.

CHAPTER FIVE

T he Tuesday-morning editorial meeting at Stratford Publishing was coming to a close. At one end of the conference table Martin Stratford sat considering, as he swirled the remaining coffee at the bottom of his cup, just how many of these meetings he had attended over the last forty years. He was anxious to get to his summer home on the North Fork of Eastern Long Island. It was mid-July, and the city was untenable. At the other end of the table his company's president, J. P. Woods, sat looking as cool and unruffled as she always did. Martin considered for a moment whether J.P. ever broke a sweat. There was never a hair out of place on the damned woman, but she knew how to run a publishing house. He'd give her that. Still, she wasn't the best-liked person in their industry, which was why he was considering someone else to sit in his chair next year.

"Devlin!" J.P.'s voice grated on her employer's ear. "What about Emilie Shann? How is her book coming? Are we going to have another three hundred and fifty pages of treacle? Or is she finally letting her heroine get screwed?"

Martin Stratford raised an eyebrow at J.P.'s crudeness. "Language, J.P.," he said in a warning tone.

"The book is coming along very well, J.P.," Michael Devlin answered coolly.

"You've seen it? Is it going to be on time? Or is Miss Prim and Proper going to be late, and have the vapors because she has to write about sex?"

Some of the young editors about the table giggled.

"Has Emilie Shann ever been late with her work, J.P.?" Devlin asked softly.

"You've seen the book? Read some of what she's written?" J.P. persisted.

"I've been in Egret Pointe every weekend all summer," he replied. "And I've rented Aaron Fischer's cottage for August. Trust me, J.P. The book is going to be good, and the heroine is going to be sexually satisfied. And we will increase her readership quite substantially for us all, with the right promotion and advertising."

"Miss Prim and Proper can sell on her name," J.P. said.

"Martin?" Devlin turned to the company head. "We've asked Emily to change her style and inject more sex into her book. We need advertising and promotion to acknowledge that change in order to attract new readers. Sales need to reflect that change when they head out to sell *The Defiant Duchess*."

"She already has a readership, Devlin," J.P. said.

"You asked her to make this change to increase her readership. Secondhand sales put nothing in our pocket, J.P., nor in Emily's royalty statements to reduce her advance. This book has to be heavily promoted first with the distributors and chains, and then with the readers. May I remind you it's the last book on her current contract? This book is going to be very big, J.P. And if we don't have Emily tied up tightly for another few books, someone is going to sign her right out from under our noses. Aaron Fischer isn't a fool. Or maybe you're looking to get into a bidding war for the author who is responsible for at least a quarter of this company's revenues."

"It's that good?" Martin Stratford turned to look at the man on his right.

"It's that good, Martin," Michael Devlin assured him. "It's the best work she's done yet. She's stretching herself, and even I'm surprised at the depth and scope of this book. The readers are going to love it. And so will our bottom line."

"Then," Martin Stratford said, "we'll take your advice, and promote. Right, J.P.?"

"If you say so, Martin," J.P. answered him. She shot Michael Devlin a hard look. "You have to go to London before your vacation, Devlin. Prunella is having difficulties with Savannah Banning. I think she misses having you near her to keep her inspired," J.P. said with a double meaning intended to insult him."

"Lady Palmer does not need me for inspiration. She has her husband. I am not going to London. I will call Prunella and learn what she has to say, and then I will speak with Lady Palmer."

"If I say you have to go to London, Devlin, you will go," J. P. Woods snapped.

Around the table the young editors were shifting nervously in their seats and trying to avoid eye contact with one another. The tension between their editor in chief, who was a good guy, and the company president who scared the hell out of them, was well-known. But until this moment they had never seen it so palpably.

"I think this meeting is over now," Martin Stratford said quietly. "Run along, people. J.P., Devlin. Stay!"

"You bastard!" J.P. hissed furiously at her antagonist. "How dare you embarrass me like that in front of staff?"

"Listen to me, you little bitch," Michael Devlin said angrily. "Don't you dare imply that I slept with Savannah Banning. For openers it isn't true, and you not only slander Lady Palmer and her husband, you slander me. Shoot your mouth off like that, and Stratford could be in for a lawsuit. And why the hell are you gunning for Emily Shanski? What did that woman ever do to you? She's important to this company."

"Children, children," Martin Stratford said in a deceptively mild tone. "Play nice. Mick is right, Jane Patricia. You started it. It ends now! And Mick, I am well aware of Emily's value to Stratford. I've always taken care of her, and she has always taken care of us. She isn't going anywhere. Do you both understand me?"

"Thanks, Martin," Michael Devlin said, the fires of his anger easing.

"I'm not so stupid as to sabotage our writers," J. P. Woods muttered.

Devlin crooked an eyebrow, but said nothing.

"I would ask you two to kiss and make up," Martin Stratford said with some humor, "but I've succeeded in this business by never asking the impossible of my employees. Mick, if you can straighten out Prunella and Savannah Banning by phone that's fine with me. Do it. I know you only travel first-class, and if I'm going to be spending my money to properly promote *The Defiant Duchess* then I have to save where I can," he said with a small smile. "Now, is it safe to leave the pair of you alone? I would like to get out to Orient in time for a late lunch. I've never been to Egret Pointe, Mick. What is it like?"

"New Englandy," Michael Devlin answered. "Charming little village, lovely, gracious homes. And the inn at East Harbor has a delightful restaurant. Aaron and Kirk's cottage looks like something out of the Devon countryside. I'm looking forward to August, even though it will be a working vacation."

"The book really is good?" J. P. Woods said.

"It's really good," Michael Devlin answered her.

"I'll look forward to reading it," J.P. responded. "I didn't think she could do it. She always struck me as overly genteel and prudish. I mean, she's in her thirties, unmarried, raised by two old ladies. What the hell could she know about the down and dirty? She was so tight with Rachel I often wondered if she wasn't a lesbian."

Michael Devlin laughed aloud. He couldn't help it. "Haven't you ever heard that old saying about still waters running deep?" he asked her. *My God!* If she only knew how wild and passionate Emily Shanski was. His dick twitched, and he struggled to keep himself cool and under control. He couldn't think about Emily without wanting her.

"Old sayings are usually nothing more than old sayings," J.P. replied.

"Not always," Martin Stratford murmured, looking at Michael Devlin curiously from over the top of his reading glasses. *Mick, Mick, what are you up to?* he wondered to himself. Was one of the best editors he knew getting involved with a writer? No. Mick was more professional than that. He would never do that. Would he? "If you two can refrain from killing each other," he said, "I'm going to head out to the Island now. Mick, keep me informed about the Lady Palmer problem. You have the number out there, or my assistant can give it to you." He stood up, and with a quick smile at them was out the door.

"The company is mine," J.P. said. "I've worked for it, and I'm not letting you come back from London and take it out from under me. Do you understand, Mick?"

"Don't get your knickers in a twist, J.P.," Michael Devlin told her. "I don't want the company. I'm an editor. A damned good editor. And that's what I want to keep doing. There will always be a job for me. Even in this corporate climate, J.P."

"I don't wear knickers," J. P. Woods said.

Michael Devlin laughed. "Why am I not surprised?"

"You really don't want Stratford?" She sounded almost anxious.

He sighed. "No, I don't. But don't tell Martin. Let him play out his little game with us, and believe that he really did make the choice all by himself. If you can't work with me I can go back to London and Random House. They never get tired of offering."

"It would be easier if you stayed," she admitted. "I know I'm not the most beloved person in this business. Besides, I can't afford to lose the editor who got Miss Prim and Proper to write sexy. How did you do it?"

"Trade secret, J.P., but maybe I will tell you one day." He couldn't laugh. He couldn't give himself away. Not now. And he couldn't hurt Emily or put her in a difficult position. "Look, I'm good at what I do. There's really nothing more to it than that. I've always been good with writers. It's an empathy thing. Look how I got Lady Palmer to get her manuscripts in on time when no one else had been able to do that."

"How *did* you do it?" J.P. wanted to know.

"Savannah's brain is usually cluttered with her stories. I showed her how to organize her time better. No magic. No smoke and mirrors. Every editor she had had before me was in awe of her. They let her get away with murder. I didn't. And as soon as we understood each other, it all fell into place," he explained. "Writers are human, J.P. But they need a little more cosseting in most cases than normal people."

"Do you cosset Emilie Shann?" J.P. asked slyly.

"As a matter of fact, she cossets me. She's a terrific cook. I'm going to miss my weekends just because of her cooking," he said. "I've had to work out harder at the gym after our working weekends." He chuckled. Information for J.P. to chew on, but safe information. It retained Emily's nonthreatening image in J.P.'s mind.

"Of course she would cook," J.P. said acidly. "Does she do trifle?"

"Trifle to die for, and her crème brûlée is incredible," he answered.

"Jesus, don't say another word!" J.P. exclaimed. "I'm going to throw up." She looked at her watch. "Crap! I've got a distributor coming in shortly." She turned sharply, and was quickly gone from the conference room without another word to him.

Well, that was interesting, Devlin thought, and he headed for his office.

"Savannah Banning is on the line from England," his secretary said. "She's in high dudgeon, Mick. She insisted on holding until you came out of your meeting."

"How long?"

"Close to five minutes now," the secretary said.

"I don't want to be disturbed," he told her, and shut the door of his office behind him, then picked up the phone. "Savannah! How are you? I understand we have a spot of difficulty. How can I help you?"

"You can help me by getting your Irish arse back to old Blighty, damn it!" Savannah exploded. "That woman is an idiot, Mick! She doesn't understand me at all!"

"I'm not coming back to England, Savannah," he said quietly.

There was a long silence on the other end of the line, and then Savannah said, "How is Emily?"

"Fine," he answered her. "We're talking about you, Savannah. Prunella just takes a bit of getting used to, sweetie. She's never worked with an American before."

"She wants a detailed outline. She says sales needs it," Savannah wailed.

"I'll call her and explain you don't waste your time with outlines," he said quietly.

"She wants to see pieces of the manuscript," Savannah told him.

"I'll tell her you deliver a completed manuscript, and not bits," Mick responded. "What else?"

"She isn't you!" And Savannah Banning began to cry.

Michael Devlin laughed softly. "I miss you too, sweetie. And I miss old Reg, and the kids, and those great family weekends down in Suffolk. But I suspect I'm back in the Colonies to stay. We're both going to have to get used to it."

"Then Martin is going to put you in charge," Savannah said.

"I hope not," Michael Devlin replied. "I like what I do, and J.P. is really more suited to run a publishing house than I am."

"You could learn," Savannah sniveled.

"I could, but I don't want to," he told her. "I just want to edit my books. I'll make it all right between you and old Pruny, Savannah. Okay?"

"Okay," she agreed. "Now, tell me about you and Emily."

"There's nothing to tell," he lied.

"Bullshit!" Savannah said.

"Lady Palmer!" Michael Devlin exclaimed. "I'm shocked. Shocked."

"I hope you've become lovers, Mick. She such a sweetie, and she needs a good man," Savannah told him.

"Savannah, do not disparage my reputation. I pride myself on being a bad boy, and you know it," he told her. "Remember all my fun miniscandals in London over the past few years. By the by, do the girls miss me?"

"Mick, you are such a silly man sometimes," Savannah remarked. "Was she a virgin? I somehow thought she might be."

"Savannah," he warned. "Remember we're on a company phone. Now if there is nothing else, I'm going to ring off. I'll call Pruny tomorrow. She'll be gone from the office by now with the time change. Say hi to Reg and the children for me. Ta." He put the telephone down while at the same time reaching for his cell and punching in the number one.

"Hello?" Emily's voice came through clear and sweet.

"I miss you," he said.

"It's only been a day, Devlin," she answered him.

"A day and a half," he corrected her. "I drove back late Sunday afternoon. Just another week, and we've got an entire month to ourselves."

"Devlin, I have to work if this book is going to be in on time," she reminded him.

"I want to be inside of you," he murmured. "I sent you that

little toy for times like this. When we aren't together, I want to play phone games with you."

"Devlin!" she pleaded.

"Get it," he said. "I need you!"

"Hold on. I hid it so Essie wouldn't find it," she half whispered.

"I thought you didn't let her in your office," he said.

"I don't, but you never know. Okay, I've got it." Emily was already feeling a twinge of excitement. The sound of his voice on the phone could make her wet.

"Take it out of the box, angel face. Realistic, isn't it?" he teased.

"Looks just like you, Devlin," she teased back.

"What are you wearing?" he asked her.

"Never got out of my sleep shirt this morning," she told him.

"Hold it in your right hand," he instructed her. "Start licking it. And use your left hand to play with yourself. I want you nice and wet, angel face," he told her as he unzipped his slacks and released his penis, which was already partly swollen with just the sound of her voice. He imagined her leaning back in her big leather chair, the sleep shirt hiked to her waist, the softness of her smooth, rounded hips against the black leather.

"Ohh, Devlin, this is so good," Emily whispered into the telephone. "Ummm. Ummm. Ummmmm." She began to suck vigorously on the dildo in her hand. It had been made to duplicate Michael Devlin's long, thick cock in full flagrante. It was made of a natural colored rubber, and spitted on a twisted rod of polished ashwood.

"Are you playing with your clit?" he wanted to know. The sucking noises were driving him wild. He could almost feel her mouth on his penis.

"Are you playing with your dick?" she countered.

"I am so hard you could break it off." He groaned.

"I'm so wet that Mr. Naughty is going to slip right in and go all the way," she replied. "I've got it ready, Devlin. Do you want me to shove it in? Do you?" Her voice was breathy with her excitement.

"Not yet. I want you to want it a little more, angel face," he teased her.

"You're going to come all over your office, Devlin, if you don't stop," she said. "Better let me fuck myself now so you can cool off."

"Bitch!" He groaned. She was right. He reached for his handkerchief to contain the spurts of cum he couldn't contain any longer.

"Ahhhhhh! Oh, God, that feels good!" She thrust the dildo back and forth in her vagina until, with a long exhalation of a sigh, she came. "But it's not as good as the real thing, Devlin, is it?" she complained. "I miss you too."

"I talked with Lady P today. She sends kisses," he told her.

"I'll e-mail her later," Emily responded. "And as lovely as this interlude was, I think we both have to get back to work, Devlin."

"Yeah." He sighed. "I've got a lunch date with some sexy new author."

"Think of me when you're with her," Emily told him.

"That's the problem. If I think of you I'll get a hard-on. We wouldn't want another woman getting the wrong idea, now, angel face, would we?"

Emily laughed. "Good-bye, Devlin," she said as she hung up the phone. She hadn't answered his question. She couldn't. But the truth was, she didn't want him with any other woman. Almost eleven weeks ago Michael Devlin had walked into her life. She had lost her virginity and fallen in love for the first time. What an idiot she was. She was in love with a man who owned a house in London, and had women with titles fighting over him. "You have finally gone around the bend, Emily," she said aloud.

She had seduced him in order to experience sex so she could write the kind of novel Stratford wanted her to write now. She had blackmailed him into becoming her lover, and teaching her all those wonderful, delicious, and sensual things she needed to know. He thought of her as business, and nothing more. Oh, pleasant business, to be sure—for both of them, if she were being honest with herself. But she had no business falling in love with a man like Michael Devlin. He was going to break her heart. But until then she was going to enjoy every minute of her time with him. Autumn was coming. The book would be finished by November, the way she was writing. And then it would be over.

Emily started to cry. She didn't want it to be over. She wanted it to go on forever and ever. Her heroines got happy endings. Why couldn't she have a happy ending? Her intercom buzzed. Emily struggled to compose herself. "Yes, Essie, what is it?"

"Rina's here. She says you were to have lunch. You didn't tell me you were having company. I was doing your grandma's silver," Essie grumbled.

"We're going out, Essie. That's why I didn't tell you to fix lunch," Emily replied. "Tell Rina I'll be down in five minutes."

"Oh, that's okay then," Essie said, and the intercom went dead.

Emily sat for a long moment. Then, realizing the dildo was lying on her desk and her sleep shirt was up around her waist, she began to giggle helplessly. Good thing Rina hadn't come up, she thought, and found her with her legs spread open on her antique desk, fucking herself while she talked dirty on the phone with her editor. She wiped the dildo down with water from her water pitcher, and replaced it in the cream-and-gold silk box it had come in before putting it back in her bottom desk drawer, which she locked. Standing, she pulled her sleep shirt down. Then she hurried downstairs to her bathroom to wash her face and hands, get quickly dressed, and run a brush through her tangled strawberry-blond hair.

"You look cute," Rina noted as Emily came down the stairs. "I like the capris."

"Where are we going?" Emily asked her.

"I thought the club," Rina said. "It's quiet there with so many kids still in camp."

"Essie, I'm going now," Emily called to her housekeeper.

They drove to the Egret Pointe Country Club in Rina's Lexus, parked, and went through the bar to the terrace by the pool, seating themselves beneath an umbrella table. The waiter brought them peach iced tea, took their orders, and disappeared. No one was swimming, and there was only one other couple across the pool at a table. Emily recognized Nora Buckley and her employer, Kyle Barrington.

"He is so dishy," she remarked to Rina.

"Isn't he?" Rina chuckled. "But as was said of Lord Byron, mad, bad, and dangerous to know. At least, that's his reputation. I hear he's broken up one marriage and endangered at least two others. And he seems to do it just for the pure sport of it. He really isn't interested at all in the women he screws. I don't know how Nora manages to work for him, but she says he's a good employer, is nice to her, and hasn't hit on her."

"I think Nora's the nice one," Emily remarked. "And so brave, after everything that happened. She's your neighbor, isn't she?"

Rina nodded. "Yes, and she is nice. Ah, here's lunch."

The waiter set down salad plates, each holding a scoop of chicken salad, potato salad, and cole slaw along with a sliced tomato. The two women ate, and Emily was unable to resist dipping into the breadbasket for a miniature blueberry muffin. Sex always increased her appetite.

Rina chuckled as her companion reached for a second muffin. "The work is going well then," she said.

"Yep." Emily nodded, smearing soft butter on the little muffin and popping it into her mouth. "I would never have thought I could write like this, but I can!"

"And having your handsome editor in your bed every weekend hasn't hurt either," Rina murmured softly. She reached for the last little muffin.

"And I'm using the Channel too," Emily admitted. "I was always an observer before, but now I put myself in the heroine's slippers, Rina. The duke looks just like Devlin, but his personality is quite different."

Rina's brown eyes widened. "You're having sex there too?" she practically whispered. "My God! I thought you looked tired lately, but I put it down to the stress of work, and having to change your style so drastically. Emily, I'm not sure you should be doing what you're doing in the Channel. Oh, I know a lot of women take lovers there because they can't be caught or get STDs or get pregnant. And after a while most women need a bit of a change from their spouses. The Channel offers us our fantasies without any of the guilt we would have in our own reality. But I think you're playing a dangerous game, Emily, honey."

Emily shook her head. "Look, Devlin is doing what he's doing with me to help me over the—you'll forgive the analogy—hump and into a new style. He's my editor. It's his job. But once the book is done it will be over. I'll just have the lovers I take in the Channel. I think he might even go back to London."

"He's in love with you," Rina said quietly.

"No, he isn't!" Emily exclaimed. And she sighed wistfully.

"Sweetie, I could be your mother. I know these things. I recognize the signs. I've seen Michael Devlin with you. I've seen both of you in East Harbor at least twice. Once you were having a cozy luncheon in a corner of the Lobster Trap. Sam and I had been antiquing and were going there for lunch when we saw you. We stayed outside on the terrace so that you wouldn't see us and be embarrassed. It was obvious you just wanted to be with each other. Then we saw you another time at the inn when we went out for the anniversary. Oh, Emily! The way he looks at you. He isn't treating you like an editor with a writer. He's treating you like a man in love. Give him a chance, and you'll see."

"It's nothing more than a business arrangement, Rina. You'll see," Emily said softly, and she blinked back the tears that were threatening to well up in her blue eyes.

Rina smiled and shook her head. "No, you'll see I'm right."

"Dessert menu, ladies?" the waiter asked, coming up beside them.

Rina gave him a jaundiced look.

The waiter grinned and handed them the menus.

"I'll take the key lime pie," Rina said quickly.

"I want the three-berry sorbet," Emily decided. "What kinds today?"

"A scoop each, strawberry, raspberry, and blackberry," the waiter answered.

"Yum! Make it so," Emily told the waiter, who grinned at her *Star Trek* reference, and went off to fetch their desserts.

The couple on the other side of the pool got up and wended their way through the large planters of New Guinea impatiens, petunias, and trailing vinca to stop at their table. Rina and Nora Buckley greeted each other affectionately, while the tall, dark, and handsome Kyle Barrington stood waiting impassively.

"You know Emily Shanski, don't you, Nora?" Rina asked.

"I remember you as a young girl," Nora said, "and I certainly enjoy your books. How is your new one coming along, my dear?"

"Very well, thank you," Emily answered, wondering how Nora Buckley knew she was in the midst of a new book.

"How are the kids?" Rina asked. "I haven't seen you in ages."

"My job keeps me busy," Nora answered. "The kids are fine. Jill starts her last year at Duke Law in a few weeks, and J.J. is going into his junior year at State. And I have terrific news: Margo has finally agreed to marry Taylor. She kept turning him down because she said she didn't want to be widowed again. Turns out he's five years younger than my mother." She laughed.

"Nora."

"Oh, I'm sorry, Mr. Barrington. We really have to go, Rina. Call me. Bye, Emily. Nice to see you again." And then Nora was gone.

"He's even dishier close up," Emily remarked when the couple were out of hearing. "But he's got cold eyes. And he makes me nervous just being around him."

"Mad, bad, and dangerous to know," Rina repeated. "But Nora seems to do well with him, and she loves her job. He's quite the expert on seventeenth- and eighteenth-century English and American furniture, if you ever want anything in the house appraised for insurance purposes," Rina remarked.

"No use insuring antiques if you love them, my grandmother always said. If they're stolen or lost in a fire, money won't bring them back," Emily said.

They ate their dessert, and then Rina drove Emily back to her house. "When do you see Devlin again?" she asked as they drove along the tree-lined road.

"Well, he won't be staying with me in August because he's got Aaron's cottage," Emily replied. "I've got the book pretty much under control now."

"But you don't have yourself under control," Rina said. "Are you in love with him, Emily?"

"Doesn't matter if I am," came the reply.

"I told you that he's in love with you," Rina continued.

"I don't think he is, and I'm not going to embarrass him by declaring myself," Emily told her friend. "My God, Rina, what a wedge that would drive between us. He could never edit me if I went all mushy-gushy on him. And he is a good editor. Best I've ever had. Rachel was good, but Devlin's better, I have to admit."

"There's a lovely hot tub at the cottage out on the back deck," Rina informed Emily. "It's very, very private too." She grinned mischievously at her younger companion. "Sam and I did it there once when the boys weren't home."

"Too much information!" Emily said laughing. "I don't ever want to think of my doctor as having sex with his wife, who's like a second mother to me."

Rina chuckled as she pulled up to Emily's big house. "Hey, I'm not dead yet, kiddo," she told Emily.

"Never said you were, Rina, and never thought it either," Emily responded as she got out of the Lexus. "Thanks for lunch." She hurried into the house.

"Your office phone rang while you were gone," Essie said. "I finished your grandma's silver, and now I'm going home." She went out the door Emily had just entered. "Sounded like your agent."

"I'll check. Thanks," Emily called to her housekeeper's retreating back.

She ran upstairs to find a message from Aaron. She punched in his private number. "What's up?" she asked when he answered.

"Good news! Good news! J. P. Woods called me today. She wants to make us a new offer." His voice was brimming with his delight.

"And you told her . . . ?"

"When I got back from Italy." Aaron chuckled. "I said there wasn't any time to negotiate anything to our mutual satisfaction right now. Your editor must be pleased."

"He seems to be," Emily replied smoothly. "We'll do some work while he's here. And I'll have him hire Essie to keep the place neat. Single straight men can be messy."

"Thank you, my darling. Tell Mick the gardener will be in once a week, so not to be surprised when Tony shows up. I probably won't talk to him before we go."

"When are you going?" she wanted to know.

"Tomorrow night," Aaron said.

"Have fun on Capri," she told him.

Aaron Fischer chuckled. *"Ciao, bella!"* he told her, and rang off.

Emily put down the phone. She had heard from Devlin this morning and Aaron this afternoon. In just a few hours the Channel would be up and running. She had a very passionate scene she wanted her duchess to play out with the duke. He has suddenly discovered her secret absences from Malincourt, and is suspicious. She must lull him into a sense of security, but he will not be soothed. And Caro uses her sexual wiles to distract her husband from learning about her secret life. Yes. Her character of the duchess had grown from a vengeful and determined girl into a powerful woman who would control her own life at any cost. It was up to Justin Trahern to save Caro from herself.

Emily had been going over some rather interesting pictures in one of her sexual research books. It offered a variety of positions she considered downright acrobatic, but some of them were quite conducive to the year 1793. Especially the one using the elegant tapestried wing chair, and another where a small silk cushioned side chair was utilized. The footstool she considered boring and a bit acrobatic. There had also been pictures of threesomes, which fascinated her, but there was no way to fit that kind of play into *The Defiant Duchess*. She giggled. But she would have to consider it for another book. Wouldn't J. P. Woods be surprised!

After their lovely lunch at the club she really wasn't hungry for the supper that Essie had left in the fridge for her to heat up. Instead Emily made herself a bacon-and-tomato sandwich with lots of mayo. Nothing tasted better than bacon and tomato when the tomatoes were in season. She had a basket of them on the kitchen table, courtesy of Essie's garden. She sat eating slowly, sipping her iced tea, waiting for eight o'clock to come so she could get to work. Well, maybe *work* wasn't quite the word she wanted.

The phone rang, and she picked it up. "Hello?"

"Just forty-eight more hours, and I'll be with you again," Michael Devlin's voice purred in her ear. "I miss you much too much, angel face."

"I already talked to you today," Emily teased him.

"Am I to be rationed then?" he demanded to know.

"I'll think about it." she answered.

"Are you working?" he wanted to know. "I can forgive you

if I disturbed the muse, angel face." His voice was warm, and the very sound of it sent ripples of excitement down her spine.

"I just took a break to make a sandwich," she told him. God, she wanted him here! Wanted his strong arms around her, kissing the side of her neck, her shoulder, his breath warm and moist on her skin. She shouldn't love him, but she did.

"Can you spend the weekend at the cottage with me?" he asked her. "I'll stop at Leonardo's in town and pick up a pizza."

"A garbage pizza?" she said. "I can only be bribed for a garbage pizza."

"Your wish is my command, lady," he told her.

"Then I'll bring the salad and a bottle of wine," she promised.

"And your little toy," he said. "I'm going to show you something new on Friday night, okay?" He rubbed himself, because just hearing her voice made him hard. No woman had ever had such a strong effect on him as Emily Shanski did. He didn't want their affair to end. He didn't want any other man fucking her. He wasn't quite ready to commit himself to her entirely, but he wasn't a fool. Michael Devlin knew it was just a matter of time before he asked Emily Shanski to marry him.

"Ohh, are we going to be bad, Devlin?" she teased, her voice suddenly very sexy.

"We are going to be very bad," he promised her. "Good night, angel face. Don't work too hard, okay?"

"I'll have some good stuff for you to read on Friday," she promised.

"Saturday morning," he said. "Friday night is already spoken for, angel face."

The phone clicked off.

Emily smiled happily. Although Devlin would never know it, she loved him, and always would. But just maybe the passion they shared didn't have to end when the book was finished. Yet it was business between them. But did it have to be all business? Could either of them be that cold-blooded? Emily knew she wasn't. Yet how was she ever to find out if there was something there besides a mutual desire to keep their careers? Didn't romance authors get to have a happy ending too? Rina said Devlin was in love with her, but was he? Really? Or was Rina just being a wonderfully romantic fool?

The big tall clock in the front hall began to chime the hour. Emily got up from the table, stuck her plate and glass in the dishwasher, locked her kitchen and front doors for the night, then headed upstairs. Undressing, she slipped on one of her comfortable sleep shirts, washed her face and hands, and brushed her teeth. Climbing into bed, she took up the channel changer and clicked her television set on. She punched in the Channel's number, and when the grand entry hall of the duke's home came into view Emily pushed the enter button firmly.

The duchess was standing in the foyer, shaking the rain from her long cape. She turned, startled, at the sound of his voice.

"Where the hell have you been for the last five days, madam?" Justin Trahern demanded of his wife.

"In London," the duchess answered.

"You detest London, and especially in season," he replied.

"Yes, I do," the duchess said. "But my uncle's valet sent for me. The earl was ill, and he feared for him."

"You detest your uncle too," the duke said.

"*Detest,* milord, is perhaps too strong a word. I neither like nor dislike him. But he is my late father's younger brother. He has no one else but me, and I have an obligation as his blood relation to help him where I can," the duchess said coolly.

"And what illness did he have? Something brought on by too much wine, bad companions, and the riotous living he pursues, I have not a doubt," Justin Trahern sneered. "The man is a lost cause. The title will die with him, for no decent woman will wed him, nor would any decent father give his daughter to Eddis Thornton, despite his ancient title. Not even a rich merchant attempting to vault his family into the nobility with a nubile and well-dowered daughter would have him."

"For which I am very grateful," the duchess replied calmly, "for I mean to have the earldom of Chetwyn for a second son one day, milord. As I am the last of the Thorntons, and you have a good relationship with both the king and the prince, we should be able to manage it once Uncle has drunk himself into his grave."

"So that is why you cosset the man," Justin Trahern remarked with not just a hint of admiration in his voice.

"Yes," the duchess answered in a cold voice.

"Do you give him money?" the duke demanded to know.

"Of course," she said. "God knows I have enough, thanks to my father. His investments in the East India Company paid off quite well. I do not give my uncle a great deal. I pay his valet, his wine bill, and just enough of his gambling debts to allow him to keep gambling."

"Thereby continuing to make him unattractive as husband material, and gently hastening his path to the grave," the duke murmured. "Very clever, my dear. You say you want your family's title for a second son, but we have not even a first son. Or daughter, Caro. And you were not in London, my dear. At least, not at your uncle's."

"How can you possibly know that, milord?" She began to ascend the stairs.

"Because I had you followed," Justin Trahern responded, keeping pace with her. "Do you think I am a fool, Caro? We haven't even been married for a year, and you are always disappearing from Malincourt. You do not take your coach, but ride out alone."

They had reached the top of the stairs, and the duchess almost ran to her rooms.

"Where do you go? Have you a lover? Someone you took when my uncle lay dying?" he wanted to know.

"I think you can have no doubt that I was a virgin when we married," the duchess said coldly. "And I am not a woman to betray her marriage vows. How dare you impugn my honor, milord?" She had reached her chamber door. "Leave me now! I am tired and cold and wet. I wish a hot bath, a tray, and my bed." She looked at him imperiously.

"You may have your hot bath and your tray, madam," he said. "But I will share your bed tonight, for I have lacked your company for many nights."

"You are intolerable!" the duchess said, and she stepped into her chamber, slamming the door in his face behind her.

Behind her the door sprang open, and the duke entered the room. "Get out!" he said sharply to his wife's maid. "Her lady-ship will call you when she needs you." He almost shoved the girl from the room. Turning, he said in a deceptively quiet tone, "Now, Caroline, you will tell me exactly where you have been, and with whom you have been consorting. If you do not I shall lock you in this room until you do."

"You wouldn't!" She gasped.

"But I would, madam. Oh, yes, I would," he responded.

"You would not understand, Justin," she said, actually using his name in her despair. "How could you? What could you know of the horror I have seen?"

"I cannot if you do not tell me," he replied in a gentler tone.

She flung herself into his arms, pulling his head down to hers and kissing him passionately. "Make love to me," she begged him. "Oh, please make love to me!"

Their clothing seemed to evaporate as they pulled the garments from each other. Naked, he swept her up in his arms and carried her to the large wing chair by the fire. And all the while they kept kissing each other again and again until both their mouths were bruised and sore from a mixture of both passion and sweetness. They cuddled together, slowly exploring each other's bodies. His big hands cupped her small, perfect breasts, kissing the nipples until they were tightly puckered, like small frostbitten rosebuds. His teeth tenderly scored the sensitive flesh of her bosom.

The duchess sighed with her pleasure as he lifted her to sit facing him and his mouth traveled across her torso. Her fingers entwined themselves in his dark hair, kneading his scalp with her rising desire to be possessed by him. Her slender legs rested on his shoulders. But as eager for her as he was, he was not quite ready to consummate their mutual passion. He licked her body, tasting the saltiness of the sea on her skin. Then, lifting her up, he impaled her onto his engorged lover's lance. She sighed again.

"Now, madam," he said in measured tones, "you will answer my questions or you will gain no further pleasure from me."

Her blue eyes widened with her shock. She could feel his thickness throbbing within her love passage. "Justin," she whimpered. "Please!" She attempted to ride him, but he held her firmly about her narrow waist, his fingers digging cruelly into her flesh. "Please!"

"Where were you?" he demanded once again. "Where?!"

"France." She gasped. "I was in France!"

"You will tell me the rest afterward," he told her, standing. "Put your legs about me, Caro." He walked across the room to her bed and, laying her down, stood over her, fucking her at first slowly, and then with more rapid strokes until she was sobbing for release. A release he was not yet ready to give her. He quickly took his own pleasure, and then withdrew from her heated body. Moving to a table with a basin and pitcher he bathed his satisfied member.

"Bastard!" she hissed at him. She was aching and unsatisfied.

"When you have told me all," the duke said, "I will scratch that naughty itch of yours, my dear. But not until then. Do you understand me?" He climbed into bed, taking his wife into his arms. "Now, why were you in France?"

"Have you heard of Lady Lavender, Justin?"

"The person who rescued the Duchesse d'Almay and her children? Of course. It was the talk of the ton several months ago. Why?"

"I am Lavender, milord. It is I and the women who work with

me both here and in France who have been rescuing the victims of tyranny and injustice. Not just the nobility, but decent working people who have been denounced to the Committee for Public Safety. All one need do is drop a paper with a name on it in those boxes they now have in Paris and every small town in France. Today we brought back a vineyard owner, his wife, his old mother, her elderly maid, and three children. On our last trip it was the Comtesse d'Islay, her maid, and the old seamstress who had sewn for the comtesse for years. And Justin, there are so many more who need our help."

He was astounded by her confession, and then he grew angry. "How dare you endanger yourself, Caro! And who are the women who work with you? You all put yourselves at risk! It stops now! Do you comprehend me? It stops now!"

"No! No!" she cried to him. "There are too many who still must be rescued!"

"I cannot have the woman I love putting herself at risk like this," Justin Trahern told his wife. "I love you, Caro! Do you understand that? I love you! Even if you do not love me, I love you! I have since the first day we met, and I learned to my grief that you were my uncle's bride. I have waited patiently to have you. I will not lose you now!"

"Ohh, Justin," the duchess cried softly. "I love you too. From the first day we met, and I was your uncle's wife. But he understood young love, and that is why he arranged for us to marry when he was dead. He knew neither of us would ever betray him while he lived. He was such a fine man, just like my father. That is why they were best friends. And that is why he agreed to marry me, so my fortune would be protected from Eddis Thornton when my father died. My uncle had the title by right of succession, but father's fortune was his to disburse as he chose. My uncle would have run right through it, and sold me to the highest bidder to feed his bad habits."

"If you love me then why do you put yourself in such mortal danger?" the duke wanted to know.

The duchess sighed deeply. "My mother was French, Justin. She was the Duke of Medoro's oldest daughter. Grandfather had no sons, only three daughters: Claire, my mother, Justine, and Louisa. Every summer my mother and I would go to France to stay with my grandfather and his family. The summer I was sixteen my father was not pleased to have us go. He said it was much too dangerous. It was the year after La Bastille. There was much unrest. But Mama assured him it was Normandy, not Paris, and that all would be well, and grandfather was ill. So we went.

"My father was right. On that first anniversary of the revolution a mob came to the château. When my grandfather protested this invasion they killed him. Some of the servants fled, but many of them, along with Mama and me, my *tante* Justine and her little boys, and my *tante* Louisa, who was just two years older than I, were taken into the cellars of the château and imprisoned. Mama's maid, however, had escaped the château. She fled directly to the coast, found passage to England, and hurried to Chetwyn to tell Papa what had happened."

His arms tightened about her, and he kissed her brow. "You need not speak of it again if it disturbs you, Caro," he murmured.

"No, Justin, you must understand why I do what I do," she told him. "The servants were terrorized into telling the most awful lies. A footman was made to say he was the father of my *tante* Justine's sons. They were taken from her. They were only three and five. Several weeks later she was allowed to see them. They spit on her and called her a dirty aristo. She never saw them again. Nor her husband, who had been in Paris with the new government, attempting to make order of chaos.

"But that was not the worst. The men in charge began taking the women servants in the night. Some returned; some didn't. They were being raped, of course. Then one day they came for me. My mother begged the man in charge to take her instead. She told them she was the wife of an Englishman, and that her daughter was English. That my father would pay a goodly ransom for my safe return, but only if I was returned untouched. They took us both, and I was forced to watch while my mother was raped over and over again. And then they brought my *tante* Justine to be raped. Each time I tried to look away they beat me. My mother and aunt both died, and I was dragged back to the cellars to weep with my *tante* Louisa. They came for her several days later, and I was again forced to watch their brutality. My youngest aunt was a virgin. When they learned that, nothing was too bestial for them. She too died at the hands of the Revolution.

"Several more days passed, and at last they came for me again. I thought surely this time it would be my turn to be raped until I died. But instead my father was there with the revolutionary captain who held grandfather's château. I was a fortunate little aristo, he told me. My father had paid a great deal of money for my safe return, and because I was English—and he spit after the word—I would be permitted to leave. Captain Arnaud. I will always remember him, and his toady, Citizen Leon. And I will not rest until I have revenged my grandfather, my mother, her sisters, and all our family on these wretches. Rescuing others from them is the only way I can, Justin. You must let me continue! You must! They threw the bodies of those they slew into a common pit. There is not even a marker to remember them. My mother's house was a great and noble one, and now it is gone. They are gone. All gone." And the duchess began to weep bitterly.

"I will help you have your revenge," Justin Trahern promised, "but this must end."

CHAPTER SIX

Michael Devlin put down the pages he had just been reading. "This is great stuff, Emily," he said. "Caro's backstory is particularly poignant. But she should have a little eighteenth-century survivor's grief," he suggested. "It will make her more likable."

"I agree. The coldness is, of course, a shield she uses to hide her grief behind," Emily said. "I need to show some of that grief to make the reader sympathetic toward her. Do you like the duke?"

"Yes. He's different from your other heroes. More masculine. He's got a bit of a hard edge, except where his wife is concerned. It's a weakness I find endearing, and so will your readers. How do you know so much about love?" He smiled warmly at her, and Emily felt herself melting, as she always did when Devlin smiled that particular smile.

"I don't know," Emily admitted. "I guess I just try to make my characters the way I wish people really were."

"Haven't you ever been in love?" he queried her.

"Once," Emily said. "Only once."

"What happened?" Devlin said.

Emily shook her head. "I guess I'm not his type," she replied. "Foolish man," he said.

Have you ever really been in love? Emily wondered. *Could you fall in love with me?* But she didn't dare to voice her question aloud. She didn't want to see the pity in his eyes. It would kill her if he pitied her.

"I have to go to Frankfurt in October," he said. "And I'm going to stop in England on the way back. Savannah and Pruny need a mediator. You could meet me in England, angel face," he suggested. "I know you like England."

"I could stay with Savannah," Emily said thoughtfully. "But it couldn't be any longer than a three-day weekend, Devlin. I'm in the home stretch, and I want this book in on time. I don't want J.P. to have any negotiating room with Aaron. She called him and offered a new contract before he and Kirk went off on vacation."

"What did Aaron say?" So J.P. had been listening to him after all.

"That he'd discuss it with her when he got back from Italy." Emily grinned.

Michael Devlin nodded. It was fair. Aaron was no dope, and he was hedging his bets with J.P.—making her want the new contract more than he appeared to want it.

"Okay," she said, launching herself into his lap. "No more business! You're on vacation. Want to try it in one of the boys' beautiful wing chairs?" Her blue eyes twinkled at him mischievously.

"If I get cum all over the tapestry neither of them will be happy with us," he said seriously. "But what the hell, angel face, I've always wanted to try it in a wing chair." Reaching down, he unzipped his pants, and his penis almost flew out.

"Oh, me, oh, my," Emily said, looking at it. "The big fella is all ready to go, isn't he? Haven't you ever heard of foreplay, Devlin?" She pulled away from him and stood up. " 'Let me entertain you,' " she sang as she pulled off her light green tank top and tossed it carelessly across the room. Then she licked her lips suggestively and shook her breasts at him. " 'Let me make you smile.' " She began to wiggle seductively out of her shorts. " 'Let me do a few tricks. Some old and then some new tricks. I'm very ver-sa-tile.' " The shorts followed the tank top. Emily was quite naked, and now she began to dance in what she imagined to be a stripper's manner, bumping and grinding across the room. " 'And if you're real good, I'll make you feel good. I want your spirits to climb.' " She wiggled her bottom at him. " 'So let me entertain you. And we'll have a real good time.' Oh, yeah!" She strutted toward him. " 'We'll . . . have . . . a . . . real . . . good . . . time!' "

Reaching out he grabbed her, and impaled her on his penis. "Oh, yeah! We'll have a real good time," he sang.

"Brute!" she said. "Oh, God, no man should feel this good, Devlin!"

He reached out and, grasping one of her breasts in his hand, began to lick it. "And no mortal woman should feel this good. You fit me like a glove, angel face. Sit still for a little bit. If you move, I'm going to come. I don't want to yet."

"I'll make it stand straight and tall again, Devlin," she promised him. Bending, she kissed his ear, licking around the curve of it. "I love fucking you."

"Let's not stay at Lord Palmer's when we're in England," he said softly. "There's a great little inn in their village. I don't want to have to share our passion with Savannah, and you know she's bold enough to listen at our door." He chuckled. He released her breast and, finding her lips, kissed her a long and tender kiss.

"The Drake's Head," she said against his mouth. "Yes, let's stay there. I'll make the reservations when you have the dates. Oh, God, Devlin! I can't take much more."

"I thought you wanted foreplay," he teased, nibbling on her ear.

"Screw foreplay! I want you, and I want us to come together!" Emily groaned. "Let go of me! I want to ride you hard, Devlin.

Very hard!" She struggled against him, tucking her legs about him, and his hands released her hips, slipping up about her midsection to steady her. She moved up and down on his hard penis, her hands on his shoulders, her eyes closing with her sweet desire for him as she leaned back.

He watched her face and was enchanted by her rising passions. A pride, almost of ownership, flowed through him. She was his lover. He had taken her virginity and taught her the joys of lust. She had proven an apt pupil. No one had ever had her but him. And no man was ever *going* to have her but him, Michael Devlin determined.

"Oh! Ohh! Ohhh!" Her little cries excited him further.

"I adore you!" he whispered in her ear, his own eyes closing with the intense pleasure beginning to build and build. And then it broke, and his cum flooded her womb with fierce force.

"Devlin!" She sobbed his name as spasm after spasm shook her from the inside out. *Damnation!* She wanted her happy ending! She collapsed against him, burying her face in his shoulder and neck.

"It just gets better between us," he said after some moments had passed.

"I have nothing to judge it by," she said, teasing him gently. But of course she did. Yet had she attempted to explain the Channel to him he wouldn't have understood. And it did get better between them every time. No man was ever going to satisfy her except the charming Michael Devlin. She could conjure up a host of lovers in the Channel, but no matter how skilled they were, none would ever be Michael Devlin—worse luck.

"I'm glad you can't judge my performance," he teased back. "That makes me the best you've ever had, angel face."

"Am I the best you've ever had?" she dared to ask him.

"Yes," he said, not even hesitating for a moment. "There are still things I haven't taught you, of course, but you are an incredibly apt pupil, my darling." He kissed her brow, and then said with some small humor, "If we are very careful I believe we can manage not to get the results of our efforts on Aaron and Kirk's furniture. Has your research been satisfactory, angel face?"

"Uh-huh," she replied, carefully untangling herself from him. "But I still prefer the bed, Devlin. What else have you got to teach me?"

He hesitated. What he was about to suggest wasn't for everyone, but she should attempt it at least once. "I think it's time you got your little asshole stuffed with my dick," he told her, looking carefully at her to see her reaction.

Emily swallowed hard. She had read enough Victorian porn to know a little of what his suggestion involved. "Do you like to do that to a woman?" she asked him slowly. She wasn't certain it was something she wanted to attempt.

"Some women enjoy it," he said candidly. "But it's one of those things where you have to trust me completely in order to experience it without fear. You may not be ready. You may not want to do it at all. But then again, you might want to try it just once."

"Would you stop if I said I didn't like it?" she asked him. "I mean, it's not like our first time, where you couldn't stop after a certain point, is it?"

"If we do it and you say stop, I will stop immediately," he promised her. "We probably won't do it entirely the first time. It's important you aren't frightened. Once we've done it you may not want to do it again, angel face, but you will enjoy it. And you will be in total control of our situation, not me."

Emily stood, considering the suggestion. She knew Devlin was trustworthy. And frankly the idea of anal sex—the very forbidden nature of it—was intriguing and tempting. Was she bold enough to try? She thought some more. *Yes!* She did want to try it, if only once. He had said she would be in control, yet shoving her ass up at him to be fucked seemed a submissive position to her, and it was considered deviant. Still . . . "I'm game," she finally said. "Scared, but game."

He nodded. He hadn't been certain she would attempt this new form of sexual pleasure, but he realized more and more that Emily was a consummate researcher. And he knew that eventually their play would show up in a book, if not this one, then the next. "Give me a moment more to recover from being ravaged by you," he said wickedly.

"I'll meet you in the bedroom. The guest room where you are staying has the same king-size bed as their bedroom. Do you think they knew I'd been visiting you?"

Devlin laughed. "I think you're probably the only woman to ever stay here, let alone get fucked here." He chuckled.

Emily shot him a grin and disappeared into his bedroom. He waited a few minutes until he heard the shower, and then, getting carefully up, followed her. Stripping off his clothes he joined her under the pulsing jets of warm water. She took up a bar of olive oil soap from Italy and began rubbing it across his broad, smooth chest. He closed his eyes with the simple pleasure her touch gave him. Her hands moved the soap across his taut belly.

"Considering your age," she teased, "you are a fine figure of a man, Devlin."

"Ouch!" He groaned. "That was low. I was only forty last month. I loved your present, by the way," he teased back. "But it didn't last."

"You can have more anytime," she offered him, her hands soaping his balls with such a delicate touch he almost squealed like a kid being touched for the first time. She turned him about and washed his shoulders, her hands sliding down his back to fondle his buttocks with soapy fingers. Then she turned him to face her again.

In response his big hands fondled her bottom, the edge of one hand moving along the crease between the twin halves. She tensed slightly, but the hand was gone before she could even protest. "Let's get out," he suggested.

They exited the shower and dried each other off before returning to the bedroom. Devlin threw back the coverlet, revealing a smooth, pale peach jersey sheet. "They make their beds as in Europe and England," he said. "I like it. No top sheet just a bottom sheet, and down coverlet." He fell back, bringing her with him. Then he rolled her off of him and cradled her on her side. "It's better to begin this slowly," he said. "We're just going to make love, but I'm going to concentrate on touching your butt and not your tits, okay? This isn't the kind of thing where I jump your bones, angel face. I've told you that you will be in control. If you say stop, I'll stop."

"Do you like ass-fucking your lover?" she asked him, curious.

"It's an interesting variation," he said slowly. "It's no fun if your partner doesn't enjoy it. I'm not into degradation. It's like any other aspect of making love: If your partner enjoys it, you are more likely to enjoy it. We don't have to do this, Emily."

"No, I want to try," she said. "The forbidden is always enticing, Devlin." She felt his hands caressing her back, touching her buttocks with gentle touches. Why were women so sensitive about their asses? she wondered. *We're all quick enough to flash our breasts at our men.* The edge of his hand was now running along the crease between her buttocks. She tensed just slightly, and he immediately moved away. *Okay. He's keeping his promise,* she thought. *But if I'm nervous when he just brushed by, what the hell is going to happen when it gets down to the nitty-gritty? Do I really want to do this? Yeah, I do. The unknown is always scary.*

Devlin loved the feel of her skin, the curve of her butt. His hand moved back to the shadowed furrow separating her buttocks. She tensed again, but as quickly relaxed as he followed the line of the crease. His hand pressed slightly, dipping into the fold of the flesh. He rubbed slowly, moving deeper, letting his hand remain there. "Breathe," he told her, sensing her nervousness. The little finger on his hand reached out to caress her anus, pressing just slightly.

"Oh!"

" 'Oh' good, or 'oh' bad?" he asked.

"I didn't realize you could be sensitive there," she said.

"It's an erogenous zone too. It's just not used a whole lot," he told her.

"Touch it again," she said, and he did. "Oh, very good, Devlin," she assured him. Then she gasped as the merest tip of his little finger penetrated her, but barely. "Ohh!"

He held the finger there for a moment, and then removed it. Over the next hour he played with her gently. He had taken a tube of K-Y jelly from the nightstand, but she said nothing. They used it with the dildo, and she could understand the need for it in this situation. He never stopped kissing her, attempting to take the edge off of her nervousness. A single finger, covered with lubricant, pressed gently against her asshole. "It's all right, angel face," he whispered in her ear as he felt her tensing up again. And when she said nothing and relaxed with his reassurance, he pressed a bit more firmly against the sphincter muscle until it slowly gave way and allowed his finger forward an inch, then two inches. He stopped, letting her grow used to this invasion. "What do you think?" he asked her softly.

She was quiet a long moment, and then she said, "I think I could take a little more. It's an interesting sensation. Not uncomfortable at all."

"My cock is a lot bigger," he reminded her. "Let's try two fingers and see how you manage, okay?"

"Okay," Emily agreed nervously as she felt the single finger being withdrawn. Then she felt the pressure again against her asshole. Slowly, slowly, and with great care he now inserted two of his fingers. The sensation was, to her surprise, exciting. "Oh! Oh, good. Oh, interesting." she told him.

He was surprised at how well she was handling this. He had assumed they would not manage this style of intercourse in one session, but now he considered she might very well be ready for it. "Want to try going all the way?" he asked her, kissing her shoulder.

"Yes," she answered him. "Yes, I do."

"Do you know the correct position to assume?" he asked her. "Is it in those books of yours?" he teased mischievously as he withdrew his fingers from her.

"As a matter of fact, it is," Emily told him, rolling over, drawing her knees up beneath her, and resting her arms on the pillows.

His penis was more than ready. He slid on a well-lubricated condom and rubbed her anal opening lavishly with the jelly. Then, kneeling behind her, he positioned his cock and began an insistent pressure he knew would force the little ring of muscle open. It gave, and he moved forward, inserting himself slowly, slowly, slowly into her asshole. She gasped as he began to fill the very tight passage, but she didn't cry off. He didn't know whether to be surprised or proud. Her trust in him was obviously total.

Oh my God! Oh my God! Oh my God! Emily whispered silently in her head. The feeling of him, of his thickness, of his mass sliding into a place she had never really considered a penis should be, was incredible. There had been a slight pinch of pain, but she had held herself very still, and he had been extraordinarily gentle. Now fully sheathed, he stopped, letting them both experience the sensation of his throbbing cock in her asshole. It was certainly unlike any sensation she had ever experienced before. "You don't even have to move." She gasped. "It's not going to take much to make me come."

"Just a little of this," he said, reaching beneath her to tweak her clitoris with a skilled and very wicked finger.

"Oh, my God!" Emily screamed softly, and then her orgasm exploded, leaving her almost breathless.

He pulled his engorged cock from her deliciously tight asshole, pulled the condom from it, and, rolling her over onto her back, slid into her vagina. Then with slow, deliberate strokes of his penis he began to again rouse the fires within her until her head was thrashing back and forth, and he could see nothing but a haze before his own eyes. Sensation! He could only feel sensation: the muscles of her vagina squeezing him hard, the heat and wetness of her. His lust grew in intensity as he sensed she was ready to erupt again. And when she did, her second orgasm even greater than the first, his passion met hers with equal force and determination as his own juices burst forth.

Neither of them spoke for several long minutes. Finally he asked, "Well? What do you think, angel face?"

"I don't think I would do it again, Devlin, but it was a trip," Emily admitted candidly. She rolled onto her side and propped herself up on an elbow, looking down into his face. "Thank you for being so gentle. I imagine with the wrong lover that would have been a very painful experience."

"It's not my favorite thing to do either," he admitted, "but some of the women I have known can come only when they've got a cock in their asshole." He pulled her into his arms. "I have to say you've got a cute one."

She felt her cheeks growing warm. "Shut up," she told him.

"Stay with me tonight," he said. His thumb brushed across her lips.

"I can't. I left all my lights on. If I don't come home until the morning someone will notice, and trust me, in Egret Pointe there will be questions, if not a cop car checking to see if I'm all right. I like that what we have is private, is ours alone."

"What do we have?" he asked her, wondering what the hell had possessed him to voice his own insecurities.

"Whatever you want, Devlin," Emily answered him. She slipped from his arms and, getting up, went into the bathroom.

He lay quietly listening as the shower ran again. A few minutes later she returned, dressed, and, giving him a quick kiss, was gone from the bedroom. He heard the cottage door close behind her, and then the *vroom* of her Healy as she pulled away and drove off down the long driveway to the two-lane country road that would take her back home again. He loved her. Oh, yeah, he loved her. He had tried, but he couldn't get a handle on how she might really feel about him. Were there still women in this world who could fall in love with the first man who boffed them? Or was he merely a research helper to Emily Shanski? The thought of any other man making love to her set his pulse pounding with anger. He loved her, but could he reasonably expect her to love him back? He didn't know. Michael Devlin had never before found himself in this kind of situation.

And as she drove Emily was wondering the same thing. He had said at one point, "I adore you." Did that mean love? He had asked her what they had. Was he testing her to be certain that she wouldn't embarrass him by girlishly declaring emotions for him that he could not reciprocate? For the first time in her life Emily Shanski regretted her lack of experience with a man. With love. She had never had a crush on anyone growing up. She had never had her heart broken, even once, because she was so busy trying hard not to be like her mother and her father. Maybe just once she could have thrown caution to the wind, but then the thought of the grans disappointment had always stopped her.

They had given up their middle years and their old age to bring her up. To love her and raise her to be the kind of person they had wanted Katy and Joe to be. But their own children had, in one foolish action, thrown aside the morality they had been raised to have. Only the grans cool heads and logic, along with the respect of all of Egret Pointe, had saved the day for them all. Had saved her, Emily thought. Yes, her parents had been married when she had been born. But they had been given a quick annulment with the cooperation of a local judge before Thanksgiving vacation. And everyone in town knew why they had married. If it weren't for the grans, Emily Shanski would have had a far more difficult life.

Emily didn't even dare consider what her grandmothers would think of these past three months. My God, after tonight, what hadn't she done with Michael Devlin? The thought, though sobering, still brought a grin to her face. It had been exciting in a taboo sort of way, but anal sex wasn't something she was anxious to repeat—even with her duke. Was she up to the Channel tonight, after what had happened? No, she was not. She was going to go home to bed, and go to sleep. After she had some Forbidden Chocolate ice cream. For some reason she suddenly needed chocolate in the worst way. She turned onto Founders Way, and drove straight down the street into her driveway. Her cell phone began to ring as she got out of the car. Smiling, she answered it. "I'm just home. Do you have radar, Devlin?"

"Are you in the house?"

"I'm opening the kitchen door now," she told him as she turned the key and walked into her house, closing and locking the door behind her. "I'm in and locked."

"Can I come over?" he asked her plaintively.

"No. I want a good night's sleep. Tomorrow's a workday for me. Good night, Devlin. Sleep tight. My pussy and I will be thinking of you." She made kissing noises into the telephone.

"My cock and I will be thinking of you both too," he promised, and made kissing noises back at her. "Good night, angel face." He clicked off.

Emily sighed. Why did love have to hurt so damned much?

August seemed to fly by. It was a hot and dry month. Devlin was at her house for breakfast on the mornings she hadn't been at the cottage overnight. They swam together at the club. He rented a small catboat for the month, and they spent afternoons out on the bay. They celebrated her birthday in bed with champagne, whipped cream, and chocolate sauce. It was clear on the peak night of the Perseid meteor showers. The moon was new, and had set by after midnight, which was the prime viewing time. They lay in a double lounge chair down on the cottage's narrow beach, watching the shooting stars. Afterward they made slow, leisurely love, dozed, and swam in the bay as the dawn broke. Emily could not remember a time in her life when she had been so utterly and completely happy.

And neither could Michael Devlin, although it was a thought he kept to himself.

Labor Day weekend Rina Seligmann insisted they join her and Sam for dinner at the club. "You've been hiding out all month," she told Emily. "You don't even answer messages, and you gave Essie all of August off, paid. How am I supposed to get my gossip if Essie isn't there?"

Emily laughed. "You aren't. This has been a private time, and even I'm entitled to one of those at least once a century. What time do you want us? Devlin is going back Sunday night to beat the Monday traffic."

"Saturday night. Eight p.m. Have you heard from Aaron?"

"I got two postcards from Capri. The last one complained that Kirk wouldn't let him stay longer, but insisted on returning to Tuscany," Emily replied.

Rina chuckled. "My brother is such a gadabout," she remarked. "I don't blame Kirk. When are they back?"

"Sunday afternoon," Emily said. "See you Saturday night."

"Do we have to go?" Michael Devlin wanted to know.

"Yep, we do," Emily answered. "Rina's my mother figure, and her brother is my agent. She's practically family. And you liked her, and Dr. Sam will keep her under control, I promise. I'm surprised she called. I thought she'd be up at Camp Cozy this weekend. Sam must be on call at the hospital."

"What's Camp Cozy?" he asked, curious.

"Rina and her neighbors on Ansley Court bought a big old house up in the mountains on a lake twenty-five years ago. The women used to go up every summer with their kids. The kids named it Camp Cozy. The men would come on weekends, or for a week or two in August. At least they won't all be at the club Saturday evening," she said.

They had taken his car that night. Arriving at the Egret Pointe Country Club, they were seated at a table overlooking the golf course.

"Do you play?" he wanted to know.

Emily shook her head. "I'm not particularly athletic," she replied.

"I beg to differ," he said with a small grin.

She laughed, and then she said, "Oh, hell! There's Carla Johnson and her husband, Rick. And Tiffany and Joe Pietro d'Angelo."

"Who are they?" he asked.

"Some of Rina's neighbors. Rick and Joe have a little law firm in the village," Emily explained. "But I thought they would be up at Camp Cozy. Rats! They've seen us." She returned Carla Johnson's friendly wave. "I'm going to kill Rina!"

"Why would you kill my wife?" Dr. Sam asked as he joined them. He gave Emily a kiss on her cheek.

"Everyone in town is here," Emily muttered. "I told Rina I didn't want to have dinner at the club tonight, but how come Carla and Tiffany aren't up at your place in the mountains? Isn't this the last big weekend of the summer for Camp Cozy?"

"There's a forest fire in the mountains near the camp," Dr. Sam explained. "It's been so dry. They've got it under control, but they asked people to evacuate just to be on the safe side. The Ulrichs are in Europe," he added as an afterthought. "You know my Rina. She works the room of people like a Catskills comedian entering the lobby of his hotel. She's probably telling those two he's your editor, and you know how Carla appreciates a handsome man." He chuckled.

"I'll give her two minutes," Emily said darkly.

Michael Devlin stood up. "Let me handle this," he said with a grin. Then, walking across the country club dining room to where Rina stood in earnest conversation with her two friends, he took her arm, saying, "Rina, my dear girl, we cannot order until you have joined us, and I for one am famished." Then he smiled at Carla Johnson and Tiffany Pietro d'Angelo. "I'm Michael Devlin, Emily's editor. I hope you won't mind if I steal Rina away from you." He turned Rina Seligmann away from the two women and escorted her across the floor.

"You got chutzpah, dearie," Rina murmured as they walked.

"Emily was getting upset. For some reason—and I cannot fathom why—she wants to keep our love affair a secret, Rina," Michael Devlin said softly. Reaching the table he seated her with a flourish, and then sat back down himself.

Rina chuckled. "I like him," she said to Emily. "You have my approval to do what you will with him, my child."

Emily burst out laughing. "That, sir, was ballsy," she told her lover.

"I agree with my wife, but don't I always agree with my wife?" Dr. Sam said. Then he turned to the waiter, who was now hovering. "I'll have the salmon with dill sauce, but I want rice, not those red potatoes you're always trying to palm off on me. Balsamic on the salad, and I want more than one of those blueberry muffins in the basket tonight."

While they ate an orchestra tuned up, and by the time they reached dessert people were beginning to dance. The music being played wasn't at all new, given the audience. There were foxtrots, waltzes, rumbas, and sambas. The Seligmanns got up to dance, and Emily smiled watching them.

"Aren't they cute?" she said. "He adores her, and she adores him."

"They're good people. I'm glad you have them," he answered.

"I'm lucky," Emily admitted. "Only in America would an Irish-Polish Catholic girl have Jewish parent figures. Sam's ancestors and my Dunham ancestors were among the founders of Egret Pointe. There has been a Dr. Seligmann here as long as anyone can remember."

"I don't think of the States as having such history," Michael Devlin admitted. "I am not going to ask you to dance, angel face, because if I do I will embarrass us both. I can't seem to hold you in my arms without getting a hard-on."

She blushed, but laughed softly at the same time. "What is going to happen with us, Devlin? This tutorial is getting out of control, isn't it?"

"I don't know," he said slowly. "I don't find that I am un-happy—rather the opposite. What about you?"

"I feel the same way," Emily said quietly. "Let's see how well we travel together. When are you going to Frankfurt?"

"Early October," he replied. "Want to meet in England on the tenth?"

"I'll make the reservations at the inn in Barrow tomorrow," she said. "How long do you want to visit with the Palmers?"

"I'd better fly back the fourteenth so I can be in the office that day," he said. "I don't want J.P. asking why I'm away so long. Since I'm going to smooth things out with Sava and Pruny, I'll call it business, and then say I wanted to check on my house as well, since I was there. Who will know you're away?"

"Rina and Essie," Emily replied. "I'll fly home the sixteenth, so Sava and I can have a little girl time together. I know I said three days, but I haven't been to England in a while, and I can call it a research trip."

"You two should get out there and dance," Rina said breath-lessly as she returned to the table. "They're playing real music."

"We're enjoying drinking our wine and talking," Emily quickly spoke up. "Besides, we don't want your friends gossiping, do we?"

"They'll gossip anyway," Rina said with a grin. "That's what we do every Monday morning: eat doughnuts, drink coffee, and gossip. We've been doing it for years. Now that we're all work-ing again we just meet earlier. And you have to admit that no one has seen you having dinner at the club with a handsome, el-igible man in years, Emily." She turned to Michael Devlin. "And I know you're eligible, and quite the man," Rina told him. "Oh, Emily is very quiet, but I see how happy she is. It would be such a pity if you were gay. Every time I see those men on *Queer Eye for the Straight Guy* I want to weep. That Kyan! So handsome and sexy. Jai . . . now Jai I would take home and mother. He's adorable."

"I'd like Carson as a best friend," Emily said. "He makes me laugh, and he's so witty. But kind too."

The evening was coming to an end. Fewer couples were dancing now. The dining room was growing quieter. Dr. Sam insisted on picking up the check, and they all left together, passing by the now empty table where Rina's friends had been sitting. In the parking lot they kissed, then went to their separate cars. The Seligmanns' Lexus pulled away first. Michael Devlin's Healy followed.

"He's in love with her!" Rina said triumphantly.

"Stay out of it, Rina," her husband warned.

"I just want her happy, Sam. She deserves to be happy."

"Yes, she does," he agreed. "So stay out of it. They are two grown people, and they will find their own way. What's meant to be will be."

"She'd make the most beautiful bride." Rina sighed.

Sam Seligmann laughed as they drove along. "My wife, the matchmaker," he said fondly. "A daughter and two sons, and you're still not satisfied. Now I know what your ancestors did back in Russia, Rina."

She joined in laughing. "So I'm a Golda the matchmaker," she said. "Sue me!" Then she grew serious. "Do you think he'll marry her, Sam?"

"You said he was in love with Emily," her husband reasoned.

"But he's forty, and never married before," Rina fretted. "Do you think she loves him?"

"You can't see it? Oh, yes, Sam! Emily loves Michael," Rina declared with great assurance. "He's her first love, and I suspect her last love. She isn't a girl to give her heart lightly. Oh, God! What if he doesn't want a wife?"

"What's meant to be will be," Dr. Sam repeated. "It's already

written in the book of life, Rina, my darling. So stay out of it!"
He turned their car onto Ansley Court.

The Healy turned into Emily's driveway. They walked together
into the house.

"Are you hungry?" she asked him.

He pulled her into his arms. "Only for you." His mouth took
possession of her, moving tenderly over her lips, tasting her with
his tongue, playing with the tongue she offered him back. "Why
are you always so delicious?" he murmured against her short
strawberry-blond hair. "I can never get enough of you." His
hands pushed up her silken skirt, caressing her hips, her buttocks. He backed her against the kitchen table, green eyes dancing mischievously. "We're going to do it on the table," he
growled in her ear. "Right now, angel face!"

"Devlin!" She gasped as he lifted her up. She was quivering
with her excitement. Tomorrow he would return to the city, and
she wouldn't see him again for almost a week. Her buttocks felt
the rough oak beneath them as he lowered her. His head was between her open legs, searching out the core of her, finding it,
teasing it. "Oh, yes! Yes! Yes! Yes!" she encouraged. Her nipples were hard and tingling. She slipped the straps of her dress
off her shoulders and freed her breasts from the fabric. He was
pulling her forward onto his cock. His mouth found her nipples.
"Oh, God!" He was inside her, moving slowly at first, and then
with a quicker and more intense rhythm. He suckled on one of
her tits hungrily as he worked them to a fever pitch. Emily cried
out as they came together in a blaze of heated passion.

What the hell is the matter with me? Michael Devlin asked
himself as he pulled himself off of her. He loved her. Did he
really want to go back into the city tomorrow morning and
spend the day away from her? But what if it didn't last? What
if it had just been a wild and wonderful fling that Emily had initiated to learn about sex? And that had been her—their—
original intent. Maybe she was one of those women who prized

their independence above everything else. He needed more time. He was too old to offer his heart to a woman, only to have her refuse him.

"Do you have to go back tomorrow?" she asked him.

"Yes," he said. "If I leave around noon I'll miss all the traffic. The Healy doesn't like idling in traffic."

"You could leave the Healy here, and take the train in on Tuesday morning," she suggested casually.

"I pay for garaging in my building," he answered her.

"Oh." She sounded disappointed.

"We have the rest of tonight, and tomorrow morning," he told her as he helped her off her kitchen table. "And if you need me to come back next weekend, I can."

Emily nodded. "I think you have to come back every weekend until the book is finished," she told him. "And after that, only if you'd like to, Devlin."

He ruffled her soft hair. "I would like to, angel face." Was the suggestion casual? Or did she mean something by it? Could she care for him as he did for her?

"Let's go to bed!" Emily suggested happily. Men were so dense. Did Devlin really think she was going to let him get away from her now that she had found him? If he loved her, as Rina said he did, he wouldn't want to leave her.

She barely had time to feed him, they lingered among the sheets so long the next day. But she wouldn't let him go until she had given him a late breakfast, and then she tucked into the Healy a bag containing several sandwiches and fresh peaches. "Call me so I know you're back safe," she said to him, kissing him sweetly on the back porch where no one could see them.

He nodded, kissed her back long and hard, and fondled her butt. "Be good, angel face," he said as he walked off the porch and climbed into the car.

"I only want to be bad with you, Devlin," she told him, and waved him off as he backed out of her drive and roared down

Founders Way. Well, that wasn't one hundred percent true, the afterthought struck her. She liked being bad with her duke. But the duke wasn't real. He was a fantasy lover. She wondered if she would take other fantasy lovers now that her writing had taken a turn for the hotter. The Channel offered such safe sex. No unexpected pregnancies. No STDs. Just utter incredible bliss. It wasn't real, but it certainly seemed like it was real when you were experiencing it. Going back into the house, she considered having the Channel tonight, but it seemed almost disloyal to Devlin to get it so soon. Couldn't she live without sex for a single night? She grinned. Now that she knew what it was all about, she wasn't sure she could.

He called her around four to say he was back in his apartment, and the Healy garaged. "It prefers your driveway to its space in the building," he told her.

"My Healy misses yours," she teased. "She liked being nose-to-nose with your Healy in the drive. How was the traffic?"

"Good, but thickening as I got near town," he said.

They talked for a few more minutes, and then he rang off, telling her, "Now playtime is over, angel face. Get back to work. I'll call you in a few days."

"Okay," she said. "And I'll see you next weekend."

"You bet you will," he promised.

Emily hung up, and then, considering the time, she dialed Savannah's cell number. It wasn't that late in England, and Sava was a night owl anyway.

"Hallo?"

"He went back to the city, and I'm alone," Emily said.

"Well, you've had a month of him now. Not tired? Not bored?" Savannah asked.

"I will never be tired or bored with Devlin," Emily answered honestly.

Savannah laughed. "I'm so glad you finally know what love really is, pet. And the sex? Still incredible? I always heard he was the best."

"God, yes!" Emily sighed. "Oh, I know that because he's my first and only lover, some people might say I didn't know what I was talking about, but I do. I guess it's an instinct, Sava. The duke may look like him, but he isn't at all like him in either personality or in the boudoir. Does that sound crazy?"

"Not to me," Savannah replied. "The gentlemen on the Channel seem to have their own personalities. I don't really understand it, but I also don't want to question it."

"I'm coming to England next month. Devlin goes to Frankfurt, and then we're meeting. We'll come down to Barrow and spend a few days. Make me a reservation at the inn in the village, will you? The best they have to offer."

"You'll stay with us," Savannah protested.

"Not this time," Emily said. "We want a romantic interlude, and we can hardly have one at the manor. Besides, you listen at keyholes, and don't deny it."

Savannah giggled. "That's how I gained my first knowledge of sex," she admitted. "Mama used to bed my father's brother every chance she could. Of course, she was a widow, but Uncle Dorian was married. Mama always left her bedroom door open except when Uncle Dorian came. I wondered why. I certainly got an eyeful and earful that first time I peeked. My nanny caught me and hauled me away, muttering about bad girls coming to bad ends." Savannah laughed. "Thank God for the Channel, for I seem to have my mama's wild libido! But I would never embarrass Reg. I do love him."

"You'll make the reservation then?"

"For when?" Savannah asked.

"We'll get there October tenth. He's leaving the fourteenth. I'll come up to the manor house then until the sixteenth, if that's all right with you," Emily said.

"That would be super," Savannah agreed. "Reg goes up to London a few days a month, and we'll have girl time while he's gone. The Channel is trying something new here in England and France, and it's a perfect time to use it."

"What is it?" Emily asked.

"It's a new channel changer. You know how they replaced our old ones with one that got us in by simply pressing the enter button? Well, now there's a new one that you can program to allow two women to enter the same fantasy at the same time! And I've been working on a wonderful idea about a Victorian bordello. You know how prim and proper the Victorians are said to have been. Well, sexually they were animals, darling! While old Reg is up in London we can indulge our most wicked little selves at the Cock and Cunt. That's what I call the place." Savannah chuckled.

"Sounds very wicked," Emily said slowly. "I don't know if that's my style, Sava. You are far more adventurous than I am."

"Emily, we hold the power in the Channel. That's what makes it so ideal for experimentation. If you say stop, it stops. Not like real life, where, when a man gets past the point of no return, you can't say, 'Whoa, Nellie,' " Savannah reminded Emily. "I know these last few months you've been a participant in the Channel and not an observer, but I also know you've probably played it safe. Try something new and maybe just a little dangerous. We'll be together, darling. Aren't you just the least bit curious to know what it would be like to have multiple partners at the same time? Or to spend the night entertaining several different cocks in your pussy? Come on, admit it. Every woman thinks about it, and given the right circumstances most of them would attempt it at least once. I've created a really fun group of gentlemen. There's Bertie and Willie, Freddie and St. Albans. And several others. More than enough to go around. Don't make a decision now. Wait until you get here. I'm really excited about this. Imagine being able to go into the Channel with your best friend."

"It is tempting," Emily considered thoughtfully.

"Devlin will be on a plane flying back to the States. Old Reg will be up in London, and you and I will be in our fantasy getting ourselves fucked to distraction. I know it's not the correct period for you, but sex is sex. You might pick up something you could use in *The Defiant Duchess.*"

"I might," Emily said.

Savannah laughed. "You are intrigued, aren't you?"

"I admit it," Emily said.

"Then we'll have to do it, darling," Savannah decided for them.

"I expect we'll be doing it a whole lot that night," Emily riposted back.

"Gracious, what a wicked thrust," Savannah said drolly.

"There will be lots of wicked thrusts that night, won't there, Sava?"

Savannah laughed. "God, I hope so! I haven't had a good orgy in ages, and you haven't had one at all. I do so want your first orgy to be fun, darling."

"I'm going to ring off, Sava," Emily said. "I'll talk to you before I come. Have the inn e-mail me a confirmation."

"Of course. I'll tell old Reg you sent kisses," Savannah replied. "You know he would fuck you if you let him, Emily. He's always fancied you."

"Well, I wouldn't fuck him. Not my best friend's husband," Emily said, a bit shocked. "Give William and little Selena a kiss for me, will you?"

"Well, just thought I'd ask now that you're well broken in and all. It's his birthday in a few weeks, and you would really make a terrific gift. I mean, another consumer something is so predictable, after all."

"Savannah! You are a dreadful woman," Emily said, half laughing. "The one woman in this world you will never have to worry about where Reg is concerned is me. As your husband he is off-limits, as far as I am concerned. I've never even made one of my heroes look like him. Ewww! Creepy. Now, kisses for the children, remember?"

"It's done," Savannah replied. "Night, darling. See you next month."

"Good night, Sava," Emily said, and hung up. She was actually relieved that Lord Palmer would be up in London while she was staying with Savannah. The last time she had been at the manor he had come into her room, and then pretended he had made an error, being somewhat foxed, as he had so quaintly put it. But Emily had known her friend's husband knew exactly where he had been going. He was a hound dawg, to use an Americanism, she thought. Savannah probably knew it too, but she did love Reg and their children, and she loved being Lady Palmer, Baroness Tilbury. And Reg, even if given the opportunity, would never leave his wife. In his way he loved her too.

Love. What a funny emotion, Emily thought. *It's physical, and it's emotional. It's delicious lust, and at the same time it's emotions for which there are no words.* At least that was how she felt about Devlin. Rina said he loved her. But Devlin had never said it. Not even in the deepest throes of passion had he uttered the word *love.* The closest he had come was to say he adored her. *Adore* meant to worship. To be extremely fond of. So he was fond of her. It was something to build upon, wasn't it?

She had entrapped him into seducing her back last spring so she might learn just what sex was all about. She hadn't planned on falling in love with Michael Devlin; nor had she even considered that he would fall in love with her. But she had fallen in love with him, and more than anything in the whole world Emily Shanski wanted Michael Devlin to be in love with her. She wanted a happily-ever-after, complete with a small but fancy wedding, a honeymoon, and two or three children. If her heroines could have it, why couldn't she? She had gotten him into bed. Now could she get him to the altar?

The telephone rang and, surprised, she picked it up.

"Emily, it's Aaron. I've been trying to get you for hours," he said dramatically.

"Aaron, welcome home! How was Italy? How was Capri?" she asked him.

"Tuscany was heaven. Capri overrated. Too many pretty boys. Dancing, dancing, dancing, and drinking twenty-four/seven. We were supposed to stay a week, but we left after two days. Kirk was right," Aaron Fischer said. "But the Blue Grotto was divine! Now, how is the book coming, and are you getting along with Michael Devlin? You seemed to be content before we left."

"We're lovers," Emily heard herself say.

There was a long pause, and then Aaron said, "Is that wise, sweetheart? I mean, this kind of a relationship between an author and editor has always been a forbidden kind of thing. What happens when it's over? Will you be able to work with each other? And how will you explain it if you can't?"

"Rina says he's in love with me, and Aaron, I am in love with him. Don't I get to be happy too?" Emily asked softly.

"Rina! I should have known! The busybody of the Western world! Don't listen to my sister, Emily. She has no touch with reality."

"The book is three-quarters done," Emily told him. "It will be in on time. I'm going to England next month for a week. I'll be down at Barrow seeing Sava."

Aaron Fischer sighed audibly. "So you don't like my concern," he said. "Sue me. I promised Emily O when I took you on as a client that I would look after you like a daughter, if I had a daughter. I reiterated that promise just before she died. What kind of a father would I be if I weren't concerned? Michael Devlin is charming, and he's a wonderful, talented editor. But he has never shown any inclination to settle down. If you understand that and can live with it, then so be it."

"It isn't just the sex, Aaron," she began. "We get on together. We like the same things, laugh at the same jokes, and he loves my cooking."

"Everyone loves your cooking," Aaron replied. "I can't believe that Mick was so cavalier as to seduce you. I thought he was more professional."

"I seduced him, Aaron. He did try to resist, but I was determined," Emily said.

"Oy vay!" her agent replied. "Well, if nothing else, the misery you're going to find when this madness is over will hopefully translate into even better writing."

Emily laughed. "You really are a wretch, Aaron. But what if he decides it's time to settle down, and he wants to marry me?"

"If Michael Devlin asks you to marry him, sweetheart, then I will walk you down the aisle at St. Anne's and give you away," Aaron Fischer said. "So maybe it wouldn't be such a bad thing," he reasoned. "Now, I just called to see that you were all right, and to tell you that tomorrow I will make an appointment with J. P. Woods for a little negotiation session. E-mail me what you've written so far so I can read it before we meet."

"First thing in the morning, Aaron. And Aaron—no one in the business knows except you and Sava. I don't want Devlin embarrassed by any gossip."

Aaron chuckled wisely. "So having seduced him, you are now setting about to stalk him and get him to the altar," he said. "Well, good hunting, sweetheart. I'll call you in a few days and fill you in on what's happening. Good night."

"Night, Aaron. Say hi to Kirk for me." Emily hung up the phone. Then, locking up the house, she went upstairs to bed. She wasn't going to stalk Devlin. No. She was going to run him to the ground and hog-tie him. It was time they were both married.

CHAPTER SEVEN

❧

"What will happen to me when you have finished the book?" Justin Trahern, the Duke of Malincourt, asked his creator. They were standing in his library.

"Why, Trahern, you'll be immortalized forever," Emily told him.

"You really ought to write another book about Malincourt," he said. "Am I not the most fascinating and interesting hero you have ever created, dear girl?"

"Well, you are certainly the most arrogant." Emily laughed.

"You are a magnificent duchess, madam," he remarked.

"I have given you a duchess worthy of you, my lord," Emily said. "Caro is the perfect woman for you. To please you I made her look like me, as I have made you look like Michael Devlin. But you are not Devlin, and I am not Caro."

"You are Caro when you are in my arms," he replied wickedly. "How else could you know the emotions she feels, dear girl?" Reaching out, he took her hand in his and drew her toward him. "Tell me where you go when you disappear from Malincourt, madam? I do not believe it is to a lover, for your own sense of honor is too great." He wrapped strong arms about her and looked down into her small heart-shaped face.

"My lord, do not ask, I beg you, and allow me to do what I must," the duchess said breathlessly. "I do not cuckold you, and with that you must be content." The feel of his hard body against hers was intoxicating. She wanted to remain safe in his arms forever. If only she could, but it was not to be. She had yet to wreak her full revenge on those who had first dishonored her mother and then murdered her. And her aunts. Especially her beloved youngest aunt, Louisa.

The duchess pressed herself against her husband's broad and comforting chest. He did not know of that summer three years ago when she and her mother had visited her grandparents in France. Her father, the Earl of Chetwyn, had not wanted them to go. The political situation in France was growing worse by the day. But her beautiful French mother, Claudine, had laughed at his fears.

"Most of the difficulty is in Paris, *mon chou*," she had said. "Caroline and I go no farther than Normandy. There has been little trouble there. Besides, Papa is in agreement with the Marquess de Lafayette and the others. Great changes are needed if France is to survive, and Monsieur le Roi and Madame la Reine must be brought around. I always felt sorry for that poor little Austrian princess who had to marry fat Louis. But everyone knows that my father, the duke, and all his extended family support the revolution. We will be perfectly safe, *ma coeur*."

And so they had sailed in the Earl of Chetwyn's yacht across the Channel to Normandy to spend a few months with the countess's parents. And at first it had been just like every other summer Lady Caroline Thornton had spent in France at the charming little château of her maternal grandparents. Her mother's two sisters had been there with her. The elder and her family lived in the Loire region. The younger was Caroline's age but for a few weeks. They were seventeen, and they spent their days out of doors riding, or walking beneath the trees in the orchards. Caroline was to have a London season next year, and the lovely Louisa had been invited to share it, as society in

France nowadays was precarious at best. The two girls giggled together as they imagined the gowns they would have, and the husbands they would soon find among the ton. The weather had been hot and sunny. It had been so perfect, and neither had even considered that it would be the last time they would be happy together.

And then one afternoon a ragged band of men had appeared at the the door of the château demanding entry. Seeing them, the duke had been hesitant at first, but then he permitted the men entry. He was a good son of the Revolution. But they had arrested her grandfather and charged him with treason against the Republic. An anonymous complaint against him had been put into the box set up by the Committee for Public Safety in their village. The duke was accused of hoarding, and of mistreatment of one Citizen Agramant. Searching the château, they claimed the supplies in the pantry were evidence of his hoarding.

The duke protested. What was in his pantry was an average supply of foodstuffs for his large family and his servants. As for Citizen Agramant, he had been in the duke's employ as a stableman. He had been caught in the pantry stealing food, and there had been a bottle from the duke's cellar beneath his coat as well. He had been whipped, ten lashes only, and dismissed from the duke's employ. Had Citizen Agramant been hungry, the duke declared, had he come to his master, the duke would have given him food from his own stores. But he was not going hungry, and the duke had evidence that the stableman had stolen from him before, and was selling what he stole in the village at inflated prices.

But the band of men would not listen. The duke was taken away, and his household imprisoned within the château. Several days later they received word that the duke had been tried, found guilty of crimes against the republic, and taken to Caen to be executed. His body was never returned to them. Upon hearing the news the duchess had clutched at her chest and collapsed. She died several days later. As their servants were now forbidden from waiting upon them, the family of women had dug her grave in the family cemetery. A coffin had mysteriously appeared in her bedchamber. No one spoke of it or asked from where it had come. The old duchess was wrapped in a shroud and put into the coffin. And her two daughters and her grandchildren had gone to request that some of their manservants be allowed to carry the coffin to the grave.

The man who called himself the captain of the ragged band, one Captain Arnaud, had looked them over, licked his lips, and then said, "For every favor there is a price, my pretty aristos. What have you to offer?"

Caroline's mother had immediately removed the gold-and-pearl chain and crucifix she wore about her neck and handed it to him. "Will this do?" she asked quietly.

"For now," Captain Arnaud had answered with a leer.

They had not known what he had meant then, but several days later Caroline, her mother, her aunts, and all the younger woman servants were taken to the château cellars, and imprisoned. Every night Captain Arnaud would come with his right-hand man, Citizen Leon. They would pick two of the young serving girls, and return them in the morning. Now and again a girl would not return for several days, if at all.

"What is happening to them?" Caroline had asked her mother.

"Better you not know," her mother had replied.

And it had been better, until the night that Captain Arnaud had pointed his thick finger at Caroline and beckoned her to him.

"Non!" her mother had said, standing up and facing their captor. "My daughter is the only child of an English lord. He will pay you a very generous ransom for her safe return." The countess had put emphasis on the word safe. "I have told you this before, Captain Arnaud. My husband will pay for all the women here. You have but to send to his yacht, which by now lies anchored in the village cove, waiting to return us to England. Ask what you will. My husband, the Earl of Chetwyn, will pay. Have you no desire to be a rich man?"

"Why is it that all you damned aristos think money is the answer? I've come to get a woman for a night's entertainment. If you do not want me to take your daughter, then come with me yourself. And your sister will do for Leon."

Lady Caroline Thornton had not known then the terrible sacrifice her mother and her aunts had made for her that night—and in the nights that followed, for Captain Arnaud and Citizen Leon delighted in degrading the two women. Yet the two sisters retained their dignity in spite of it all. Her mother managed to write a note to the earl, and with the aid of the château cook it reached the yacht captain, who sailed immediately for England. And the Earl of Chetwyn had come immediately to rescue his family from the hands of the Revolution.

But it had been too late. Now bored with the two sisters, Citizen Leon had had them restrained by his men as they were taken from the cellars to the main salon. They were then forced to watch as the youngest of them, Louisa, had been raped first by Captain Arnaud, then Citizen Leon, and finally the other six men in their ragtag band. Her aunt had at first struggled and screamed to her sisters and then to the Holy Virgin to save her. The taking of the girl's virginity was a painful event, made more so by her eager rapist. Her pitiful cries had set Caroline's *tante* Justine into a frenzy of hysterical fury. She fought against her captors wildly, and then to their surprise she managed to break free. Snatching a knife from one of the men's waistband, she stabbed him to death before she was subdued by the others and her own throat was slit.

By now Caroline was numb with her fear of what was to come. But then, to her surprise, she was returned to the cellars of the château. She did not see her mother again. One of the serving women returned in the morning and told her that they had strangled *pauvre* Madame Claudine, but not before the countess had been forced to endure every possible indignity a man might visit on a woman. She had been raped over and over again, and beaten. As for her *tante* Louisa, she had not survived long after Caroline had been taken from the chamber. Now Caroline was alone. But Captain Arnaud did not point his fat finger at her again. And several weeks later she was led from the cellars to the château's elegant salon, where she found her father waiting with the captain. A ransom had been paid, and she was free to leave France.

The Earl of Chetwyn, while heartbroken at losing his wife, never knew how she had really died. He had been told she and her two sisters had suffered from the damp and cold of their prison. And Caroline had never told her father the truth. How could she? And if she could not tell her father, how could she tell her husband? How could she explain that when she disappeared from Malincourt it was to travel to France on her father's old yacht, which now belonged to her? Would he understand that she was the rescuer, Lavender, whom all the ton was talking about, and that at least half a dozen of her close friends were Lavender's Ladies? She had a mission to rescue those poor souls caught up in the Terror of the Revolution. It didn't matter if they were aristocrats or bourgeoisie. But most of all she wanted her revenge upon Captain Arnaud and Citizen Leon. But she had yet to be able to find them again. They had disappeared from her grandfather's château.

"Tell me where you go, Caro," the duke said once again.

She looked up at him with desperate eyes, and shook her head. "You must trust me, milord," she told him.

"How can I when you do not trust me, my love?" he asked, anguished.

And then there was the sound of a tinkling bell, and Emily awoke in her bed. The television screen had gone to snow, as it always did when the Channel closed for the night. She gazed briefly out of her window. The leaves were turning, and in just a few days she would be off for England. Devlin had left for Frankfurt last Thursday, and she missed him. Sighing, she closed her eyes and willed herself to sleep. She had a busy few days ahead of her, and in the morning she would rewrite the scene that had just played out in the Channel. It was much better than her first draft. It seemed she was hardly asleep when Essie was shaking her awake.

"Honestly, Emily," she said, "you've got to stop all this burning of the midnight oil, girl. It's past nine o'clock. The phone in your office has rung twice now. Can I fix you some breakfast? I'm washing windows today, and getting the slipcovers off in the living room. October is my turnover time."

"Bring me a yogurt and an English muffin up to the office," Emily said, swinging her feet over the edge of the bed.

"Coffee?" Essie asked as she turned to go.

"God, yes!" She stumbled into the guest bathroom and started the shower. Essie was right: She had to stop burning the midnight oil. Essie, however, would have been shocked to know why she was burning it. With Michael Devlin away, Emily had discovered a need for daily sex that she had never anticipated. Ever since he had gone back to the city after Labor Day and his visits were limited to the weekends, her insatiability had been growing. She was in the Channel every night he wasn't with her, sporting with her duke. And then in the morning she would translate it into pages for the book. Emily was frankly amazed by her own appetite for fucking.

She stepped into the shower. Just thinking about it made her hot as a firecracker. She slicked the body wash over herself and thought it felt like a rough tongue. Her nipples grew tight, and an ache began between her thighs. A hand moved to push between her labia to play with her clitoris. It felt so damned good, Emily thought with a sigh, and then she caught herself. Her hand reached out, quickly turning the shower lever all the way to the left. She gave a little yelp, and winced as the icy water hit her, but it sure as hell took her mind off of endless sex. This had

to stop! She needed Devlin—not just on the weekends, but forever after.

Just two more days until she flew to England. Emily packed. England in autumn in Suffolk. She'd need her riding pants, which
were put away, but she knew where to find them. They would
need a slight alteration. Her boots and a tweed jacket, and two
pairs of slacks, sweaters, one little black dress, because she
knew they would eat out at least once, and her London Fog
raincoat. Savannah would have Wellies if the weather was
mucky.

She paid a visit to Lacy Nothings and stocked up on a few
outrageous items: two garter belts, one in black, and the other
a wild magenta with matching stockings; and four very naughty
teddies, one a very hot pink, one red, one cream, and the other
black. She also bought a pair of wicked black stilettos with
rhinestone studded heels; and she couldn't resist a pink feather
boa.

The local girl totting up her purchases looked at her somewhat askance. "These all for you, Miss Shanski?" she said, one
eyebrow just slightly raised. Emily was known to love beautiful
lingerie, but some of these items were positively raunchy.

"For my friend Savannah Banning. I'm going to England to
visit her tomorrow," Emily said. "She just loves all the things I
have from the shop, and she's got a birthday coming up soon."

"Ohhh," the salesgirl said, smiling. Now it all made sense.
She had read Savannah Banning's novels. "Yeah, some pretty
naughty stuff in this lot." She grinned. "Hope Miss Banning
likes 'em."

"I'm sure she will," Emily lied. Why did people think only
someone like Savannah Banning would wear racy lingerie? But
she knew the answer to her own question. Emilie Shann wrote
romantic love stories with chaste heroines and manly heroes
who only alluded to sex. Well, not anymore! And she almost
giggled aloud.

The flight was perfect. Emily always flew first-class. Like pretty lingerie, it was one of her weaknesses. She could afford it, and she liked being able to stretch out her legs. And she always booked the entire row, so she didn't have to talk if she didn't want to talk. A young stewardess in first class was a fan, however. She oozed compliments, and practically swooned when Emily agreed to sign her copy of *Vanessa and the Viscount,* which she just happened to have with her. The senior stewardess, who had flown with Emily before and knew her habits, nodded to her passenger with a sympathetic smile. Then she murmured quietly in the younger woman's ear, and the rest of Emily's flight was a peaceful one. Lord Palmer's car was there to meet her. The drive down to Barrow, in Suffolk, was smooth.

"I can't believe you're here!" Savannah Banning squealed, flying from her house to greet her guest. She was an extraordinarily beautiful woman with a mane of midnight black hair, gardenia skin, and gray eyes. "Did you stop at the inn and leave your bags? Devlin phoned from London. He'll be down by teatime, and he's meeting you here." She stepped back and looked at Emily. "Oh, God, you really are in love with him!"

Emily laughed. "I am," she admitted. "Now all I have to do is bring him up to scratch, as they say in my novels."

"I read what you e-mailed me, darling," Savannah said, and she smiled her little cat's smile. "Your fans are in for both a shock and a treat, Em. I love *The Defiant Duchess.*"

"Give me a quote then," Emily said. "That should please J.P."

"Screw J.P.! The woman is a dreadful bitch, but if she knew you got what she didn't I suspect she would explode in a puff of her own nastiness, darling!" Savannah laughed. "Is he good? Really good?"

"Savannah, we had this conversation before, and I have no real comparison," Emily said, laughing. The two women linked arms as they went into the house.

"Is there a similarity to the duke?" Savannah wanted to know. "I thought we'd wait for tea until Devlin gets here."

"There is, and there isn't," Emily said as she settled herself into the cushions of a flowered sofa. "Trahern seems a bit rougher, but then, he is eighteenth-century, Sava."

"Actually I think he's quite dreamy," Savannah murmured. "And so in love with his defiant duchess, darling. It's a wonderful book, Em. It will make you oodles of money." And at Emily's look of disbelief, Savannah Banning giggled. "I know, I know." she said. "Authors don't make money. Publishers make money."

"If it weren't for the early books I couldn't have my simple small-town lifestyle," Emily said. "When was the last time you saw royalties?"

"Oh, let's not talk about publishing," Savannah replied. "I think I hear a car." She got up and went to the bay window of the room. "Yes, Devlin is here."

Emily felt her heart jump. He was here. Would he feel the same way he had felt before he left for Frankfurt almost two weeks ago? Did she? The door to the lounge opened, and oh, yes, she did! Emily launched herself at Michael Devlin, whose handsome face was suddenly wreathed in a broad smile at the sight of her.

His arms closed tightly about her. "God, angel face, I've missed you," he said, and then he was kissing her.

"I'll go and check on tea," Savannah said diplomatically, wondering if they even heard her as she left the room.

"I can't wait," Devlin growled in her ear. He unzipped his fly.

"Neither can I!" Emily moaned as he turned her about, bent her over the padded arm of the couch, and yanked her skirt up. "Oh, God, yes!" she sobbed as his long, thick penis pushed into her. His hands held her steady as her hips moved in rhythm with his. He stopped for just a moment, and the throbbing of his talented cock made her dizzy with her own heated desires. "Make me come, Devlin," she begged him. "I have missed you too. Oh, yes! And yes again!"

He had become an engine of lust with her. He felt himself growing harder than he could ever remember. He plumbed her depths first with slow, almost majestic strokes of his dick. She whimpered with her need, and so he increased the tempo until he was moving with increasing rapidity, and he could feel her orgasm approaching. He slowed himself, and she protested, but, laughing, he first kissed and then nipped at the nape of her neck. "Be patient, angel face. I want it to be extra good for us this time." Then he began to thrust harder and harder, until she was crying out to him with her need for release. He gave it to her, his come spurting in thick gobs into her vagina. Then with a groan he fell forward briefly, his hands reaching around her to clasp her breasts.

Lord Reginald Palmer, Baron Tilbury, had come upon the scene shortly after it had begun. He smiled and watched as Michael Devlin fucked the adorable Emily Shanski, his own dick getting harder and harder. The scene seemed to go on forever, and he was sorely tempted to pick up where the Irishman had left off. But then his wife was drawing his penis from his riding breeches, kneeling down, and sucking him off. "Good girl," he murmured low as she swallowed every bit of his salty cum.

"I heard you come in," Savannah said softly. "You're a very naughty boy, Reg, spying on Emily and Mick." She stood up and smoothed her dress down.

"He covered her like one of my stallions with a mare," Lord Palmer replied admiringly. "No hesitation at all. And damned if she didn't seem to quite enjoy it, Sava. Didn't know Emily fucked. Do you think she would enjoy a threesome with us?"

"Already asked, darling, but she said no. Thought it would make a nice birthday surprise for you. Unfortunately you're married to me, and that makes her uncomfortable. Sorry about that. Now I've told Roberts to give us ten minutes and then serve tea. We're fortunate he didn't come upon us, but, of course, it wouldn't be the first time." She took his arm. "I think they're finished now," she said, peeking through the door to the lounge, which hadn't been quite shut. "Let's go in. Emily, Mick, look who's just come in from the stables." She led her husband into the room.

Emily was flushed rosy, but she managed to stand up from the couch, where she had just been sitting. "Reg, how nice," she said as they kissed each other's cheeks.

"You are radiant, Emily, my dear," Lord Palmer replied. There was just the faintest scent of sex about her, and it was very erotic, he thought. He turned to Michael Devlin. "Mick, how are you?" Dumb question. The man had the look of a well-fed tabby, and why not? He was fresh from a boisterous fuck with a lovely woman.

They were barely seated again when Roberts appeared, accompanied by a little maid and carrying a large silver tea tray. He set it down on the butler's tray. "Shall I pour, m'lady?" he asked Savannah.

"Yes, but just first cups, Roberts. Then you and Agnes may go," she answered. She glanced at the tray. Watercress, cucumber, and beef-and-cheddar finger sandwiches. Scones, clotted Devon cream, and strawberry jam. A plate of Mrs. Munson's miniature lemon curd, and mince meat tartlets. Another plate of thin-sliced dark fruitcake. A bit skimpy, but it would do. Tea was a bit late, after all, and there was dinner to consider.

"Didn't they feed you on the flight?" Lord Palmer asked Emily innocently.

"Your English air makes me extra hungry," Emily replied, snatching the last beef-and-cheddar sandwich from the plate. "Sava, this mustard is delicious. Where do you get it? Is it French?"

Master William and Miss Selena were brought into the lounge by their nanny, a starchy-looking older woman, to greet the guests and then bid their parents a good night. They were fresh from their baths, and in pajamas and nightgown. Selena, her mother's miniature, was shy, for she hardly knew Emily, but she did recall Michael Devlin, and was soon curled up in his lap.

"Her mother's daughter," Emily said with a smile.

William, however, remembered his godmother. He put his arms about her neck and kissed her cheek. "Did you bring me a gift?" he asked her.

"It's at the inn, and I will have it for you tomorrow," Emily told him.

"What is it?" he wanted to know.

"It's a surprise, William," she replied.

After fifteen minutes Nanny announced it was time for Master William and Miss Selena to depart. Their supper would be waiting for them in the nursery. The children bade their parents and their guests good night, and left the lounge without protest.

"They have beautiful manners," Emily remarked. Then she glanced at her watch. "I think we have to be going, Sava. I'm exhausted with the time change."

"I thought you would remain for dinner," Savannah protested.

"Not tonight," Emily replied. "I need my rest. It's after eleven at home." She stood up.

"I rented a car," Michael Devlin said, and he stood too. "We know our way back to the inn."

"We'll ride tomorrow about ten," Savannah said. "Join us?"

"I brought my breeches," Emily answered her. "Do you still have that lovely gray gelding I like? He's such a sweetie, and has a nice gait."

"I think we keep him just for your visits, my dear," Lord Palmer said. "I'll see he's saddled and waiting for you. How about you, Mick? That mean black fellow you always seem to favor?"

Michael Devlin nodded. "Perfect. Savannah, my love, thank you for a delicious tea. Reg, we'll see you in the morning." He took Emily's hand, and together they left their hosts. "I've rented a Jag," he said as they came out of the house and helped her into the car. "Shall I order supper in the room?"

"Yes," she agreed, knowing she could look forward to a night of bliss in his arms. "And champagne, Devlin."

"What are we celebrating?" he asked her.

"Being in England," she replied lightly. *Having your cock in my pussy again. Being in love with you,* she thought to herself.

Savannah had arranged for them to have a charming little suite consisting of a small lounge and bedroom, both with fireplaces. The bed was large and hung with flowered curtains. The bathroom was small, but serviceable. Their bags had been unpacked for them by the maid. Emily smiled, wondering what the poor country girl must have thought of all her naughty lingerie. They ate a simple supper and drank their champagne before the fire in the lounge. Then they slept for a while in the big bed, awoke, made tender love, and slept again. When morning came they lay together for a time, watching as the sun crept into the garden outside of their bedroom windows.

"I really did miss you," Michael Devlin said to her. He was holding her hand. It had been lousy without Emily, and he had realized with shock that he didn't like being without her at all. He needed her, which was difficult for him to admit, for Michael Devlin had never needed anyone—especially a woman. But he needed this woman. Still, while she seemed to enjoy the passion they shared, and was an enthusiastic bed partner, she had never indicated that she cared for him. Maybe she didn't. Maybe it was just all about the sex, and hanging on to her career. Well, he could live with that if he had to, couldn't he?

"I missed you too," Emily admitted. "It was so wonderful in August when we could be together all the time. I'm glad you asked me to meet you in England, Devlin." She snuggled against his shoulder. "Rina's afraid you're going to ruin my reputation."

"I certainly hope I am," he teased her. "Ruining you is a most enjoyable pastime, angel face." Then he leaned over and kissed her slowly and sweetly.

Emily sighed with her happiness as their lips touched. But then, as the kiss began to grow more serious in its intent, she pulled away. "We promised milord and milady that we would ride with them at ten," Emily said. "We have to get up. I need my breakfast, Devlin. Knowing Sava and Reg we'll be gone for several hours, and won't see food again until teatime." She slipped from his arms and from the bed.

They showered together, dressed, and went downstairs to the inn's little dining room for breakfast. They were just in time, the hostess told them as she announced that there was only scrambled eggs and sausage left, plopped a rack of toast on their table, and asked if they would have coffee or tea. When they had eaten they drove through Barrow village and several miles on to Tilbury Manor, where Lord and Lady Palmer were waiting for them at their stables with the horses.

As they mounted their animals Devlin noticed Lord Palmer admiring Emily's ass, which looked particularly fetching in her taupe riding breeches. He felt a sharp prick of anger. He knew the Palmers' predilection for threesomes. He'd been invited once to join them himself, but he'd refused. The bastard had no right looking at Emily like that—like a damned fox contemplating a particularly delicious chicken dinner. And then Michael Devlin realized with surprise that he was jealous. He was jealous! Jealous because he loved her. And she was going to damned well love him or he'd know the reason why.

It was a beautiful day, and they rode for several hours. Savannah had arranged for Roberts to bring a picnic luncheon to a designated spot beneath some willow trees in a meadow by a winding stream. When they finally returned to the stables, Reg's cell phone rang, the ring tone playing "Rule Britannia." After a few terse words he went into the house, followed by his wife, who called to her guests to come in for tea.

Emily caught Devlin's arm and drew him back into the darkened stables. The horses had been unsaddled and rubbed down, their feed bins filled. There were no stablemen in sight. "My clit's been rubbed back and forth all day," she whispered in Devlin's ear. "I have always wanted to be fucked in a stable. Would you like to screw me here in a darkened stall on the hay?" She licked at his ear, and then nipped the lobe. Then she unzipped his riding pants and drew his penis out. Kneeling before him she pulled his pants down and began to play with him, nuzzling and licking his balls, twisting her head to take them into her mouth. Her tongue rolled them about slowly within the wet warmth.

Michael Devlin drew a sharp breath. Where had she learned to do that? Her sexual manuals, of course. But dear God, she did what she was doing very, very well. "Not that I don't appreciate the offer," he ground out, "but you'll have to get out of your pants, and getting back into them if someone comes in won't be easy."

Emily released his balls. "No, I won't," she said. "I made a little alteration to my breeches, Devlin. I told you, I've always wanted to be fucked in a stable à la Lady Chatterly. Trust me." Then she licked up and down his penis a few times before taking him into her mouth and suckling him.

His fingers dug into her scalp. "I'm perfectly willing to be the gardener to your Lady Chatterly," he groaned, "but I don't want to come in your mouth, angel face."

She nodded and continued her glorious torture of his cock, which swelled and lengthened until Emily began to gag slightly.

"That's enough," he said low, pulling her up. "Now, madam, show me how I am going to fuck you with your damned pants on." And she took his hand and drew it down to her crotch, pulling the fabric there apart. "Where the hell did you find these breeches?" he asked, both surprised and delighted as they slid to the hay.

"I sew," she murmured, guiding his penis to her very wet cunt. "God, I am so hot for you, Devlin! I don't think I can wait too long."

"Let's get your legs up over my shoulders," he said. "I want to go deep."

And he did, thrusting harder and faster into her until she screamed softly with her orgasm, and he came so hard that they both shook with the force of their pleasure.

"Ohh, that was incredible." Emily gasped as she began to come down again. "It was even better than I thought it would be."

"Glad to be of service, madam," he replied weakly. "You are becoming insatiable, angel face. And I love it."

He adored her. He loved sex with her. Was it possible he had real feelings for her? Of course he did. He loved her. "We'd better pull it together," she said finally. "Sava is no fool, and she'll have figured it out already. But I don't want Reg leering at us when we come in for tea."

"Agreed." Devlin stood up, pulling Emily with him. "Don't forget to close your breeches. How did you make that alteration, by the way?"

"Velcro," she told him with a grin.

He was still laughing when they entered the manor house lounge for their tea.

Savannah was alone, and appeared extremely annoyed. "Reg has to go back up to London tomorrow," she said. "That damned woman," she added, looking as if she might cry. And Savannah Banning never cried.

"What woman?" Emily was at once sympathetic.

"Gillian Brecknock, that so-called actress," Savannah said.

"I thought he gave her up when you were married," Emily said.

"So did I, but it's obviously been going on all along," Savannah said bitterly.

"Oh, Sava, I'm so sorry." Emily put her arms about her friend.

"Oh, don't worry. I'm no Lady Di. I'll never divorce him. And the truth is that he does love me. But he's like all these damned Brit toffs: He's got to have his little bit on the side and think he's keeping it a big secret from the wife because it adds

excitement to the relationship for him. I could ruin it by caus-
ing a scene, but I won't. At least I know who he's with when he's
with Gillian. I know what she is. And I know he had the opportunity to marry her before he even met me, but he wouldn't.
I may be an American, but I'm Southern aristocracy, I'm famous
for writing racy novels, and I'm rich. It gives me more points
than an actress who began her life in Liverpool and still lapses
into the dialect when she gets angry. Reg is a snob at heart, you
know, and I've done my duty as a nobleman's wife. He's got an
heir and a daughter, and the little stick went pink the other day
when I peed on it, so there'll be another next June. That's why
I'm so weepy. Hormones running rampant," she concluded with
a weak grin.

Emily hugged Savannah. "Oh, I'm so happy for you! Even if
he is a pig!"

"You should have kids," Savannah said softly.

"You have to have a husband to have kids," Emily replied.
"At least I do."

"Then you're ready to get married," Savannah persisted,
looking past Emily to Michael Devlin and fixing him with a
hard stare.

"If the right man asked, yes," Emily said.

At that moment Lord Palmer came into the lounge. "Did
Sava tell you?" he asked them. "I have to go back to London tomorrow. One of my clients is in need of my services," he told
them smoothly. "Let's skip tea, Sava, and take Emily and Mick
out to dinner. That charming little French restaurant that
opened up a few months ago on the other side of Barrow would
be lovely, don't you think? It's called La Belle Auberge."

"What a brilliant idea, darling," Savannah said, smiling at
her husband.

"Then we'll go back to the inn to dress, and we'll meet you
at the restaurant," Michael Devlin said. "The concierge will tell
us how to get there."

"Perfect!" Savannah agreed. "I'll make the reservations.

Eight o'clock all right?" She reached up, and pulled a piece of straw from Emily's hair. "Don't be late," she told them with a wicked grin.

"How long do we have?" Emily asked her lover when they had regained their rooms at the inn.

"A little over three hours," he said. "Why?"

"I thought you would like to see something I bought before I left," she replied innocently, but a little smile played at the edges of her mouth.

"Is it naughty?" he asked her.

"Yes," she said, "but how naughty depends upon you, Devlin."

He nodded, seating himself in a wing chair by the lounge fire. "I will await your pleasure, angel face," he told her with a smile. He loved how she was suddenly seeking out things to please him. Was it because she cared for him, or was she just re-searching again? How the hell could he ever really know? And yet she had said quite plainly to Savannah that she was ready to marry and have children. But was he? Yes, he loved her the way he had never really loved another woman. But was he ready to give up his freedom, and stick to one woman for the rest of his days? And when he married it would be forever. He was Irish, for God's sake.

Emily went into the bathroom and quickly showered. Thor-oughly dried, she now put on the black garter belt, rolled on a pair of black stockings with tiny diamantés scattered all over them, and slipped on the black teddy. It barely reached her belly button, was held up by thin little silk straps, and had tiny heart cutouts that allowed her nipples to thrust out through the fab-ric. Slipping her feet into the black silk-and-rhinestone stilettos, she gave her strawberry-blond hair a quick brush, looked at her-self in the floor-length mirror on the closet door, and smiled, pleased.

"Close your eyes, Devlin," she told him. "And ready or not,

here I come!" Then she walked out into the other room, stood before him, and said, "Okay, you can open your eyes now." She had struck a provocative pose, her butt sticking out.

His open eyes widened with appreciation at her appearance. "Yes," he drawled slowly. "Very naughty indeed, angel face. Now stay where you are, because I found a few things in a shop in Frankfurt that should give us a little fun." He stood up, going back into the bedroom to reemerge a moment later. There was a leather glove on his right hand. "This," he said, showing it to her, "is a spanking glove. See the tiny little prickers on the palm? The outfit you're wearing just screams, "Spank me," and so I'm going to spank you, angel face." He held out his hand. "Over my knees with you!" He pulled her down, and without another word began to spank her adorable bottom. He thought about Lord Palmer eyeing it earlier, and his hand fell harder.

At first the prickly glove simply stung. Then it began to burn, and her flesh grew warm, especially her clitoris. The spanking seemed to excite the sentient little nub of flesh. She squealed and wiggled, attempting to escape the glove, but Devlin's hand was firmly planted in the small of her back, restraining her. Finally she could bear no more, and begged him to cease. He did at once, putting her on her knees and pulling his engorged penis from his pants.

"Suck!" he commanded her. "Take me all the way." And she did, letting his come slide down her throat. But she was still filled with her own lust.

She looked up at him, pleading. "Devlin?"

He stood and pulled her with him, leading her into their bedroom. "Lie down," he said. Then his hand went into his pocket, and he drew out two tiny, smooth ivory balls, rolling them about in his palm. "Inside each of these is a tiny drop of mercury," he told her. "When they touch each other the effect is going to be quite stimulating. Open your legs for me," he told her, and when she had he slowly inserted each ball into her vagina, pushing them well up into her body. "Now get up and walk across the room for me in those wicked trashy shoes that are so perfect with the teddy and garter belt."

Emily slipped her legs over the bed and, standing, began to walk. Suddenly she stopped and gasped. Her body was suffused with a rush of heat. "Oh, my God!" she exclaimed. She took a few more steps. "Devlin, these are pure torture." Not only that, but her ass was still burning from his leather glove. The combination of the two was murder.

"Then they're doing their job," he replied. "By the time we get back from dinner you should be more than ready to be fucked, angel face."

"You expect me to keep these things inside me while we're having dinner with Savannah and Reg? If the way I'm feeling now gets any more intense, even Reg Palmer is going to look good. Do you have any idea what they are doing to me?" She looked outraged. "Damn it, I am ready to be fucked right now!"

"I know what they are supposed to do to you," he answered her, "and obviously they are. But trust me: It will be much, much better after dinner. But," he taunted her gently, "if you don't think you can manage it then I'll take them out."

He was throwing a challenge at her. She slowly walked back across the bedroom. "No," she said. "I'll manage." But how, she wasn't quite certain. Every time those damned little balls hit each other a wave of sensual sensation rolled over her, and all she wanted was his big cock in her pussy.

Devlin pulled her into his arms and began to slowly kiss her. "Good girl!" he said softly. "You won't be sorry, I promise you." He slipped his hand beneath the sheer silk of the teddy and fondled a breast.

"Go to hell!" she snapped, and pulled away from him. "I'm going to take a nap before we have to dress for dinner."

"Me too," he replied with a grin.

"Not here," Emily said. "You can't have your cake and eat it too, Devlin. Nap in the lounge."

"Okay," he said, just slightly chastened, and he left her.

Emily escaped the subtle torture of the ivory balls for a brief time while she napped. She found a comfortable position and remained in it. He awakened her with kisses, and for a moment she forgot the little spheres—until the first wave of lust hit her. She stripped the teddy off and slipped the little black dress on. It had a scooped neckline to show off her breasts, cap sleeves, and a flirty ruffled skirt that just brushed her kneecaps. She slipped her feet into a pair of black silk heels, ignoring the deliciously trashy stilettos. She could only imagine what Lord Palmer would think if he saw her in those. Sitting at the little dressing table, she opened her jewel pouch, but Devlin came up behind her and slipped a delicate gold chain with a small diamond heart about her neck.

"I found that in Frankfurt too," he said softly, kissing her shoulder.

"How can you be such a bastard one minute, and so nice the next?" she asked him, admiring the chain and the diamond.

"Do you like it?" he asked her.

"Of course I do! It's beautiful," Emily said.

"How can you be so prim and proper one moment, and so carnal the next?" he asked, smiling down at her.

"My orgasm later had better be the best one I've ever had, or you're toast, Devlin!" she threatened him. "These damned little balls are wicked torture. At least my butt isn't burning anymore."

"We'll take care of your cute little ass later, and you'll come like you've never come before, I promise you," he said, drawing her up and to her feet. "We had better go. It's at least a twenty-minute drive, the barman said. I went down while you napped, and asked."

The Jag sped through the night, the countryside around them dark but for the occasional lights from a cottage. Finally they reached La Belle Auberge, parked, and went in to find Sava and Reg already there. Emily thought at one point that she was going to scream as the little balls banged together over and over again. There was a tiny dance floor, and Reg insisted on dancing with Emily. He held her so close she could feel his hard-on, and the damned thing felt good, considering the silent torture she was enduring. Finally the music stopped, and Emily excused herself to go to the ladies' room. Savannah followed.

"What's the matter?" she asked Emily. "You look pale."

"I'm walking around with two little balls stuck up my cunt," Emily said.

"Oh, my God! He made you wear them out to dinner?" Savannah's gray eyes were wide. "Oh, sweetie, you are going to come like no tomorrow later! Those things are wicked, wicked, wicked. Devlin is more adventurous than I thought, considering he turned us down like you did. Reg usually never asks other men to join us. He's jealous of other men who hover around me. And, of course, he likes to be sure my children are his. He only asks other women. He asked Devlin to join us because he knew I think he's hot, and I suspect he'd done something especially bad that I didn't know about, and was trying to soothe his conscience. We had better cut this evening short."

"Not until I've had dessert," Emily said. "I need the most chocolaty of chocolate mousses, and I need it now!"

Savannah began to giggle. "I hope Mick is prepared for endless fucking," she said. "It's going to take several long hours to scratch that itch he's given you."

"Even your randy Reg looks good to me right now," Emily muttered.

"You'd hate yourself in the morning." Savannah cackled.

"I know," Emily said, wincing, and her best friend laughed harder.

The two women returned to the table, and dessert was ordered. Emily ate two plates of chocolate mousse, complaining when she saw the first serving that it was way too little. She washed them down with champagne, and then announced she was ready to go back to the inn. Outside, the two women air-kissed each other, and Lord Palmer insisted on giving Emily a kiss on the cheek, which was no more than an excuse to squeeze her ass as his arm slipped about her waist and he pulled her close. He still had the hard-on. Well, at least Savannah was guaranteed a good night as well.

They began the drive back to the inn, but Devlin suddenly pulled off the road into a stand of trees. The engine had barely died when he was yanking her into his arms and kissing her hungrily. "He had a hard-on when he danced with you. Did he rub it against your pussy?" Devlin demanded.

"Yes," she whispered in his ear. "He still had it when he kissed me good night, and he squeezed my butt. Are you jealous, Devlin?" she teased him, the tip of her tongue outlining the inside of his ear seductively.

"Did you want him?" His voice was rough, angry. "Did you think about what it would be like to have his cock up your cunt, angel face?"

"I only want you, and instead of taking me back to our room, where we can fuck each other's brains out, you're raving at me in the car like a jealous lunatic. The thought of Reg Palmer as a lover disgusts me. If he were the handsomest, most charming man in the world I wouldn't screw him. He's my best friend's husband, and I do have some standards," Emily said icily. "Now start the damned car and let's get back. I am so hot for you right now I could die, Devlin!"

He groaned. "I'm sorry," he said. "I get jealous when I see him imagining himself with you."

"Why?" she demanded softly.

He wasn't certain he had heard her. "Why?" he repeated.

"Yes, why do you get jealous?" Emily said.

Why? Because he loved her, that was why! But he couldn't seem to get the words out of his mouth, and remained silent.

"Do you like me, Devlin?" Emily said gently. "Do you get jealous of other men because you like me?"

"I think so," he admitted to her. "Yes, damn it, that's it!" He sounded to himself like a moron. What the hell was the matter with him that he couldn't tell her that he was in love with her?

That he had never before loved a woman the way he loved her? But he couldn't say it, because if he did it would mean more to Emily than just a casual affair. Loving Emily meant forever. It meant children. It meant happily-ever-after, and Michael Devlin wasn't quite ready to admit that he had the same needs as other men: a desire for a mate, for offspring, for a warm place to come home to. And what if she didn't love him? What if it really had been all about the sex, and nothing more? About her career.

"Turn the key in the ignition, Devlin," she said to him. "If you don't get those damned ivory balls out of me soon I'm probably going to kill you. And incidentally, I like you too." There! She had said it. And she had heard him say it. He liked her! Was *like* shorthand for *love*? Men always found it hard to use the word *love*. Was *like* better than *adore*? When they got back to the States she was going to begin to put the pressure on Michael Devlin. She didn't want him just as a lover anymore. She wanted him as a husband, but getting confirmed bachelors to commit to forever-after was never a simple thing. Aaron had said their relationship was a forbidden one. But it didn't have to be. Why couldn't real life be as easy as her novels? She could manage the Duke of Malincourt, the Earl of Throttlesby, and their ilk. But could she manage to get a proposal of marriage from Michael Devlin? If she couldn't she was going to die an old maid, because Emily Shanski was not a woman to give her heart away more than once, and Devlin already had it.

CHAPTER EIGHT

"How does it work?" Emily asked Savannah. They were curled up together on Lady Palmer's large bed. Lord Palmer was in London, and Michael Devlin was flying back to New York even as she spoke. Emily could hardly wait to follow. Two nights ago she and Devlin had engaged in the most incredible sex. She wanted more.

"Actually, it works just like the old one, except if you click the enter button twice, both of us can enter the same fantasy," Savannah explained. "They're just trying it out with a few good customers worldwide. I haven't attempted it with a friend yet, but I thought this would be a great time to try it."

"I don't know, Savannah," Emily demurred.

"Now that you know what sex is really all about," Savannah said, "aren't you just the tiniest bit curious to know the perverted side of it? I know you, Emily. If Devlin doesn't propose you'll never marry, and you probably won't take another lover in or out of the Channel. This is your chance to experience some naughtier aspects of sex."

"Devlin and I have had oral and anal sex," Emily replied. "And he likes to spank me now and again."

"Ever had multiple partners?" Savannah replied. "Of course you haven't. There are things you should experience, if only once. You know you have the right to refuse or say no. And I'm going to be there too."

"Where?" Emily asked.

"London, 1870. I've created this fancy brothel called the Cock and Cunt. I peopled it with a Madame Rose, pretty whores, and lots of randy gentlemen. Only wealthy gentlemen can afford the Cock and Cunt. We'll be two of the girls. You'll be Molly, and I'll be Polly. We're cousins, and the men are all mad about us."

"I suspect I shouldn't ask," Emily said, "but what are we wearing?"

"Well, to begin with, we both have long, curly hair down our backs," Savannah said. "Do you want to change your color? I like my black hair, especially with my fair skin. Actually, I think your coloring is perfect."

"What are we wearing?" Emily asked again.

"Not a whole lot." Savannah giggled. "We have black silk stockings that are gartered at the thigh, and colorful short silk robes with sashes."

"How short?" Emily wanted to know.

"They barely conceal your pussy," Savannah admitted.

"Sounds very provocative," Emily noted. "I think I should have a narrower waist and bigger boobs, though. What do you think?"

"Tiny waist and curving hips," Savannah replied. "Very fashionable, Em! And we'll be twenty. It's a perfect age! Then you'll do it with me?"

"I shouldn't," Emily said, "but a couple of hours without Devlin and I find myself getting very horny, Sava. I don't know what the hell has come over me; I seem to want sex all the time. Sometimes I think I would have been better off to remain a virgin."

"No, you wouldn't have!" Savannah said. "Look, sex is fun.

And sex on the Channel is not just fun; it's guilt-free. These fantasies are our secrets. We don't share them with the men we love, or even most other women. Men have their secret fantasies too. And some not so secret, like old Reg up in London boinking Gillian tonight. She's such a cow. I don't know what he sees in her, Emily."

"The forbidden," Emily said sagely. "Aaron says my relationship with Devlin is something forbidden." She sighed. "I never thought to fall in love with him. And if I'm in love with him, should I be cavorting on the Channel with other men?"

"The men we're going to cavort with are fantasy men. They don't exist in our reality, Emily. No guilt," Savannah repeated. "Besides, Devlin hasn't committed himself to you yet. And God knows, he's had plenty of other women in his time. He's your first," Savannah responded softly. "We'll have a great deal of fun, I promise you, and you know you can stop it anytime you want. But you won't want to stop, I'll wager."

"If I did, would I spoil your evening?" Emily wanted to know.

Savannah shook her head. "No, you wouldn't. I understand from the brochure I got that we can go into the Channel together, but we don't have to return together. Curfew, of course, is the same. We'll wake up here. We're the toast of the Cock and Cunt, Miss Molly. The men all adore us, and we're Madame Rose's special pets because of it." She tilted her head to one side. "Are you ready for a wicked adventure?"

Emily laughed. *Why not?* she thought. *In my reality I would never be unfaithful to Devlin, particularly if we marry. This is probably the only chance I'll ever get to be a wild child. And having Savannah with me is just perfect. She can always get me to attempt things I might otherwise never try.* "I'm ready," she said.

Savannah pointed the channel changer at the large plasma-screen television. She clicked the on button. She clicked the proper numeral. And there on the screen an elegant parlor came into view. The couches were upholstered in ruby-red velvet. They matched the heavy curtains covering the windows. The furniture was dark mahogany in the Empire style, with bright brass fittings. Some of the tabletops were of marble. The carpeting on the floor was of thick wool in the Oriental style. Everything was expensive and of the best quality, from the Waterford chandelier hanging from the center of the gilt plaster ring of fruit upon the ceiling to the decanters on a mahogany sideboard to the heavy gilt-framed paintings on the wall, which offered tasteful scenes of gods, goddesses, satyrs, nymphs, and centaurs in various sexual pursuits.

In the middle of a large settee covered in purple-and-turquoise-striped satin sat a large, voluptuous woman in a beautiful bright green silk gown with a low neckline that showed a generous amount of her big snow-white breasts. Emeralds and diamonds sparkled around her neck and at her ears. Her red hair was drawn back in a chignon, which was decorated with creamy camellias. "Where are Miss Molly and Pretty Polly?" the woman said in a slightly rough voice that belied her elegant appearance. She looked about the large parlor, which was filled with several well-dressed gentlemen and a number of scantily clad young women.

Savannah double-clicked the enter button. "Here we are, Madame Rose," she answered as she and Emily walked into the parlor.

Madame Rose looked both women over critically. "A prettier pair of soiled doves I ain't never seen," she said, smiling at them. She had big teeth, and they were faintly yellow with her age, for Madame Rose had seen a good half century. "Come and sit with me, my dears. I expect some of your regulars will be here soon enough tonight, and you'll be kept as busy as two little bees servicing their randy cocks in your juicy cunnies." She cackled. She patted the settee where she sat.

"If we sit down the gentlemen will see our pussies," Savannah simpered. Within the Channel in her guise of Pretty Polly she had lost fifteen years off her face. Her breasts were high and conical in shape beneath her short little robe of black silk. The color flattered her fair, creamy skin.

"They'll see your pussies soon enough," said the madam with a chuckle, "and a pretty one it is, my dear. All those thick black curls. I am amazed that you and Miss Molly are related in the first degree of cousinship. You do not favor each other at all in either features or personality."

"Yet we are both fine whores, are we not?" Savannah said. "And you would not have had Miss Molly had I not convinced her to join me."

"True, true," the madam agreed. "And you are both excellent girls, obedient and adventurous, although Miss Molly must often be convinced. How the gentlemen love strapping her plump bottom until she agrees. No one can cry as well as Miss Molly," the madam said approvingly, and she patted Emily's round pink knee.

Emily had been silent from the moment they had entered the Channel. Her surroundings were fascinating. The idea of being a whore in a brothel was intriguing. She was wearing a sheer pale lavender silk robe that came just to her thighs. She might as well be naked, she thought, yet the garment suited her current state.

Suddenly a party of boisterous gentlemen entered the parlor. They were dressed in formal evening wear. Flinging their cloaks and hats to a little maid, they looked about them. Spying the two young women with Madame Rose, they made directly for the pair. The leader of the group snatched up Madame Rose's hands and kissed them. She simpered at him.

"Bertie, you naughty boy, I know what you want, and you shall have it," she said with a wide smile, showing all her teeth.

"We want both of them, Madame Rose. There are six of us tonight, and we will need these two delicious wenches to keep us well entertained. May we have your special big room, or is it already taken?"

"I told you I knew what you would want." Madame Rose cackled. "I have saved the big room for your party. You will find champagne, well iced, and lots of toys awaiting you. Miss Molly and Pretty Polly have been eagerly awaiting your arrival," she assured the group. "Go along now, girls, with your fine gentlemen, and entertain them well," she ordered Savannah and Emily, pushing them gently from their places at her side.

"Come, sirs," Savannah said, taking the hands of Lord Albert Bowen and Sir William Cunliffe.

The Honorable Frederick Sinclair slipped an arm about Emily, grinning down at her lecherously. "Come, Miss Molly. I am longing for your kisses."

"And where would you like those kisses to be, Master Freddie?" Emily heard her alter ego asking. Then she giggled and patted his trouser front.

They reached what was known as the big room, and the gentlemen stripped off their coats and vests. Champagne was poured, and they drank liberally.

When the first bottle had been emptied, Lord St. Albans said, "Open your robes, girls, and display your treasures for us to see."

The two women obeyed, revealing their generous breasts and well-furred pussies. Emily was rather fascinated by the amount of pubic hair she suddenly had: tight red-blond curls that overflowed from between her thighs. Her breasts were large and round, with very prominent nipples. St. Albans cupped one of her breasts familiarly, tweaking a nipple, and it immediately stiffened for him.

Baron Everhard licked his lips slowly, and then said, "I want to see you two girls standing facing each other and rubbing your titties together."

Each girl cupped her breasts in her two hands, and then, moving to face each other, began to rub their nipples against one another. Emily's nipples puckered again, and the men chuckled. She blushed, but Savannah just grinned mischievously at her and, leaning down, kissed Emily's right nipple.

"Move closer to each other, girls, put your arms around each other, and rub your pussies against each other," St. Albans told them.

The men watched, two of them growing visibly excited by the little scene before them. Savannah leaned forward and kissed Emily's lips. Her fingers lost themselves in her companion's pubic curls, and Emily's eyes widened in surprise.

"Let's have a girl fuck," one of the men suggested. "It's always a good way to begin a long evening of fucking, frigging, and sucking."

"Capital idea, Johnnie!" another enthused.

"Wait!" St. Albans said, his eyes glittering with his lust. "Why should we waste time watching the ladies when we could be fucking them ourselves? On your back, my adorable Miss Molly."

"Oh, sir, I am hardly ready for that fine man cock of yours," Emily murmured, eyes wide, a single finger in her mouth, making her appear quite innocent.

"Then you shall have Master Dildo and a little bottom birching to warm you up for me, my darling," St. Albans told her. "Gentlemen, if you two would take Mol's legs and bring them up and back so I may have perfect access to her cunny."

"She'll need to be prepared for the dildo," Sir William said. "Let me!" And, straddling the daybed, he leaned forward, and, drawing Emily's nether lips apart, he began to lick the pinkish flesh with a very skilled tongue.

Emily gasped with surprise, for she was being aroused by this strange man, and she wondered if that was right. But the tongue caressing her was most adept, and when he nibbled on her clitoris she could not restrain her squeal of pleasure.

Sir William got up, laughing, and removed himself from between Emily's legs. "Now, St. Albans, give her a bit of the birch, and she will be quite ready for you."

Emily yelped as St. Albans brought the birch rod against her plump buttocks once, twice, and a third time. Then, taking the dildo, he carefully inserted it into Emily's vagina, whipped her three more strokes of the rod, and then began to move the dildo back and forth, slowly at first, and then with increasing rapidity.

Savannah lay down by her friend's side and murmured into her ear, "Pretend to come or he'll be at it all night. Just close your eyes and moan. Thrash your head too."

Emily closed her eyes. The leather dildo was more irritating than exciting. "Oh! Oh! Ohh! Ohhh!" Her strawberry-blond head rolled from side to side. "Ohhhhhhhh!" She stiffened her body and made herself shudder. "Ohhhhhhhhhhhhhhhhhh!"

St. Albans pulled the dildo from Emily's cunt. The bulge in his trousers was enormous. "Give Pol a good treat, boys, while I reward our Miss Molly with what she really desires," he said, unbuttoning his trousers to release his penis which, to Emily's eyes seemed even bigger than the nine-inch leather dildo. "Now, darling," he said, slipping between her thighs, "you have been such a good girl I'm going to let you have a taste of the real thing." He kissed her lips, his auburn mustache tickling her.

"Oh, sir, you are so very big," Emily said.

He chuckled indulgently, pleased by her observation. "Let's see how well you can take a ten-and-a-half-inch cock." He began to push into her.

Emily wrapped her legs about his torso, and he grunted his approval. He was indeed very big, but to her surprise—or was it delight?—she took him in easily, purring in his ear with pleasure as he began to fuck her lustily. His enthusiastic movements were arousing her, and without another thought she let herself enjoy the pleasure he was giving her, and that she was obviously giving him. She began to whisper in his ear, "Oh, sir, you are a bull, and I your little heifer. Oh, sir, I can feel your big balls slapping against my bottom. What a lover you are, sir! Yes! Yes! Oh, yesssssss!" She nipped at his ear and then, sticking her tongue into it, pushed it back and forth in time with his movements.

St. Albans groaned with delight. The evening had only begun, and it was, he decided, a great success. Miss Molly and Pretty Polly were the finest whores he had ever encountered, and there was going to be so much more to come. His thrusts became more intense, and then as he felt her coming he loosed his juices into her with a yell.

Across the room Savannah was lying upon a chaise while Lord Bowen fucked her enthusiastically and she sucked strongly upon the Honorable Frederick Sinclair's big cock. Baron Everhard had his penis in Bertie's asshole, fucking him in time with Bertie's thrusts into her own pussy. The evening had begun quite well, Savannah observed. She watched as Sir William went over to where St. Albans lay with Emily.

"Let someone else have a go, St. Albans," he said.

"She needs a restorative, Willie," St. Albans said. "Mol is a wonderful fuck, but I can see she wants some champagne."

"Very well," Sir William agreed. "I'll get it for her."

Emily did not know until afterward, but the champagne was well laced by Madame Rose with aphrodisiacs to keep the desires of her whores and their patrons up for several hours at a time. The longer a patron spent with one of her girls, the more money she collected. Of course, in the case of certain girls, like Molly and Polly, they were sold for an entire night's entertainment, which included a midnight supper of champagne, raw oysters, and chocolate truffles; and a breakfast of eggs, country ham, kippers, toast, butter, jam, and tea.

Sir William handed Emily a glass of champagne. "Drink it down, my pet," he said. "After all I have seen so far this evening, I am more than ready to fuck you."

"Oh, sir." Emily giggled. "You are very naughty, but I will do my best to please you, I promise." She gave him a mischievous smile.

"If I am naughty," Sir William said, "then you must birch me, my pet, and I shall be even naughtier for you. Would you like to whip my bottom, Miss Molly?"

Emily was amazed by her reaction to this suggestion, and her own behavior as well. She put a thumb in her mouth and, sucking upon it, looked coyly at him from beneath her lashes. "Can I whip you hard?" she halflisped at him.

His amber eyes glittered with anticipation. "As hard as you can, my pet. After all, bad boys need to be well birched if they are to perform well."

Now Savannah joined in the play. "He must be stripped naked," she said. "All of you must strip naked. Clothing inhibits one from fully joining in our little games."

Obediently the men took off their garments, and as they did the two young women folded the clothes and put them in a large mahogany cupboard on one side of the room. Then, going to the big basket of toys on the marble table with the round brass feet, Savannah took out a black leather collar decorated with brass studs from which hung a short brass chain. Wordlessly she handed the collar to Sir William. He looked at her questioningly.

"Put it on at once!" Emily said in a hard voice, falling right into the spirit of the game. "You will regret any further disobedience, Willie. Polly, choose a birch for me. One as thick as Willie's own index finger."

Gathered about them, the other men in the room grinned at one another.

"You should have the punishment bar, girls," Baron Everhard suggested. "Shall I fetch it for you now?"

"Ahh, the baron seeks to curry favor with you, Molly," Savannah said with an arch smile. "You will have to reward him for his good behavior."

"Oh, I shall," Emily promised with a little smile. "Yes, James, fetch the punishment bar from the cupboard like a good boy."

Grinning, Baron James Everhard walked across the room, opened the cabinet, and pulled out the required item. He drew the device across into the center of the chamber and, bending, locked the wheels so it would remain steady. An adjustable bar covered with lambs wool that was covered with silk rested between two narrow pilasters. Savannah led Sir William to the bar by his leash, which was then removed. He was bent forward, and the bar fitted to a height that would allow the lordling's bottom to be well displayed for his whipping. His arms were drawn out on either side of him and shackled so he could not flee. His legs were spread wide and shackled as well. He was quite helpless and ready to be punished. Savannah handed Emily the birch rod.

"Now, sir," Emily said in a stern voice. "You have admitted to being naughty. You will confess your fault, and then I shall decide how severe your punishment will be. What have you done, sir? The truth now!" She flourished the rod, which made a fierce swishing sound.

The other men looked to one another, grinning and nodding.

"I caught my cousin Eloise and her maid, Tansy, fondling each other's titties, licking each other's cunnies, and frigging each other. I threatened to tell on them if Eloise did not suck me to a stand, and then let me fuck her maid, but when the maid came too quickly, I buggered Eloise until I finally came. She is very angry at me."

"Did you request her permission to ass fuck her, William?" Emily said seriously.

"No," he said in a petulant tone. "I was far too angry at her wench for coming before I did. Eloise was lying on the bed. She laughed at me, so I rolled her over and just did it to her." He chuckled wickedly. "She squealed like a little piglet when my come filled her up."

"Well," Emily remarked, "you have certainly been a very, very naughty fellow. One does not ass-fuck a lady without her permission. Had it been the servant that would have been a different matter. After all, it was the maid who was at fault, not her mistress. You will have ten strokes of the rod, and then I shall decide if that is enough." Emily said, bringing the birch down on his plump buttocks. He yelped, his body jerking as much as it could as she continued on. When ten red stripes had bloomed upon his pale flesh, Emily asked Savannah, "Is he ready, Pol? Or must he have more?"

The other men looked to Savannah, who had seated herself before Sir William's penis, and watched as it began to rise with each stroke of the rod.

"I think he must have five more strokes, Molly, and I think it will help him if I can lick those big, hairy balls of his. Too much of the rod and he will falter entirely."

Emily began to slowly administer the final five strokes while Savannah attended to Sir William's balls with a wicked tongue. When the last blow had fallen and his friends rushed to undo Sir William, Savannah remained, licking him. But once freed, Sir William pushed Emily to the floor, fell upon her, and began fucking her vigorously. She wrapped her legs about his thick torso and enjoyed every minute of his attentions.

"Champagne!" Savannah sang out quickly, when Emily and Sir William moaned with their orgasms. "We must have more champagne! Then Emily and I must bathe before we continue on, good sirs. We still have much of the night ahead of us, and my cousin and I have not yet been fucked by all of you. I cannot count the night a success until that has happened."

"Oh, we shall all enjoy your bountiful charms, my pets," St. Albans promised.

He was, Emily observed, the leader of the group. He stood naked and quite at ease among his friends. He might very well have been at his club. "Is he going to be your next hero?" she murmured to Savannah who was now pouring the gentlemen their champagne. "He's very handsome and most commanding, I think."

"No, not this St. Albans," Savannah replied. "I'm planning on using an ancestor of his in my next book. It'll be a Renaissance setting. Henry the Eighth or Elizabeth. I haven't decided yet. St. Albans is a marquess's heir. I'm going to write about the ancestor who first got the earldom. The other title didn't come until Charles the Second."

Seeing that everyone now had a glass of fresh champagne, Emily lifted her own glass. "Drink up, good sirs! Polly and I don't want you to flag before the night is over."

The gentlemen laughed and raised their glasses, toasting Polly and Molly, the two finest whores in England.

"Can't speak for the rest of the world because I ain't never been nowhere," the Honorable John Stevenson declared as he drained his glass.

The two women insisted on bathing alone, for they knew that if they allowed the men to join them, all would be lost. Savannah was very particular where cleanliness was concerned, especially after such a round of sexual activity. Emily agreed. Hot water had been brought into the bath next to the big room, and they washed themselves thoroughly. Then, calling the gentlemen to them one by one, they bathed their private parts. They had no sooner finished the ablutions when a knock sounded upon the door, and it opened to reveal two footmen and two little maidservants.

The young men were dressed in tight breeches of dark black satin, and cream-colored vests that were embroidered with a floral design. They wore no shirts, and their arms were bare, their chests visible. Their penises hung out of their breeches, and the rear of the pants had circular cutouts revealing their tight bare buttocks. One of them carried a silver tray, and the other had his arms full of champagne bottles.

The little maids who accompanied them were dressed only in tightly gartered black stockings with ruffled white lawn aprons tied with large bows. Each wore a frilly lawn cap upon her head and calf-high black boots upon their feet. The maids at the Cock and Cunt, but for some older women who supervised, were usually whores in training whose virginities were auctioned off when they reached the age of sixteen. They bustled in now, smiling, one announcing, "Madame Rose thought you might enjoy a small repast now, sirs. There are raw oysters and champagne for the gentlemen, and chocolates and champagne for Miss Molly and Pretty Polly." She curtsied.

"Are you tired yet?" Savannah said softly to Emily. "Do you want to end this fantasy now? The gentlemen have been most enthusiastic tonight."

Emily shook her head. "No," she replied. "The champagne and the chocolates will reinvigorate me, Sava. Besides, I am curious as to what is to come. We have yet to use that enormous bed, which is surely large enough for all of us."

"We're about to use it." Savannah chuckled as the Honorable Frederick Sinclair and Baron James Everhard came to lead her by the hand to the bed. Lord Bertie Bowen and the Honorable John Stevenson came for Emily. St. Albans was recovering, and Sir William was swallowing down the last of the raw oysters.

Lying on the bed, Emily kissed Lord Bowen's lips as her other companion lay behind her, fondling her large breasts. Lord Bowen's fingers played amid her pubic curls for a few moments before pushing past her nether lips to find her clitoris. She continued kissing him, her tongue playing hotly with his tongue. She was just faintly aware of Johnnie Stevenson stroking her bottom with seductive touches. She murmured and pressed back against him. His cock was hard, and, encouraged by her, he rubbed it down the valley between her buttocks.

Then Lord Bowen was lifting one of her legs and bringing it over his torso as he slipped his thick penis into her cunt. Emily felt her ass being pulled open, and her other companion rubbing her fundament with some sort of cream. Then he was pushing into her. She whimpered slightly, but he was already fully sheathed, and his hands were back upon her breasts. "Ohh," she exclaimed as the men began to gently ream her from both ends. "Ohh! Ohh!" Would they find that certain spot? Oh, God, yes! They were working it from both sides, and it was incredible.

"You can take two, my dear," Lord Bowen said.

"And later you will take three," Johnnie Stevenson said, grunting as he worked in rhythm with his friend. "That's it, Mol, push your little ass back nicely onto my cock as Bertie fucks your pretty pussy. How tight you are!"

Lord Bowen groaned with the pleasure he was receiving, and Emily, feeling the two penises almost rubbing against each other as they stroked that sweet little spot within her thought she was going to die of satisfaction. Could you die in the Channel? Could you die of incredible and wonderful sexual satisfaction? She didn't care. And then to her utter amazement they all came at almost the exact moment. She was being spermed from both ends, and it was unlike anything she had ever known before. She tore her lips from Lord Bowen and shrieked with pure delight. Then she fainted.

"Magnificent!" St. Albans said as he observed the trio. "The girl is a perfect whore, gentlemen. Give her some champagne and help her to recover. I must have her again. What an adorable ass she has. I have never seen better."

"Give her time to recover, St. Albans," Savannah said. "She has never before taken two men in that fashion. She has fucked and sucked, and she has been buggered. But she has never been fucked and buggered at the same time. It was an incredible performance, and even I am amazed that she did it so well."

"And she'll do it again!" St. Albans insisted. "I want her ass this time!"

"And I want her pussy," Freddie Sinclair said. "I haven't had a taste yet at all."

"Take me first," Savannah begged. "It will give Molly time to recuperate. Why should she have all the fun?" She turned onto her knees, thrusting her buttocks up. "Is this not worthy of your cocks, gentlemen?"

Sir William grinned. "I'm a fool for a tight ass," he said.

"And Pretty Polly has the juiciest cunt I've ever known," the baron said.

The two men quickly had Savannah impaled on their engorged penises, and they all enjoyed themselves greatly before a mutual orgasm that left both men in a weakened state, for Savannah had squeezed both her vaginal and rectal muscles until both men were so filled with lust that their come burst forth in fierce spurts. She, however, felt merely refreshed. What a pity Reg would allow them to have only another woman in their bed. The things a girl could do with two men were delightful, she thought, and far more interesting than what two women might do together. She would do this again in the Cock and Cunt. It was her favorite fantasy on the Channel to date.

Emily gradually regained consciousness and was plied with more of the champagne laced with aphrodisiacs. She was thirsty, and drank it down gladly. This evening was certainly an eye opener where sexual activity was concerned. She had seen pictures of much of what they had done in her research books, but in the reality of the Channel these things were far more exciting than on a printed page.

"What time is it?" Willie Cunliffe asked.

"Three thirty," St. Albans said, "and time for me to have Miss Molly's ass for myself. Are you recovered, my pet? As you can see, my poker is quite ready for you."

"I want to do it differently," Emily said. "I want three cocks this time. I've never before done three at one time."

James Everhard chuckled as he lay sprawled among the pillows in the middle of the bed. "Come onto my lance then, Mol. St. Albans can have you from the rear, and Freddie will have your mouth."

"Ohh, yes!" Emily agreed, and straddling him, lowered herself onto his penis. It was every bit as large as St. Albans', and slid into her vagina easily. Leaning forward to facilitate her second lover, she felt St. Albans slowly pushing into her ass. The two men began to move in concert, and when they had established a rhythm Freddie Sinclair pulled Emily's head up by her hair, and Savannah guided his cock into Emily's mouth. She began to suck upon him, but the young man had been so aroused by just watching her with the baron and St. Albans that he came almost immediately. Emily, however, understanding his embarrassment, kept him in her mouth, sucking hard upon him and covering his faux pas.

Savannah was, in the meantime, sucking upon the Honorable Johnnie's cock while Lord Bowen fucked her lustily, to be replaced eventually by Sir William. And then the two women heard the clock on the mantel striking the hour. Each regretted the time, but there were strict rules regarding the use of the Channel. They allowed their final orgasms to wash over them, and as the pleasure died they woke up together in Savannah's bed. Turning to look at each other, they burst into laughter.

"You are the best and most awful friend a girl could have," Emily said, grinning. "I have never known a night like that. I never expect to know a night like that again, Sava. I don't believe I could survive another night like that. What a wicked imagination you have to have created such lusty men as those six."

"We could go again," Savannah tempted her. "I know I will."

"No, thank you very much," Emily replied.

"Was it as good as with Devlin?" Savannah wanted to know.

"No," Emily said honestly. "I'm not such a dope that I don't know you can get sexual pleasure with a man you don't love as long as you're having fun. But it's entirely different when you love a man, and you know it. I've had a taste of wickedness, Sava, but it will suffice me for the rest of my life."

"But you seemed to enjoy the multiple partners," Savannah said.

"I did, but you couldn't go on like that in the real world. A night like that would kill a healthy woman. And sex without emotion . . . well, it just isn't right. At least not for me, Sava. Call me old-fashioned, but there it is. It was a fun night, but I don't want to do it again. I don't think I could justify it to myself if I did."

Savannah nodded. "I don't think I'll be taking the Channel's new service myself. I've had it two months now. I never wanted to use it before tonight. I don't really need it. I can visit the bordello on my own. But it was quite an experience, wasn't it?"

"And you pregnant with your third child!" Emily scolded.

"Nothing I do on the Channel harms that," Savannah said. "I asked."

"Who did you ask?" Emily wanted to know.

"Haven't you met Mr. Nicholas, who created the Channel? He's absolutely charming. He invited me to tea once before he moved on to his other interests. There's some woman running the Channel for him now. This double-click thing was her idea, I guess. I never met her, but I did meet him. I clicked on one night and there was this text message for me. I was invited to tea by Mr. Nicholas. Well, I couldn't resist, Emily, so I went. He asked me how I was enjoying it, and some other questions. All very harmless, and he had the most delicious chocolate biscotti. Actually, we didn't have tea. It was sherry. It was a wonderful sherry, but when I asked him where I might get a bottle he apologized and said it was bottled for him expressly. I've never seen him again, but I think he liked me," Savannah concluded. "He said that if he could ever be of help I was simply to leave him a message, and he would help me. Wasn't that nice? Maybe I'll ask him if he can do something about Gillian Brecknock. I wonder if he could. I hate it when Reg goes to see her."

Emily nodded. "Sounds a bit odd," she said. "But nice." She yawned. "I have to get some rest if we're going up to London day after tomorrow, Sava." Turning away from her friend, she curled up and was soon asleep. Lady Palmer quickly joined her.

＊　　＊　　＊

The two women spent the next day relaxing, riding out into the autumn countryside, and playing with Savannah's children. They went to bed early, and the following morning were up early. Tonight Emily would be flying home, and the two friends were going up to London for a few hours of shopping before Lord Palmer's chauffeur would take them out to Heathrow. In late afternoon they stopped in at Claridge's for tea.

"Put us somewhere discreet," Savannah said to the maître d'. "We don't wish to be disturbed by fans, Charles."

"Of course, Lady Palmer," the maître d' said, leading them to a table in a corner where they might observe the room without necessarily being observed. "High tea?"

Savannah nodded. "Perfect!" she said.

"I'll send the waiter over immediately," the maître d' replied with a bow, and he hurried off.

"I love having tea here," Emily said. "It's so genteel, even today."

"Yes," Savannah agreed. "Well, are you ready to finish *The Defiant Duchess* after your little interlude here in England?"

"The whole thing is in my head and ready to be written. Poor Trahern will be very disappointed to know our time is almost over and done. He's been a most charming character, and I've actually enjoyed interacting with him. I think I would have felt guilty about it, except I made him look like Devlin." She chuckled.

"Will Mick recognize himself?" Savannah was curious.

"No," Emily said. "You describe a character on the pages of your manuscript, and you see him or her one way, but every reader sees them a little differently. Devlin hasn't recognized himself. It's odd. I've come to like Trahern. He's been more a friend and a confidant for me. Given the nature of what I do, I don't really have a lot of friends. Rina Seligmann is in her late fifties, and more a surrogate mother to me. You're in England." Emily laughed. "And the truth is, I don't really have a great deal of time for friends."

"I know what you mean," Savannah agreed. "If it weren't for Reg and the children I'd be pretty much alone. I'm just barely involved in village life, but only because of him and the kids. And I don't really have any close women friends except you, and as you pointed out, we're an ocean apart. Well, that's the life of a successful writer, isn't it? We live for and are consumed by our work. It's a lonely business."

"But you manage to do it even married with children," Emily remarked, and then her eye caught a couple entering the room. The woman looked familiar. "Oh, my God!" she said, and forced herself not to stare.

"What is it?" Savannah wanted to know.

"Your husband just came in with a woman who looks suspiciously like Madame Rose," Emily said, her fingers fumbling for her teacup. "Thinner, but same face and blazing red hair."

"Oh, that's Gillian Brecknock," Savannah said casually. "Reg's little friend."

"She looks older than him," Emily observed from beneath lowered lashes.

"She's twelve years older, sweetie," Savannah replied with a small grin.

"Why does he do it? I can see he loves you and the kids," Emily said.

"Well, I wondered that myself," Savannah answered, "when I found out he was coming up to town to see her every now and again. He swore to me when we married that he had given her up, but as he obviously hadn't, I hired an investigator to find out for me what was going on. Gillian styles herself an actress, but she hasn't had a play in five years, and she hasn't done a film in eight. She needs to support herself, and Reg is just one of a number of friends she has who suffer from what I call naughty-boy syndrome. Gillian has become a dominatrix. It's all very discreet. A number of very prominent men go to her for what is referred to as correction. She's obviously very good at what she does. I was shopping here in town about a year ago and saw them together. That's when I got suspicious, but I suppose it's harmless, and I know Reg loves me, so I simply pretend I don't know, like the wives of all the other men for whom Gillian serves a purpose. However, she was Reg's girlfriend before she became what she is, which makes it a little different. He handles her investments, and now and again she calls him."

"And you manage not to kill her?" Emily said. "I'd be furious, not to mention jealous of a woman like that."

"Oh, I have my little ways of getting even just to remind her who's really in charge of Reginald Charles George Arthur Palmer," Savannah said as she popped a miniature lemon-curd tart into her mouth and ate it. "You'll see when we go out."

The two women finished their tea and prepared to leave for the airport. Savannah stood up. She smoothed her cream-and-beige tweed skirt and the cream cashmere turtleneck she was wearing, checked her lip gloss, and fluffed her shoulder-length ebony curls. Then, sliding from behind the table, she gave Emily a wink and charted their path to take them directly by the table where her husband and Gillian Brecknock were now seated. Emily followed, swallowing back the giggles bubbling up in her throat.

Savannah stopped directly in front of the table. She smiled brightly. "Darling! What a coincidence! Em and I had just finished our tea when I saw you. Gillian, what a surprise. You're well, I hope." She bent and air-kissed the woman as her husband stood up from his seat at the table.

"Very, darling," Gillian Brecknock replied in her plummiest tones. "You look wonderful for someone who lives in the country. I do adore tweed, but one just doesn't wear it in London these days."

"This is my best friend, Emilie Shann, the novelist," Savannah introduced her.

"Charmed, Miss Shann," Gillian Brecknock replied, offering Emily four limp fingers. "My mother adores your novels. When is the next one coming out here?"

Lord Palmer looked very uncomfortable, Emily noted, pleased. He should. He was such a pig. "I'm really not certain," Emily answered the woman.

"Reg, my love," Savannah said brightly, "I've got the car, and I'm running Emily out to the airport. Are you coming home tonight? I can come back and pick you up. I have a wonderful surprise for you." She hesitated, and then continued. "Oh, I just can't wait for you to come home! I have to tell you now! We're expecting again!"

Lord Palmer grabbed Savannah and kissed her a lingering kiss. "What fantastic news!" he exclaimed. "Yes, I'll wait for you here at Claridge's, darling. Shall I book us a room for the night so we can celebrate?" he asked her.

"Oh, darling, what fun! That's brilliant," Savannah responded. "I'll come back to the hotel after I drop Emily. But no champagne for me now that I'm preggers again." She laughed. She gave her husband a kiss and, sliding from his embrace, smiled at Gillian Brecknock. "So good to see you, darling. Ta!"

"Good-bye, Miss Brecknock," Emily said. "My housekeeper just adores your old movies on the telly. So nice to have met you. When I tell Essie she'll be thrilled." And, turning, Emily followed Savannah from the restaurant.

They both burst into giggles as the hotel doorman signaled Lady Palmer's car, and they climbed into it.

"What are they serving in there, m'lady? Never thought tea was that funny," the family chauffeur asked, grinning in his mirror at the two women, who were caught in the throes of their laughter.

"Just a particularly silly jest, Jim," Lady Palmer answered, and she pressed the button that put up the privacy window between driver and passengers.

"That was fun!" Emily said.

"I know," Savannah replied. "It's almost too easy with Gillian. Is Essie really a fan of the bitch's?"

"Essie wouldn't know Gillian Brecknock if she fell over her," Emily responded, "but after that remark about her mother enjoying my books I couldn't resist having my revenge. Wait until Mama reads *The Defiant Duchesss*." She giggled.

"I really am going to miss you," Savannah said.

"We'll always have e-mail," Emily teased her friend. "And the phone."

"Not the same, but it will have to do, I'm afraid," Savannah said.

"It's been the most wonderful week." Emily sighed. "But that manuscript is going to be in on time, and Merry Christmas to J. P. Woods. Devlin says the advertising and promotion are really spectacular. They have a whole bunch of interviews arranged for me. I can do the radio stuff at home, and we'll do a dozen or more on television from a studio in the city. It sounds really exciting."

"And you'll have Mick pitching the book hard," Savannah said. "Emily . . ." She hesitated, but then went on: "I don't want you to get hurt. You've done what you had to do to write this book. But if it doesn't go any further then you mustn't be heartbroken, sweetie. He's a great affair, or so the women I know who've been with him have said; but I'm not sure he's more than that. Oh, damn! I know you love him, but too often these things don't work out. You have to be prepared for it. And you don't want to lose him as an editor. He really is the best. I'm going to be working with him again. I could not tolerate old Pruny, and I called Martin. My manuscripts are going to New York now, and Mick will do them. They're published there anyway, and with the computer it's so easy now. Not like the bad old days." She put her arm around Emily. "You're going to be all right with this, aren't you?"

"Rina says he's in love with me," Emily said softly.

"Well, I have to admit I did see a difference in him when you were together," Savannah admitted, "but I just don't want you being blindsided and hurt if he does the usual Mick thing and goes off with some other woman."

"I'm not going to let him," Emily said quietly. "He's mine, and I'm not nearly as tolerant as you are, Sava. I'm not one of my early heroines. I'm every bit as tough as my defiant duchess. Devlin is mine, and I mean to keep him."

CHAPTER NINE

Emily came through customs to find Michael Devlin waiting, and her heart skipped a beat. "You're supposed to be at work," she said to him as he kissed her mouth.

"I took the day off," he said with a grin. "Give me your bags. I'm taking you home, angel face. I called Rina yesterday and told her to cancel your car service."

"I'd much rather ride with you," Emily replied with a smile.

"How was the flight?" he asked.

"I slept most of it," she admitted. "Remember, I left at eight their time. Sava and I had tea at Claridge's, and then she took me to the airport. I bought you something at Harrod's. I hope you don't mind," Emily said. "It's just a sweater, but it had your name written all over it."

He helped her into the car. "You don't know my size," he said.

Emily laughed. "I've figured out all of your sizes by this point, Devlin," she teased him. "It's a sweater, for heaven's sake, not a pair of trousers or silk boxers. You don't have to take it, you know. I can give it to my oldest half brother for Christmas."

"I didn't say I didn't want it," he began.

"Oh, shut up and drive," Emily told him. "I've had it with traveling, and I want to go home. We've got two hours ahead of us, given the traffic. My flight was full of business people who want to get into the city for a full working day, and it's rush hour."

"We're going in a different direction," he reminded her, and put the Healy into gear, pulling out of the arrivals parking lot.

They escaped the airport congestion and swung onto the parkway. It was closing in on the end of October, and the leaves were almost at peak. It would be a glorious weekend, and with luck the weather would hold. It had been a perfect day coming in. The sky was a clear blue and the sun bright. It didn't seem possible she had been gone just over a week. They were both quiet as he drove. He seemed to sense her need for it.

Emily brightened, however, as they came off the parkway onto the local country road that meandered into Egret Pointe. The village was decorated for autumn. The tall trees along Main Street where the old-fashioned shops were located were surrounded by cornstalks tied with bright orange ribbons. At their feet were piles of pumpkins and gourds, along with small baskets of apples. A banner was hung across the street announcing the Egret Pointe Harvest Festival, which was being held the coming weekend.

"Wanna come?" she asked him. "We raise money for the hospital at the festival."

"Yes," he replied. "How?"

"The proceeds from it all go to it. We've got booths selling handiwork, jams and jellies, baked goods, knitted goods, birdhouses," she explained. "I even have a table selling my author copies, personally inscribed, of course. And there's a big harvest supper in a tent. And, of course, the Dr. Sam Dunk. That always raises a pretty penny."

"What's the Dr. Sam Dunk?" he asked her, smiling at her enthusiasm. He turned onto Colonial Avenue, and then Founders Way.

"Dr. Sam sits over a tank of Jell-O," she said. "You get three balls for two bucks. If you hit the mark right, Dr. Sam goes into the Jell-O. At this time of year the gelatin is a bit warmer than water, but he usually gets the sniffles anyway. He's an awfully good sport about it. His great-grandfather started the hospital, you know. There's always been a Dr. Seligmann in Egret Pointe."

He pulled the Healy into her driveway. "You love this town, don't you?"

Emily nodded. "I gain my strength from living here," she said. "When do you have to go back? Not right away, I hope."

"I'll drive in tomorrow morning," he said, leaning over to kiss her. "I missed you, Emily." His big hand cupped her face, and he kissed her again, this time lingeringly, longingly. "I didn't like having you on the other side of the pond."

"I missed you too," she told him. "As nice as it was to be with Sava, I missed you, Devlin. Maybe we shouldn't be apart again."

"Maybe not," he agreed. Then he got out of the car. "I'll get the bags. I hope you bought something outrageous for Essie in London. I think she's expecting it."

"I never forget my friends," Emily told him. "And I bought a lovely teddy bear for her new grandchild, and two sets of old-fashioned wooden soldiers for her grandsons. They don't make tin ones anymore. Something about the lead content. I asked."

He took her bags in and up to her room. Emily wanted a quick nap before lunch, and so Michael Devlin went upstairs to her office in the widow's-walk room to make some calls while she napped. He made a point of saying that was where he would be, for Essie's benefit, and sure enough the housekeeper trudged up at one point to see if he needed anything. He thanked her and said he was just fine, grinning at her retreating form. He knew from having been raised in his own small Irish village that people were probably talking at this point, but no one here—except Rina and Dr. Sam, of course—really knew what was happening between Emily Shanski and her editor from New York.

What was happening? Michael Devlin asked himself for the thousandth time. He was in love with her, and he knew now that he had never really been in love before. He was going to have to make a decision sooner rather than later. Was forty too old to get married for the first time? He had never lived with a female except his grandmother, although there had been several invitations over the years from women whom he had dated. But it hadn't felt right to him. They hadn't felt right. This was different, however. Picking Emily up at Virgin Atlantic this morning, driving her home, planning to spend the night, and driving into town in the morning—that felt right. But was he ready for a lifetime of moments like that? Yeah, he finally thought he was, but he'd give it a few more weeks before making a final decision. Forty wasn't the end of the world for a man.

They ate lunch out on the side porch: bowls of Essie's thick corn chowder, home-baked bread and butter, warm apple Betty with heavy cream.

"I'm going to get fat eating like this," he said with a smile.

"No, you aren't," she assured him. "You're too active. We'll go for a walk after lunch down by the beach."

"I thought we'd take a nap." He leered at her, waggling his bushy black eyebrows.

Emily laughed. "Not until Essie goes home, Devlin. I'd like to keep the town guessing awhile longer, if you don't mind."

He laughed aloud. "Agreed."

Essie came out to collect the dishes. "You want me to get something out of the freezer for supper?" she asked.

"Lamb chops," Emily told her.

"Chops?" Essie cocked her head to one side.

"Mr. Devlin is remaining the night. I've been away a week and missed our working weekend, Essie. We have to catch up if the manuscript is going to be in on time. You know I've never missed a deadline."

"And you ain't ever had an editor working with you on weekends either," Essie observed. "I think you should know people are talking, Miss Emily."

"Oh, I'm sure they are, Essie," Emily agreed, "but no matter the talk, I still have to get my work in on time. This book is a little different, and I needed my editor's help."

"Mrs. Seligmann says it's going to be sexier, like Miss Savannah's books," Essie noted, a faint hint of disapproval in her voice.

"Yes, Essie, it will be sexier," Michael Devlin spoke up. "It's what the reading public wants, and Emily has got to go with the flow if she wants to keep working. But it's nothing like Savannah Banning's novels, I promise you. I edit both women."

Essie nodded, obviously satisfied. "I'll get the chops out," she said, taking the dishes and departing the porch.

"She's very protective of you," he noted.

"She was Gran O'Malley's last housekeeper," Emily replied. "I couldn't do without her. Not with my lifestyle, Devlin. I'm amazed how well Savannah manages, especially with children. She's a wonder."

"She manages because she's Lady Palmer," he said. "She's got a cook who has a kitchen maid, a housekeeper, two maids, a chauffeur, and a nanny for Wills and Selena. She's just like you in that her work is her rationale, and she has the time for it. A lot of writers don't, you know. They have to balance everything in their lives—house, husband, kids, maybe a second job, and their writing. You know as well as I do that to be successful in this business you need a strong work ethic, the luck of the devil, the hide of a rhino, and a devoted and detail-oriented guardian angel."

Emily laughed aloud. "I don't think, Devlin, that I've ever heard it described so aptly. Now I know why you are such a good editor, other than your talent at it. You've put yourself in a writer's shoes. That's pretty terrific."

"Yoo-hoo!" Rina Seligmann came out onto the porch.

"I didn't hear you drive up," Emily said, getting up and hugging the older woman.

"I wanted to make certain you got home all right," Rina said. "Hello, Mick. Have you called Aaron? He worries like an old woman." She chuckled, sitting down in a wicker rocker. "I told Essie to bring me an iced tea. It still isn't that cold outside."

"I'll go in and call him right now," Emily answered her. "Then Devlin and I are going for a walk. Want to come?"

Rina Seligmann looked as if Emily had just asked her to take a stroll over a bed of hot coals. "No," she said. "I'll leave the exercise to you two."

Emily grinned and hurried into the house. Essie arrived with the glass of iced tea and returned inside. Rina Seligmann looked at Michael Devlin.

"So?" she said.

He laughed. "If anything happens I don't doubt you'll be the first to know, Rina," he told her.

"If? So you're thinking about it?" she returned.

Michael Devlin sighed. "Rina, I'm forty."

"Mick, you're scared," she answered him.

"I suppose I am," he agreed.

"Don't you dare hurt her," Rina said.

"How do I avoid it at this point?" he asked her.

Rina nodded. "Maybe you shouldn't have let it get this far, Mick. But then again, maybe you should have. I can see you love her, and I know she loves you."

"She hasn't said it," he remarked.

Rina Seligmann laughed helplessly. "Mick, women usually don't say 'I love you' first. They wait until the man has said it. They don't want to be rejected or act too soon or feel they've made fools of themselves." She sighed. "Same thing with men, I suppose. Well, what's going to happen is going to happen, as my Russian grandmother said when the Cossacks razed her village. Just keep in mind you love her, and she loves you, Mick. It would be a shame to waste all that love because of pride."

Emily came back onto the porch. She was practically bouncing. "I spoke to Aaron, and wow! J. P. Woods must really think *The Defiant Duchess* is going to be good. She's made us a marvelous offer. She wants to read the manuscript, though, before anyone signs on the dotted line."

Michael Devlin nodded. "That's fair," he agreed. "How about if you print me out what you've got tonight, and then I'll bring it in with me in the morning?"

"No," Emily said. "I've got two more chapters to write, and I never allow a partial manuscript to be read. Most people don't have the imagination to know what's coming next, Devlin. They get ideas in their heads, and then when it doesn't turn out the way they thought it would, they don't like what you've done. No. Whole manuscript or nothing. I can have it done by Thanksgiving. You're coming for dinner, aren't you?"

"Am I invited?" he teased her with a smile.

"Uh-huh," she said with a smile.

"If you two are going to take a walk," Rina remarked, "you'd better get going. Sun sets early this time of year. I've gotta get home myself." She stood up. "I'll take my own glass in to Essie. Go on now."

Hand in hand they followed the trail beyond Emily's back lawn and through the woods down to the beach. The trees above them were ablaze with color, but unlike New England hues these had the muted tone of a Degas canvas. The reds had an almost pink shading to them, the yellows were clear, and the gold more of a tobacco hue. Squirrels rummaged over the woodland floor, seeking out nuts. At one point she and Devlin spotted a red fox going about his business. Reaching the beach, they walked for a short distance. The beach plums had been pretty much picked clean by those with a preference for jam, or by the deer and raccoons. The waters of the bay lapped gently against the sand. They spoke little, just enjoying the beauty of the late afternoon, and each other's company. Finally they turned back and, reaching the house, found Essie preparing to depart for the day. She waved at them as she trotted off down the sidewalk.

Inside the house they found a fire going in the den next to the kitchen. The chops were defrosted, and set neatly upon the broiling pan. From the smell the baking potatoes were already in the oven. The remainder of the apple Betty was covered and on the counter. Emily opened the fridge and saw a bowl of salad waiting.

"When the potatoes are almost cooked I'll do the chops," she said.

"Come and sit down," he called to her from the den, and she joined him, crawling onto his lap and kissing him gently. His arms slipped about her, and she laid her head on his shoulder happily. This was where she belonged. In her house. In Egret Pointe. In Devlin's embrace. It was a perfect moment. Air travel was always so amazing, she thought. This time yesterday she and Sava had been having tea at Claridge's in London.

"I like today's now better than yesterday's now," she told him.

His heart beat a little faster. "Do you? What were you doing yesterday?"

Emily told him, including seeing Reg with Gillian Brecknock, and what Sava had told her about the woman. "I can tell she's a perfect bitch," Emily remarked. "But do you think there's enough there for a book, Devlin? Born in Liverpool poverty, claws her way up to be a film and stage actress, now a dominatrix to the rich and discreet."

He chuckled. "Possibly. I'll Google her and see what else there is, and if it's worth making an offer. I'd probably have to go to London myself to do it," he teased Emily. "Do you think she'd dominate me if I asked nicely?"

Emily butted her head into his shoulder. "Villain!" she accused. "If you want your bottom smacked I'll be happy to oblige."

He burst out laughing. "Would you now?" he said. "Do you

want to make me your sex slave with a leather collar and leash, angel face?"

Suddenly the memory of Sir William, and the bordello came into Emily's head, and she felt her cheeks growing warm. "No," she said. "I think I can make you behave without resorting to that, Devlin." *Lord!* Was it only three nights back that she and Sava had been Pretty Polly and Miss Molly? It would show up in one of Savannah's books eventually, she knew, and she giggled into his shoulder.

He turned her so he could kiss her, and one kiss blended into another as he cradled her in his arms. Oh, she had missed him! She wanted him here every night. Snuggling in his embrace while the smell of potatoes baking filled the air was hardly the most romantic picture in the world, but recently thoughts of domesticity with Michael Devlin were overwhelming her. Why wouldn't he say he loved her? Rina said he did; she sensed he did. And yet what if Rina was just a romantic, and Emily's instincts just wishful thinking? She didn't want to ruin a good author-editor relationship and get stuck with some bright-eyed, eager twenty-something for an editor. She was beginning to understand why this kind of a relationship was forbidden. Emily pulled away from her lover. "The potatoes are almost done," she said. "I've got to get the chops on. Do you mind if we eat in here on trays with the fire?"

"No. What can I do?"

"You can toss the salad, fetch and carry," she told him.

When the lamb chops were done Emily turned off the oven and slipped the apple Betty in to warm. Together they carried the food and a bottle of wine into the den and ate while Frank Sinatra played on a CD Devlin put into the player. The fire crackled, and it was all very cozy. And after dinner they put a DVD in and watched *Casablanca*. Emily cried when Bogart intoned, "Here's looking at you, kid," and sent Ingrid Bergman off with Paul Henreid. Devlin chuckled as Bogart and Claude Raines, who played the French police inspector, strolled off together into the mist, planning their own war against the Nazis.

"Time for bed, Devlin," Emily said, stretching as she stood up. "If you're going to be a commuter tomorrow you'll need to start early."

"How early?" he asked her.

"You should probably roll out of here no later than seven. I know you don't have to be in at nine on the dot," Emily told him. "I'm going to take a bath before I go to bed."

"Can I join you?" he asked softly, a single finger running down the bridge of her nose. "Then I won't have to shower in the morning."

"Yes, you will," she told him with a smile. "And yes, you can join me."

He scrubbed her back with a large sponge as they sat together in a tub filled with bubbles. They lay back together, his hands cupping her breasts as he murmured lascivious suggestions into her ear and kissed the side of her neck, which suddenly smelled of lilacs. He sniffed. He smelled of lilacs. Michael Devlin began to laugh. "Did you put scent in this water?" he asked her.

"Bubble bath doesn't come unscented," she told him dryly. She could suddenly feel his penis beneath her, and she drew a slow, deep breath, turning herself about so that she was now facing him. The palms of her hands slid up his smooth chest to rest lightly on his broad shoulders. "I like it when you smell like a flower, Devlin," she said, her mouth brushing teasingly over his.

"Do you now?" he answered softly, his green eyes narrowing, his hands slipping about her waist.

"It but adds to your charm," Emily said. "Oh, yes, Devlin! Yes!"

He was lifting her up and then lowering her onto his penis. He leaned forward, pressing her against one of the curved ends of the large oval tub. Her legs came up and fastened about his torso. He fucked her slowly, deliberately, in a leisurely manner, until her eyes were closed and she was moaning with her pleasure, her nails digging into his back. When she had attained a small orgasm he pulled away from her, and, in answer to her puzzled look, he said, "I want to have enough left for when we get into bed."

They got out of the bathtub, drying each other off with thick towels. His erection remained, and Emily found she was almost weak with her anticipation, she wanted him inside her again so badly. What was the matter with her? Was she turning into one of those sex addicts the gossip shows were always promoting? He didn't ask if she wanted to go to his room. He just led her to her own bed and they got into it.

He kissed her slowly, and Emily sighed with happiness as she kissed him back. She loved the feel of his mouth on hers. His tongue ran teasingly along her lips, and then slipped into her mouth. She played with it, her own tongue brushing against his. Her hands caressed his lean, hard body. His fingers brushed over her breasts, and then his tongue was tracing the outline of her nipples and dipping into the valley between her breasts. His dark head rested on her as he began to suckle on one of her nipples.

Emily made little murmuring noises of obvious contentment. One of his hands slipped between her thighs, playing with her pubic curls, fingers pressing between her nether lips to find her clitoris, which was already swelling with rising excitement. He teased her until she was squirming with her eagerness, and he was satisfied she was moist enough to take him easily. Then he mounted her and slid his thick penis into her wet vagina.

"Oh, God, yes!" Emily cried out unabashedly. "Oh, Devlin, that feels so good."

"Look at me," he said softly. "Open your eyes and look at me, angel face. I want to see the look in your eyes when you come."

"I can't," she whispered.

"Yes, you can," he told her. "And I want you to see the look in my eyes when I come. I want you to see everything you do to me. Any woman can give you a hard-on, Emily. But you can find paradise with only one woman. Now open your beautiful big blue eyes for me, angel face."

Look at him while he was fucking her? It had never occurred to her. She had just let herself get swept away. Could this be better? Emily opened her eyes and looked into his. He began to move on her, slowly at first, then with increasing rapidity. To her surprise the sensations were even greater. They were incredible. She could feel his thickness and the length of him more acutely. And then she was getting lost in his intense green gaze. She gasped with surprise and struggled to pull herself back, but she couldn't. She saw in his eyes what he couldn't say to her, and her heart was near to bursting. Did he see the same thing in her eyes? How could he not? And then the passion threatening to overwhelm her did. Eyes locked on his she reached orgasm, the shudders racking her body until she almost fainted with the pleasure they were gaining from each other, and that she saw in his own eyes. And when it was finally over they lay silent in each other's arms. There were no words left except the few neither of them could say. The three words that both Emily Shanski and Michael Devlin each wanted to hear from each other: *I love you.* They slept.

In the darkness just before dawn he brought them tea, and as the sun slipped over the horizon he kissed her lips and left her. She heard the distinctive roar of the Healy as it pulled out of her drive and went down Founders Way turning onto Colonial Avenue. Gradually it died away, and Emily fell back to sleep, only to be awakened by the ringing phone.

"It's after nine a.m., angel face," his voice sounded in her ear. "You've got work to do. Get going. I miss you."

"This is the second time this morning that you've wakened me, Devlin," she said.

"I liked the first time better," he replied. "I've got a full day, so I'll call you tonight when I get home."

"I don't suppose you'd like to commute back to Egret Pointe?" she suggested.

"Yes, I would, but I won't. I've got early meetings Tuesday and Friday, and a breakfast meeting with a group of distributors on Wednesday. I'll see you Friday night, angel face. Now get your pretty ass up and start writing."

"Okay, okay," she responded. "Geez, I've never had an editor who was such a slave driver," Emily pretended to complain. "Or such a good lay."

Michael Devlin burst out laughing. "Get to work!" he told her, and rang off.

Smiling, Emily got out of bed, her fingers brushing the faint indent still in the pillow that his head had been upon. Then, dressing, she called down to Essie, "I'm up! Breakfast, please!"

"Up or down?" Essie called back.

"Up," Emily decided as she headed for her office. Just two more chapters to go. She ate the scrambled eggs with cheese that Essie produced, and drank her morning juice. Then she started to work. The last two chapters would almost cost Caroline Trahern her life, but her husband, the duke, would not only save her, but help her to attain the revenge she needed in order that the tragedy darkening her life could come to its final end. So that the duke and his defiant duchess could live happily ever after. It was not going to be an easy transition. And there would need to be one more very hot love scene at the conclusion in which both Justin and Caro would finally admit their love for each other. If it were only that simple, Emily thought wryly.

The passion that she and Devlin had shared last night had been different from any they had shared before. She knew it. And she knew he knew it too. From the moment he had picked her up at Kennedy there had been a new intimacy between them. The quiet time together they had shared. Fixing dinner.

Eating before the fire, and watching an old movie afterward. He had been like a kid while she loaded the dishwasher, scraping the last crumbs from the glass pan that had held the apple Betty, and eating them with a grin on his face. And in bed afterward he had made love to her so tenderly. She had felt like a woman very cherished. And yet he still had not once uttered the word *love*. It was the only thing wrong with the picture.

Devlin returned that weekend for the Harvest Festival, which was set up in a farmer's field just outside of the village itself. They walked among the booths, and she bought him a knitted scarf, and he bought her a birdhouse. They ate corn dogs and drank cider, and he discovered that Emily had a fancy for pink cotton candy. He stood watching as she sat at a card table beneath an awning and signed books. They had spent so much time alone that he had never realized how charming she was with other people. She seemed to know everyone in the town, and they her.

He chuckled as a woman, obviously not a local, stood watching Emily for several minutes. Finally she walked up to the table. She put on her glasses and read the sign on the table that said, *Best-selling Author Emilie Shann Will Sign Your Book for You.* ALL PROCEEDS OF THE SALES GO TO EGRET POINTE GENERAL HOSPITAL." The woman picked up a book and turned it over, reading the back cover copy.

"You write this?" she asked.

"Yes, I did," Emily said.

"I don't read these kinds of books," the woman remarked, replacing the book on its pile. "You write all of these?" She gestured at the other titles in their neat piles.

Emily nodded. "If you don't read romance," she said, "you might buy a copy for a friend or your local library. All the proceeds from the book sale are going to our local hospital. I live here. It's one of the ways I help the hospital."

"So it would be like a charity donation?" the woman asked.

"Yes, it would." Emily smiled.

"Could I get a receipt?" the woman wanted to know.

If he had been sitting there, Devlin thought, he would have strangled this bitch, but Emily just smiled again.

"Of course you can," she said. "I'll write it myself. Who would you like the book inscribed to, ma'am?"

"I'll think about it," the woman said. "You here all day?"

"No. Just a few more minutes," Emily murmured as the woman walked away.

"How do you keep so calm?" Devlin wanted to know. "I'd have killed the cow!"

Emily laughed. "All part and parcel of being an author who writes popular commercial fiction. There's no glory in it, Devlin. Look how well I did though. I got rid of all my copies of *Vanessa and the Viscount, A Special Season, Marrying Miss Moneypenny,* and *The Vicar's Daughters.* I imagine next year we'll do even better, as I have turned to the dark side," she teased him, and now it was his turn to laugh.

They ate dinner under the large tent set up for the meal. There was country ham, sweet potato casserole, creamed corn, cut green beans, rolls, and butter. For dessert, dishes of baked apples were brought to each place by the various church ladies and teenagers who helped. The apples swam in heavy cream, and were rich with brown sugar and cinnamon. There was coffee or tea.

"Decaf's in the pot with the green edge," Emily told him. "There's hot water if you want tea. But it's only Lipton's."

They sat with Dr. Sam and Rina, who introduced Michael Devlin to their neighbors on Ansley Court. And afterward Emily and Devlin drove home in the Healy with the top down beneath a large, almost-full moon.

"Is that the harvest moon?" he asked her.

"Nope. Harvest was September. This full moon will be the Hunter's Moon," she explained.

"But it was a Harvest festival," he said, puzzled.

"The Indians didn't celebrate until after the harvest was all in and everything set for the winter months to come," Emily said. "Then in October they hunted meat to be butchered, hung, or salted for the winter. Life was one long round of hard work back then. Still is, but, of course, the work is different. Did you like Rina's neighbors?"

"Yes," he said. "They're very nice. I thought Mrs. Buckley a bit mysterious, though. Pleasant, but standoffish."

"Oh, Nora Buckley. She's a widow. Her husband was divorcing her and taking everything. He had a hot girlfriend, but then Nora got sick. Long story short, he beat up the girlfriend, she filed charges, he was nasty with the judge, who denied bail, and he died of a coronary in jail that same night. Nora and her two children were saved from disaster. She works in a very elegant little antique shop on Main Street. The owner is extremely hunky too, and it's rumored he likes the ladies."

Devlin felt a bolt of jealousy shoot through him. "Would you like to fuck him now that you know how?" he asked her bluntly.

"Nope," Emily said calmly, but her heart was thumping with excitement. Yes, he loved her! *Damn!* Why couldn't he just say it, and be done with it? "He's not really my type, but I can appreciate that he's good-looking, just like you can appreciate a beautiful woman when you see her, Devlin." She smiled softly in the darkness.

He made love to her that night with a fierceness he had never before displayed. It was as if he were branding her with some mark that could be seen only by another man. They ate brunch at the inn with Rina and Sam the next day, and then Devlin drove back to the city. He called her later in the week to tell her he had to fly to Europe on business.

"You're still coming for Thanksgiving, aren't you?" she asked him.

"Yes, but I'm not certain I'll get out to see you before then," he answered her. "Everyone is excited about the sea change you've made. I know you don't like anyone looking at your work before it's finished, but I've shown the first three chapters to a couple of people. J.P. is suddenly ecstatic with what's she's read, and crowing that it was all her idea, and she just knew you could do it."

"You're why I can do it," Emily said softly.

"Let the bitch revel in her own glory, angel face," he replied. "You were a good writer to start with, and you're just getting better with new direction. They've decided to release *The Defiant Duchess* in April both here and in England. It's short notice. April was your pub date here, but we'll have to scramble to get it out in England at the same time with less than six months' lead time. And you know the English editions have different covers."

"I think the American cover would do nicely for both editions," Emily said to him. "It's beautiful, and other than the barest glimpse of bosom it's tasteful enough for England. Caro in her green riding outfit standing, with the duke in the background and the sea behind them. It's elegant. They could change the lettering to make it look different."

"It's a good idea. I'll see what they say," he told her. "Emily . . ." he hesitated.

He was going to say it! He was going to say it! Her heartbeat accelerated. "Yes, Devlin?" *Say it! Hurry up and say it!*

"Take care of yourself while I'm away, angel face. I'll call you when I can," Michael Devlin said. What the hell was the matter with him? He had wanted to tell her he loved her and he would miss her.

"Okay," she responded, disappointed. Why couldn't he say it?

"I'll miss you," he managed to get out.

"Me too," she said. "Good-bye, Devlin." No use dragging it out.

"Bye, angel face," he replied softly, and hung up.

Emily put down the phone with a sigh. This was getting ridiculous. Suddenly she started to cry, and when she finally stopped she picked up the phone again, called her cable company, and ordered the Channel. She needed a friend. Not Rina, who loved her like a mother. Or Savannah, who was far too wrapped up in her own life right now. She needed someone who would sympathize with her and comfort her. And maybe even help her to decide what she was going to do next. She wanted Michael Devlin for a husband, and she was getting damned tired of waiting for him to come around and say what she saw in his eyes every time he made love to her these past few weeks. Words she sensed on the tip of his tongue. Until he could say them she was going to be driven crazy wondering why. Sometimes love stank, Emily thought.

She finished up her work for the day, went downstairs, and had the supper that Essie had left for her. She took a bath, smiling at the lilac fragrance that perfumed the room. Then, sliding into a sleep shirt, she climbed into bed. When the clock in the hall struck nine p.m. Emily picked up the channel changer, pressed the on button, and then programmed in the Channel. Almost at once the duke's library came into view. She hit enter, and there he was waiting for her.

"Caro, my love!" he said, coming forward to take her into his embrace. Then he stopped. "What on earth are you wearing?"

"No, Trahern," she said firmly. "No Caro tonight, damn it! Emily tonight. It's a sleep shirt. I need a friend, and you are elected."

The Duke of Malincourt looked somewhat horrified by her words. "A friend? My dear girl, men are not friends with women," he told her.

"Maybe not in your century, but in mine it happens all the time. My mother and father were best friends. You know what almost ruined that friendship? Sex. Me. But Mama went on to become a gonzo lawyer who married a man who became a senator, and together they produced two children. As for dear old Dad, he became a pediatrician with a nice Irish wife and three kids. I was raised by my grandmothers."

"Dear girl, I don't understand half of what you are saying to me, but I can see you are wretchedly unhappy. How can I help you?" He motioned her to a chair by the blazing fire, sat down, and drew her onto his lap.

"It's your doppelganger," Emily said with a sigh.

"My what?"

"The guy in my reality who looks just like you, Trahern," she explained.

"What is his name?" the duke wanted to know.

"Michael Devlin," Emily answered him.

"Irish. The Irish are always trouble, dear girl. Dispense with whatever services he provides for you. 'Tis the best advice I can offer you."

"I'm in love with him, Trahern! I want to get married!" Emily wailed.

"Ahhh," the duke said as understanding dawned in his green eyes. "Has he said that he loves you, dear girl?"

"Not in so many words. Sometimes I think he's going to say it, and then he can't seem to get it out," Emily said. "What the hell is the matter with him? Everyone says he loves me. And I sure as hell love him!"

"Have you told him so, dear girl?" the duke asked her.

"Of course not," Emily replied. "Women don't tell men that they love them until men tell women that they love them."

"Well," the duke said wryly with a small smile, "at least that much hasn't changed in the centuries separating our worlds. What does he do, this Michael Devlin?"

"He's my editor," Emily replied. "And he's a really good one."

"So you have something in common," the duke noted.

"Yes," she agreed.

"And he is your lover?" the duke inquired.

"Yes," Emily said softly.

"Is he as good in bed with you as I am, or have you endowed me with his qualities?" the duke wanted to know.

"Trahern! This is not just about sex. It's more for both of us, but I just can't seem to bring him up to scratch," Emily complained.

"Well, oddly I'm not particularly surprised by that," the duke remarked.

"You aren't?" This was interesting. "Why not?"

"You're too independent a woman, dear girl," the duke told her candidly. "Other than making love to you, is there anything else this man can do for you?"

"I don't understand," Emily said, puzzled.

"You earn your own keep, do you not? You own your own house. You manage your own funds, I would assume, as you are close to neither your father nor your stepfather, and you are certainly of a legal age to do it. What is there that Michael Devlin can do for you that you do not do for yourself? Men do not always think only with their cocks, dear girl, and a man has his pride, y'know."

"If it were this century I would agree with you, Trahern, but in the twenty-first century women in my country, even here in England, take care of themselves. We don't need to be cosseted and wrapped in cotton wool," Emily told the duke.

"More's the pity, dear girl," the duke murmured softly. "Perhaps if you were not so formidable a young lady, your Mr. Devlin would act upon his instincts and sweep you off to the parson. Even in your century the men surely want to be needed."

"In my century men sell their seed for pocket money at universities," she told him.

The duke actually paled at her words. "Tell me no more," he said.

"You're a man, Trahern. Surely men haven't changed that much in the past three centuries. Tell me what I can do so that

Devlin will tell me he loves me. After that I can handle it just fine," Emily said.

"I have not a doubt that you can, dear girl. I honestly don't know what to tell you except to tell him how you feel and that you need him. A man who avoids declaring himself to the woman he loves is often as skittish as a colt in a pasture. He needs to be reassured, for one of the two things a man fears most is rejection by the woman he loves," the duke explained.

"What's the other thing?" she asked him mischievously.

The duke chuckled. "I believe you already know the answer to that, you minx, although it has certainly never happened to me."

"Perhaps I should make it so," she teased him.

"Dear girl!" he exclaimed shocked.

Emily slipped out of his lap. "I feel better now," she said. "I'm going back."

"You don't want to remain?" he asked her softly.

"Not really, Trahern. I don't honestly feel like stepping into the duchess's slippers tonight. I need to think."

"Don't think too much, dear girl," he said to her, rising to take her hand in his and kiss it. "Too much thinking could lead to disaster."

"Good night, Trahern," Emily said to him, and suddenly she was in her bed again, staring into the duke's library, which was still visible on her television.

"Good night, Emily, my sweet," he called to her from the other side of the television screen, and Emily clicked the off button, watching as the glass darkened.

In the days that followed Emily worked as she had never worked before. Although the book was not due in until year's end, she had promised Devlin it would be there right after Thanksgiving. While Aaron Fischer had worked out the terms of her new contract with Stratford, J. P. Woods wanted to read

The Defiant Duchess herself before she signed off on the money involved, which was almost double what Emily had been getting. Carol Stacy, the publisher of *Romantic Times BOOKclub Magazine*, had been pressing Emily on those terms and the advance to be paid in the new agreement, but Emily never discussed such things, even with friends like Savannah.

Thanksgiving was coming, and Emily always had a dinner party as her grandmother Emily O had had before her. There were a few more pages and an epilogue to write, but Emily put her work aside to prepare for the holiday. She went out to the local farm with Essie, and together they picked several pumpkins for pies, a half bushel of McIntosh apples, another of mixed pears, both white and sweet potatoes, broccoli, two stalks of Brussels sprouts, carrots, beets, parsnips, a large bag of onions, and a couple of heads of cauliflower. Emily had a small root cellar where she would store the cold crops over the winter. She liked her veggies fresh, even if she did appear to be like Bree on *Desperate Housewives* sometimes.

Together she and Essie prepared the pumpkin filling for the pies. They cut up the apples for the apple pie. Emily made her Irish grandmother's poultry stuffing, using homemade bread crumbs, Bell's poultry seasoning, and onions and celery sautéed in butter. The turkey, all twenty-two pounds of it, was fresh from another local farm. Emily made the sweet-potato casserole with lots of butter, brown sugar, cinnamon, and maple syrup. She cut the broccoli into individual florets, and sliced the parsnips into small rounds. While she put the pies together Essie made up two guest rooms: one for Devlin and the other for Rachel Wainwright, who was coming from Connecticut. Rachel had come for Thanksgiving for over ten years now.

Devlin called, but not as often as she had hoped. She thought he sounded tired, and even distant. When he called two days before Thanksgiving to announce he would be in London for the next few days, Emily felt the tears coming. She hadn't seen him in several weeks, and it was not just the incredible sex she missed; it was Michael Devlin.

"Why not? What happened?" she asked, her voice choking.

"The woman who's been renting my house had a fire in the kitchen. It was Harrington's day off, and instead of using the electric kettle for her tea she turned on the gas. Then she got a phone call, forgot the kettle, the water boiled off, and the kitchen caught fire, the damned stupid cow!" He sighed. "Jaysus, I miss you, angel face! What's for dinner besides the traditional Yankee turkey?"

"Parsnips." Emily sniffed. "I was making you parsnips."

"Turkey and parsnips, huh? Is that strictly traditional?" he teased her. Oh, God, she was crying. Why was she crying?

"Turkey, stuffing, sweet-potato casserole, broccoli with Hollandaise, parsnips, apple and pumpkin pies," she recited. "Oh. Gravy, cranberry, rolls, butter."

"I wish I were going to be there," he said, genuine regret in his voice.

"Will you be home for Christmas, Devlin?" She was struggling not to sound weepy, but she did.

"I promise you that whatever happens, I will be home for Christmas, angel face," he told her. "And we will spend it together."

"Will I see you before then?" Why did she sound so needy? Men didn't like needy women. Well, Trahern thought they did, but not in this time and place they didn't, she was sure. "When will you be back, Devlin?" There, her voice was stronger.

"Probably not until just before Christmas," he said. "Martin wants the London office reorganized, and he's decided that since I ran it for five years, and I was here, now was as good a time as any. He's going to announce his semiretirement before the year's end."

"Will you get his position?" she wondered aloud.

"I don't want it, and I've told him that in no uncertain terms.

I'm an editor first and foremost, angel face. I like working with writers. Martin will still hover in the background enough to keep J.P. in line, but the truth is, she really deserves the post, and I've told her so. Haven't you noticed lately that her attitude toward me—toward you—has changed?"

"I haven't talked to J.P. in a couple of years," Emily said. "I hide behind Aaron."

He chuckled. "I'm going to go, Emily. It's past midnight here, and I'm exhausted. I just got into London yesterday. I apologize again for missing Thanksgiving."

"It's your loss, Devlin," she told him. "Night."

"Good night, angel face," he said.

She cried after he hung up. *Damn! Damn! Damn!* Well, it wasn't as though she weren't going to have a tableful on Thanksgiving Day. And Rachel was arriving tomorrow. It would be fun seeing her old editor and catching up. Emily suddenly realized she hadn't spoken with Rachel since April, until two weeks ago, when she had called her and reminded her she was expected for Thanksgiving as usual.

Essie came Thanksgiving morning to help Emily get everything started. They had set the table together the day before. Now the turkey went into one oven, the apple and pumpkin pies into the other. The sweet-potato casserole came out of the freezer to defrost. By afternoon it would be ready to be heated. The broccoli was in the steamer waiting to be cooked, the parsnips in their pot.

"I'll be going now," Essie said. "Have a good day, Miss Emily."

"You too, Essie. Happy Thanksgiving. I'll see you on Monday."

"You don't need me tomorrow?" Essie asked.

"Go shopping like all the other crazy people," Emily said with a smile.

The door closed behind Essie, and hearing Rachel Wainwright coming down the stairs, Emily pulled a pan of her sweet rolls from the warming oven. "Morning, Rachel," she said. "I've got your sweet rolls and coffee."

The two women sat down at the kitchen table and gossiped. Rachel's main concern was whether Emily was working well with Michael Devlin. She assured her former editor that she was. At four o'clock that afternoon Emily's other guests arrived: Rina and Dr. Sam, Aaron Fischer, and Kirkland Browne. They came in from the cold late afternoon sniffing appreciatively, greeting their hostess and Rachel Wainwright.

"Where's Mick?" Aaron immediately asked as Emily settled them in the living room before the roaring fire.

"Stuck in London," Emily explained, and then told them of the conversation she had had with Devlin two nights ago.

"He always did enjoy London," Rachel said. "I doubt he's lonely. I have friends in the London office, and the stories they told me . . . !" She laughed. "He's probably looked up a few of his birds, as he always called them. And no doubt they're happy to see him."

Emily looked slightly stricken, but then, recovering, she said, "Savannah told me a story of some girl who thought she had him roped and tied, and then he showed up at her birthday party with some model. There was a fight, and someone got shoved into the birthday cake."

"Oh, yes, I recall that story. The model was Lady Soledad Gordon Brumell. She goes just by her first name. You've seen her. She's the model for Helèna Cosmetics. Tall. Fair. Black hair and very blue eyes. And the disdainful look. Attitude, they call it today. In my day it was just plain sulkiness. They all seem to have that look nowadays."

"Emily's new novel is going to be very big, Rachel," Aaron Fischer said in an attempt to change the subject. "They're going to release it simultaneously in England and the United States. And such promotion they've arranged for it. I haven't seen promotion like this since the early days of romance literature."

"Like what?" Rachel wanted to know. She seemed pleased for Emily.

"Posters of the cover as giveaways. Floor and counter dumps with headers. Emily will be at BookExpo in New York in June for a big signing. They've got radio and television interviews scheduled. And Stratford is holding a raffle in all the big chains. Ten winners get flown to New York during BookExpo, all expenses paid, to have lunch with Emily at her favorite restaurant. And the grand-prize winner gets ten days in England, all expenses, etcetera, etcetera, etcetera. No one's done anything like that for a romance author in years. Oy! I'm forgetting. She's going to do breakfast with several distributors, at least those who are left, in February. Valentine's Day, I think."

"My goodness," Rachel exclaimed. "Do I get an ARC to read soon?"

"I just have a few pages to go," Emily said. "It will be in to New York next week." She stood up. "I've got to go and check on the turkey. It should be almost done. Rina, come and give me a hand, will you, please?"

When the two women had left the room, Aaron Fischer looked to Rachel Wainwright and said, "Rachel, I think there is something you ought to know."

And Rachel's eyes grew wide with a mixture of shock and surprise as Emily's agent explained what was happening between Mick Devlin and Emily.

"But he's a ladies' man," Rachel said when he had finished. "Mick never struck me as a man who was going to marry and settle down. But then, I never saw a man in Emily's life either. She's too much of a writer."

Dr. Sam chuckled at this observation. "She can't be a writer and a wife too?" he asked quietly. "She's in love."

"But what about Mick?" Rachel asked.

"According to my Rina, he's in love with Emily," Dr. Sam replied.

"From your lips to God's ears," Aaron Fischer said. "I

wouldn't admit this in Rina's hearing, because I would never hear the end of it, but she does have an instinct for these things. The problem is, he's been a bachelor for forty years. Can he find the chutzpah to propose?"

"Christmas is coming," Dr. Sam said. "Hanukkah's coming. It's a season of miracles, my friends."

"It's going to take a miracle," Rachel Wainwright said. "But why not?"

And the three men in the room nodded in agreement.

CHAPTER TEN

It was the first week in December, and *The Defiant Duchess* was finished at last. Caro and her duke had been reunited and would live happily ever after. The duchess had gained her revenge by finally trusting in her husband to aid her. It was a good story with fully developed and likable characters both major and minor. The villains were deliciously evil and got their proper comeuppance, because good must always triumph over evil. And, most important, there was lots of steamy sex. Emily was surprised at how easily a more sensual story line had been incorporated into her novel. It really hadn't spoiled a thing, once she had learned from delicious experience what real love, both emotional and physical, was all about.

She had gone over the chapters in her computer, making small corrections: adding a line here, deleting one there. Finally satisfied, she burned two CDs and printed out five paper copies of the five-hundred-page manuscript. Normally she would have printed out only four. Putting two large rubber bands about the first copy, she taped a small Post-it note to it that read, *Dear J.P., I know how patiently you have waited for the final manuscript of* The Defiant Duchess, *so here is an early Christmas present. As ever, Emilie Shann.* Then, placing the manuscript in a box, she wrapped it in Christmas paper decorated with fat dancing Santas, and tied it with a large red silk ribbon. She kept a paper copy for herself, sent one to Aaron, and directed the last two along with a CD to Devlin's assistant, Sally. She had been e-mailing Michael Devlin at Stratford's London offices the final pages as she completed them. The entire finished manuscript would be awaiting him upon his return to the States.

Some authors celebrated the successful completion of a manuscript by going out to dinner. Some went off on little vacations planned weeks before. Emily Shanski cracked open a bottle of her favorite wine and opened a double box of Mallomars. Then, sitting in her den before a roaring fire, she listened to Mozart and unwound. Christmas was coming, and she had a great number of things to do. There were Christmas cards, both personal and business, to write. There were presents to buy. There was a very special Christmas dinner to plan for, as Devlin had missed Thanksgiving.

Already the village of Egret Pointe was in the holiday spirit. There were little pine trees with white lights in round red wooden tubs along Main Street. And all the shop windows were beautifully decorated. This year each had a miniature scene of a country Christmas in a past era. Egret Pointe's shop windows all followed a single theme each year in imitation of the store windows on Fifth Avenue in New York.

The weather was cold, but so far there was no snow, and for that Emily was grateful. She far preferred a green Christmas. She thought the composer of "White Christmas" should have been boiled with his own Christmas pudding, as Mr. Scrooge had once declared regarding the whole holiday. Emily loved Christmas, however. She just didn't like snow. For some reason it depressed her and always had. No one understood it, least of all Emily. Sure, snow was magical when it was falling. And the next day, when it sparkled on all the eaves and roofs in the bright sunshine, it was pretty. But the day after, when it wasn't gone and it sometimes stayed for weeks—oh, how she hated that! So every year Emily hoped for an El Niño and a mild winter that would lead into an early spring. Nothing was nicer than daffodils in bloom on St. Patrick's Day.

Several days after she had sent off the manuscripts, her office phone rang. As she was writing Christmas cards at her desk, she answered it.

"Ms. Shann? One moment for J. P. Woods," a young voice said.

There was a click. Another click.

"Emily? Sweetie, I was up all night reading! It's a triumph," J. P. Woods crowed. "Mick said it was, but we've invested so much into promoting this book I couldn't rest easy until I had read it myself. You've outdone yourself! I am so pleased." Emphasis on the last sentence. "And Aaron has probably told you that we've worked out a wonderful contract. Stratford isn't about to lose its brightest star."

"Thank you, J.P." Emily said. She really didn't like the woman, but this wasn't personal, after all. It was, to quote a certain megamillionaire, business.

"And you're happy working with Mick Devlin? We want you one hundred percent happy, Emily."

"He's a wonderful editor, J.P. I will admit to being upset when Rachel retired, but even I have to admit Devlin is a better editor. Yes. I am happy working with him. I hope to do many more good books for Stratford with him," Emily replied. "I want to thank you for putting me with him." *Even if you did have an ulterior motive, you bitch. You didn't care whose career you destroyed in your pitiful attempt to get even with Devlin for turning you down all those years ago. I wonder what you would think, bitch, if you knew I've been fucking him for months. And he is good!*

"I thought long about it," J.P. said. "But editors like Mick Devlin are few and far between. Martin and I felt you deserved the absolute best. And I was right," she crowed. "I just knew you could change your direction and produce a hotter book."

Emily gritted her teeth listening to J. P. Woods. Then she said, "Savannah Banning is willing to give me a quote, J.P."

"Wonderful! I was thinking of asking her. You're friends, aren't you?"

"Yes," Emily answered.

"And did she give you some advice on how to do a sexier novel?" J.P. tittered.

"As a matter of fact, she did," Emily said. *She suggested I seduce my editor, and I did, and we all see how well that worked out.*

"I don't suppose you'd share her secrets with me?" J.P. said coyly.

Emily forced a laugh. "Now, now, J.P. Trade secrets have to remain secret."

"Of course they do, and as long as they produce the results they did, Emily, I am more than satisfied," J.P. replied, all business once again. "Now, Emily, Stratford is having its Christmas party on December twenty-third, and we want you to come. The heads of several important book distributors will be here. We want you to present them with some rather special ARCs we're putting together now. Martin is sending a car for you. Sally or my girl will e-mail you all the details."

She didn't want to go into New York, especially two days before Christmas. The traffic would be horrendous. But this was a command performance, and Emily knew it. "I'll look forward to it," she told J. P. Woods. "And thank you for calling me. I'm so glad you enjoyed the book, J.P."

"I did, Emily. Good work! I'm now looking forward to what you'll do next for us. Good-bye." There was a click, and J. P. Woods was gone.

Emily set the phone back in its charger. *Damn, and double damn.* Now she would have to have everything done before the twenty-third. It was going to be a push. But it would be her first Christmas with Devlin, and she wanted it to be perfect. She had pretty much decided that if he didn't tell her he loved her, she was going to break the cardinal rule of dating women: She was going to tell him that she loved him. What could happen? He'd bolt and run? Well, that was always a possibility, but maybe, just maybe, if Rina was right, it would give him the balls to tell her that he loved her. And once they were over that hurdle there would be a future for them. And Emily Shanski wanted that future with all her heart and soul. She had two weeks to go.

She managed to finish the Christmas cards by the ninth. They were in the mail by the tenth.

"Right on time, Em," Bud Cranston down at the post office said as she handed him the shopping bag of Christmas cards over the counter. "You're like clockwork—December tenth, every year. Pat wants to know if you've got another book coming out soon. She says she's ready for one with the long winter ahead."

"Tell her next spring. Sorry," Emily said with a smile. "Merry Christmas, Bud, to you and the family. The kids okay?"

"Off the wall waiting for Santa." He grinned back at her, giving her a wave as she stepped aside to allow the next customer up to his window. Bud Cranston had gone to high school with Emily Shanski. Who knew she'd turn out to be a best-selling author? But Em never changed, he thought with a smile. She was still a nice small-town girl who always had a friendly word for you.

Now it was time to Christmas shop, and Emily did as much of her shopping locally as she could. The rest she purchased from catalogs. Now, as the gifts began to pile up in the den, she set about wrapping everything. Rina and Dr. Sam came by on the weekend, and they all drove out together to the Christmas tree farm to buy their trees, picking from among those already cut. Emily had never, since she was a little girl, had the heart to go out into the field, point at a living tree, and have it cut down.

If it was already cut, that was a different thing. Her grandmothers had always laughed and said she was too softhearted,
and she always agreed she was. Sam grumbled as he and the
farmer's helper tied the three trees to the top of the car. Emily
always bought two: a great big eight-footer for her living room,
and a small table tree for the den window.

The trees were stored outside the kitchen door in buckets of
water and sugar. On the twenty-first Emily and Essie set them
up in their stands. Emily would spend the next few days decorating the two trees. She had come down with a cold that day
at the tree farm. It had been cloudy and drizzly, but at least it
wasn't snow, she thought thankfully. Despite the romantic song,
white Christmases were very rare in Egret Pointe. But the beautiful blond weather forecaster in the city was predicting a seventy percent chance of snow late on the twenty-second, curse
him.

"Good thing we're getting out of here in the morning," Essie
said to Emily. "But I hate to leave you when you're sick, Miss
Emily. And especially at Christmas."

"You've had this Florida trip with your son and his family
planned for close to a year, Essie. I'll be fine. Mr. Devlin is coming," Emily reassured her housekeeper.

"Well, if you're sure then," Essie said, knowing even as she
spoke that Emily would never ask her to cancel her plans, "I'll
be going now. The car service is picking us up at six o'clock in
the morning. By this time tomorrow I'll be lying by the hotel
pool," she finished with a grin.

"Do a lap for me," Emily told her, and hugged the older
woman. "Merry Christmas, Essie. I'll see you January second."

"Thanks for my Christmas gift, Miss Emily," Essie said,
pulling on her gloves.

"I thought a little cash would be more appreciated than a
flannel nightie this year, considering your trip," Emily replied
with a grin.

"It is," Essie agreed. "Merry Christmas to you, Miss Emily. I hope you get just what you really want. And say hello to that handsome Mr. Devlin for me," she finished with a broad wink as she hurried out the door.

Emily closed the front door, the large green pine wreath on it rustling faintly as it shut. Her cell phone began to ring. Emily pulled it from her pocket and flipped it open. "Hello?"

"Hello, angel face!" Michael Devlin's voice purred into her ear.

"Devlin! Where are you? Are you home yet?" she asked.

"London still. Something has come up. I'll tell you all about it when I get home, but I'll be with you for Christmas, angel face, come hell or high water. I should be back just in time for Stratford's Christmas party Friday. Is it snowing yet?"

"God, no!" she said. "I'm dreaming of a sunny green Christmas, but they are predicting snow late tomorrow and into Thursday. Hopefully the AccuTracks, the Dopplers, or their Ouija boards don't know anything, and we'll get rain."

"Madame Scrooge, I presume," he teased her.

"Did you find a real Christmas pudding, Devlin?" she asked.

"At a little shop I know where they make it themselves," he answered. "It's already packed in my suitcase."

"Don't let them confiscate it at customs," she warned him.

"I had them box it, and then wrap it in some rather garish holiday paper complete with a big floppy bow," he told her. "I'm telling them it's a present for my maiden aunt."

"Perfect!" Emily replied. "Every customs agent has at least one maiden aunt."

"Emily? I miss you. These last weeks without you have been lonely for me. And I've missed Egret Pointe. Will they still have the windows up that you told me about by the time I get there?" He sounded almost wistful.

"They don't take them down until the day after New Year's, Devlin," she answered him. He had missed her! He was lonely without her! Now why the hell couldn't he get the rest of it out? "I've missed you too," Emily said, "but I've been busy. The house is all decorated inside and out. Garlands and wreaths up. Two trees. The one in the den is all finished. I'm working on the one in the living room. We're having an open house on New Year's Eve, Devlin. Will you still be here, or do you like your city celebrations?"

"Publishing is closed down Christmas week," he told her. "Can I stay the whole week with you? Or maybe you would like to come into town and stay at my place?"

"Stay with me," she said softly, meaningfully. "Besides, you live in a studio apartment, Devlin. You've said yourself there's barely room to swing a cat, and I'm much bigger than a cat."

"What will the neighbors think?" he asked her.

"To hell with the neighbors, Devlin," Emily said.

He laughed low. "Can you be a good girl until I get there, angel face?"

"If I can be a bad girl once you're here," she told him mischievously.

"I've got a big present for you," he teased her.

"And I have just the perfect place to put it," she responded.

"You're making me hot," he told her.

"I'm putting my hand in my pants," she said. "Oh! I'm already wet, Devlin. That's what the sound of your voice does to me."

"I'm in bed," he replied. "I've got my dick in my hand. It's already getting hard, because that's what the sound of your voice does to me."

"Make yourself come," she murmured seductively. "I'm going to make myself come. I'm already playing with my clit. It feels so good, Devlin. Oh! Oh! But I wish it were your tongue there, and not my finger."

"I'm polishing my cock to a fine stand," he said. "But I wish it were in your juicy cunt, angel face. I'm going to fuck your brains out when I get home." He heard her breathing coming faster in his earpiece.

"Oh! Oh! Oh! Ohhhh!" she exclaimed. "God, that was good! But not as good as you, Devlin."

She heard him groan. "Jaysus! What a waste of good cum! I've had to use two handkerchiefs. Damn it, I want you, angel face! I don't want to have any more dirty-talk phone sex with you over the transatlantic cable."

"Then get your cute Irish ass home, Devlin," Emily said.

She heard him chuckle, and then he responded, "As fast as I can, angel face. Just a few more days. Good night, sweetheart."

"Good night, Devlin. Dream of me." She made kissing sounds into the phone.

To her delight he made the same sounds back, and then the line was dead.

Emily flipped her cell shut. Just the sound of his voice, the knowledge that he was coming home soon, made her happy. Home. He had referred to Egret Pointe as home. She felt herself smiling, and then she sneezed. *Damn!* Her cold was getting worse, and she still had the big Christmas tree in the living room to finish decorating. Tomorrow, Emily thought. She'd finish it tomorrow. Tonight she would eat some of Rina's chicken soup and just go to bed.

The next day Emily struggled up, and completed decorating her big Christmas tree. Good thing, she considered, that she and Essie had begun it yesterday, and the top half had been finished. She didn't think she could have climbed up on the ladder, but fortunately all she had left had been the bottom half. She took the ornaments carefully from their wrappings. Most of them were antiques that had been in her family for over a hundred years. Her favorite was the skinny Father Christmas that had always been referred to as the seasick Santa.

But she was still feeling lousy. She had the tree finished by early afternoon, and considering that she had to go into the city tomorrow, she decided to rest. She was coughing now, but as much as she disliked having to make the trip, it was business, and it was important she be at Stratford's Christmas party. Aaron would be there. Devlin would be there. That would be the hard part: pretending they were just editor and author.

Her appetite was finicky. She finished Rina's soup and made herself a peanut-butter-and-jelly sandwich with a glass of warm milk. When she had eaten she went upstairs and swallowed some cold tablets. Looking outside, she saw it had begun to snow. Maybe it would snow so much she wouldn't have to go into the city, Emily thought. Crawling into bed she fell into a deep sleep. It wasn't even eight o'clock.

It was still snowing when she awoke the following morning. She felt a little better, and so she took some more twelve-hour cold medicine to get her through the day. Looking at the clock she thought, *In another twelve hours I'll be home.* It made the day ahead of her just a little bit less onerous. She showered, washing her hair, then drying herself and her hair thoroughly before stepping out into the bedroom. Even so, a chill swept over her. The chime from the hall announced nine o'clock. She had plenty of time. Wrapping herself in her pink fleece robe, she went downstairs, and made herself a bowl of apple-and-cinnamon oatmeal. The heavy cream she poured on it made it taste even better, along with the hot tea she drank.

Having eaten, Emily trudged back upstairs and got back into bed. She didn't feel great, but she felt better. Aaron called to make sure she remembered the car would be there for her at noon. She had at least two and a half hours before she had to get dressed. She set her clock for eleven fifteen, and when it rang Emily awoke to bright sunshine. The storm had blown itself out. Looking out the window, she saw the street was already plowed, which meant the parkway would be plowed too—worse luck.

With a sigh she turned to get dressed, slipping on a pair of pure silk cream panties and a matching lace bra. She was not going to the Stratford Christmas party without her underwear, and Devlin was just going to have to live with it. She couldn't decide whether she should wear a wrap dress or slacks, but given the snow she decided on her cream-colored wool slacks and a matching cashmere turtleneck. She pulled thin cashmere socks over her feet and slid into a pair of ankle-high Ferragamo boots in a rich chocolate-brown leather. Simple makeup: a little periwinkle-blue eye shadow, mascara, blush, and lipstick. Good, tasteful jewelry: an elegant gold-and-silver pin on the left side of her sweater, matching earrings in her ears, and Emily O's beautiful silver repoussé bangle on her right wrist, her own gold Seiko on her left wrist.

She took a small clutch in cream leather. In it she fit a little brush, a lipstick, a tiny spritzer of her favorite scent, sunglasses, tissues, a single credit card, a packet of vitamin C drops, and her cell. Looking in the mirror, she fluffed her hair with her brush. She had seen it look better, but she had a cold, and it would probably look fine for the day. Hurrying downstairs, Emily took her long camel-hair wrap coat from the closet, checked the pocket for a pair of gloves, and, reaching up onto the shelf, pulled down an Irish wool tam-o'-shanter. She had a cold, she rationalized again. She needed to keep a hat on until she got there. Didn't everyone say you lost most of your body heat through your head?

As if on cue the doorbell rang and, opening it, she greeted the chauffeur. "Morning! Hope the drive wasn't too bad."

"Nah," he answered her. "Parkway is clear, and so are your roads. You got a good little highway department out here in the boonies. I'm Frankie. You ready to go, Miss Shann?"

"Did they send lunch in the car, or should I make a sandwich quickly?" she asked.

"You must be somebody real special," Frankie said. "There's a little hamper in the back for you. You just tell me when you want to stop and eat."

"I'm used to eating on the run," Emily said. "You don't have to stop for me, but thanks." She put on her coat, cinching the sash to close it.

He helped her into the car, set a thick fleece lap robe over her knees, and, gaining the driver's seat, pulled out from the curb. A sudden wave of weariness swept over her. Emily closed her eyes and dozed. When she opened them again they were on the parkway, and she realized they were almost into the city. Glancing at her watch she saw it was one thirty. She had slept for an hour and a half. She felt better for it. Opening up the hamper, she pulled out a thermos. A label on it said, *Chicken Soup*. She opened it and poured some into the self-contained cup. It was delicious, and still quite hot. There were two miniature croissants wrapped in clear wrap. They were filled with thin slices of Havarti cheese and ham. She wolfed them down, wondering why, when you were sick, someone else's food always tasted better. Closing the hamper, she wiped her mouth, pulled out her lipstick, and put on fresh.

Around them the traffic was horrendous. Of course—it was two days before Christmas. Only an idiot brought his car into the city two days before Christmas. The world was obviously full of idiots, Emily decided as the cars around her honked noisily.

"Jerks!" Frankie the chauffeur said. "Whatta they think? Honking's gonna make the rest of the traffic disappear in a puff of smoke?" He swore under his breath as a black limo with black windows tried to cut him off, gunning the town car to keep his own place in the line of trucks, buses, and cars. "I got orders to pick up a Mr. Fischer," he said to her. "You know him?"

"He's my agent," Emily answered. *Good*. They would have a few minutes alone to talk before they got to Stratford.

Aaron was waiting at the curb in front of his building as they pulled up. He got into the town car and went to kiss her cheek, but Emily pulled away, putting up a cautionary hand as she did so.

"I've got an awful cold," she told him.

"You shouldn't have come," he exclaimed. He put a hand on her forehead. "I think you have a fever. What did Sam say?"

"I didn't call him, Aaron, and don't fuss at me. I will when I get home. But you know as well as I do that this is a command performance. I took some cold pills last night, and again this morning to get me through. J.P. called me herself to issue the invitation. The good news is that she's ecstatic about the book."

"I know," he replied, sitting back. "She wants you to sign the contracts today."

"No. Not today. After the New Year," Emily told him. "After Martin has made his announcement, and I am sure that Devlin will stay. He wants to remain editor in chief, and J.P. will be named Martin's successor under those circumstances. I have to be sure she isn't holding any grudges. I know every editor at Stratford. There isn't one I'd be comfortable working with except Devlin."

"So this is love," Aaron said dryly.

"No. It's business, pure and simple," Emily told him.

"But you love him," Aaron remarked.

"Yes, I do. But one has nothing to do with the other," Emily insisted.

"If you say so," Aaron said with a small smile. "Can Kirk and I hitch a ride to Egret Pointe with you tonight? Hanukkah at Rina's. Then we're going to stay a few days at the cottage. I called your Essie to open it up, but she didn't call back. Is she all right?"

"She's in Florida with her son and his family for Christmas," Emily explained. "Better call Rina before we get to the party, and she'll arrange it." She settled back in her seat and closed her eyes again, listening as Aaron made the call, imagining Rina's sharp comments to her brother for waiting until the last minute.

"Did you know Emily is sick?" Aaron asked his sister.

Emily's eyes flew open, and she shook her finger at her agent.

"What do you mean, sick?" Rina was demanding to know.

"Sounds like a pretty bad cold to me," Aaron replied. "Sam should look at her tomorrow. She'll call him."

"If she's sick she shouldn't be in the city," Rina said.

Emily, knowing what Rina would be saying, grabbed Aaron's phone from him. "I had to come. I took cold medicine. I finished your soup, and I'll be home and will go to bed in a few hours. Okay? Don't scold Aaron. He didn't know." She handed the phone back.

"She looks beautiful for someone at death's door," Aaron teased his sister.

"The pair of you are impossible," Rina muttered. "I'll call my gal and see if she can get over to the cottage. You did have an oil delivery made, didn't you? Never mind. I'll call. Really, Aaron, you and Kirk need a keeper. I'll see you both tonight."

Aaron Fischer closed his elegant little cell and slipped it back into his pants pocket. "My sister, Rina, the boss of the world— but I did forget to call for oil," he admitted sheepishly. "I would think there would have been enough to heat the place tonight, though."

"All the businesses except the IGA close at noon on Christmas Eve in Egret Pointe," Emily told him. "Oh, here we are, Aaron. Showtime! Smiles, everyone!"

The town car glided smoothly to a stop, and Frankie got out, hurried around the vehicle to the passenger-side door, and opened it up. Aaron climbed out, and the chauffeur extended a hand to Emily to help her alight. "I'll be here when you're through," he told them. "Mr. Stratford arranged it so I can wait for you right where I am. He's got some pull, I'd say."

"He's a generous man," Aaron replied meaningfully.

"Yeah, he'd have to be to have pulled this off at Christmas," Frankie agreed, nodding.

Stratford Publishing occupied three floors of the office building in which it was located. Martin Stratford paid the building management an extra stipend to have one elevator among the bank of them exclusive to his publishing house. He didn't like to wait, and he didn't want his employees or authors having to wait. And he paid a uniformed elevator man to run his private elevator.

"Merry Christmas, Miss Shann, Mr. Fischer," Bill said. "You'll be coming for the party, I'm thinking." The elevator man was a small Irishman of indeterminate age with the face of a leprechaun, who had somehow, after fifty years in the United States, still managed to retain his Irish brogue. He knew everyone who did business regularly with Stratford Publishing, as well as all its employees. He was a holdover from another era, but Martin Stratford felt that the private elevator and its uniformed operator gave him a certain kind of cache he was loath to do without. And the truth was, it did. "I'm hearing wonderful things about the new book, Miss Shann," Bill volunteered as the elevator sped up its cables to the twentieth floor.

"Thanks, Bill," Emily told him.

The elevator had been discreetly hung with an elegant, fragrant green garland. There was a wreath with a red plaid bow hung over the mirror in the rear of the car. They reached their destination quickly, the doors opened, and they stepped out into the foyer of the executive floor. More fragrant green garlands. Wreaths had been placed discreetly here and there. A large Christmas tree was set up to one side of the receptionist's desk decorated with faux Victorian ornaments and strands of both popcorn and cranberries, and complete with a blue-and-silver Star of David topping it.

"Oy vay," Aaron murmured under his breath.

Emily giggled. "I think they're trying to be ecumenical," she said.

"I wonder where the solstice and the Kwanzaa displays are set up," he answered her. "Hello, Denise," Aaron greeted the receptionist.

"Happy holidays, Mr. Fischer, Miss Shann. The party has already started down in the boardroom. Can I take your coats?" She came from behind her desk to accept their outdoor garments. "I didn't let them block the closet with the tree," she confided. "Oh, Miss Shann, that's a great outfit. I love the sweater. Is it cashmere?"

"Yes, a friend knitted it for me," Emily told the receptionist.

"Gee, I wish I had friends like that," Denise remarked.

"You don't get to come to the party?" Aaron asked the girl.

"Not until four o'clock, Mr. Fischer. Ms. Woods says everyone should have arrived by four o'clock. I don't mind. I'm reading the ARC for the new Savannah Banning book. It is so hot!" She grinned.

They laughed and made their way to the boardroom, which was located on a corner of the building and had a skyline view on two sides. J. P. Woods spotted them immediately as they walked in, and came forward. She was smiling toothily, and Emily thought she had never in twelve years seen J. P. Woods smile quite like that. It was a little frightening. J.P. had grown her hair long. It was still red, and fixed into an elegant chignon. She was wearing a Tudor-green silk wrap dress that outlined every inch of her figure, which Emily had to admit was damned good, wondering at the same time whether J.P. had had her breasts done. They were pretty perfect-looking tits for a woman in her late forties. She had to work out too, Emily decided.

"Emily! Aaron!" J. P. Woods had reached them, and they all air-kissed. "Happy holidays to us all," J.P. purred. "We are so pleased with *The Defiant Duchess,* as I told you the other night. It's going to be very big. We have your new contracts all ready and waiting for you to sign today."

"Oh, not today, J.P." Emily said.

"Not today?" J.P.'s colorless eyes narrowed. "Why not today?"

"Mercury is in retrograde," Emily said with a perfectly straight face. "I never sign any documents when Mercury is in retrograde, J.P. It would be disastrous."

"I wasn't aware you were into astrology," J.P. said sharply.

"Well, I don't check my chart before I get up every day,"

Emily answered her, "but I do have it done each year, and Mercury retrogrades four times a year. It's always a time of Murphy's Law. Things just go wrong. We'll take the contracts with us, and I'll sign them when the stars are aligned properly—right after the first of the year."

J. P. Woods looked somewhat chagrined by Emily's explanation, but she also knew it wouldn't look particularly good to get into a quarrel with the author over what was really a trivial matter. But she had hoped to make a big show of Emily's signing today, and she was disappointed.

"Now, where are these important distributors you wanted me to meet?" Emily said brightly, turning J.P.'s thoughts back to business.

"They should be here any minute," J.P. said. "One is from the Midwest, the other out of Atlanta, and the third from California. He's the one you want to really schmooze," she advised. "But come along now, the two of you. Martin is sitting on his throne over there just waiting for you two to pay him homage." J.P. tittered.

They made their way across the large boardroom, which had been emptied of its conference table and chairs which had been replaced by a few smaller round tables and folding chairs. There was a deejay playing at one end of the room, but the music was merely for ambience. Young waiters and waitresses in black pants and white shirts passed around trays of canapés. There was a bar set up at the other end of the room. As they moved across the space people parted for them, and Emily smiled to herself. Everyone, it seemed, had an eye out for J.P.

Martin Stratford, seeing them approaching, arose from his comfortable chair and came forward, hands outstretched. "Aaron." He nodded to the agent, but it was Emily's small hands he took in his own. "My dear, beautiful as ever. And you are truly a wonder. We are all very, very pleased with *The Defiant Duchess.* Thank you." Still holding her hands in his, he raised them to his lips and kissed them giving her a courtly bow as he did so. He was a tall, handsome man in his late six-ties, with beautifully styled silver hair and piercing blue eyes. He was dressed impeccably in a dark suit, white shirt, and silk tie with a military stripe, which was held neatly in place with a gold tie pin. There were gold oval cuff links in his shirt cuffs, and just the barest hint of expensive men's cologne about him. Martin Stratford had the elegance of an old-time movie star, and the same sort of charm as well. But he was a very smart man.

Emily retrieved her hands, smiling. "Your blessing is very important to me, Martin, and J.P. called me the other night to tell me how much she had enjoyed the book. Knowing that I have the approval of both of you is wonderful."

"It was Rachel who was holding you back," J. P. Woods said. "I just knew with the right guidance you could do a more sensual book for us, and do it well. Didn't I say that, Martin?" J.P. smiled brightly.

"Your faith in Emily has always been something of a wonder to me, J.P." Martin Stratford said smoothly. He wondered if Emily knew the truth, and hoped she didn't. He didn't want to see this lovely young woman hurt. "Will you be signing your new contracts for us today?"

J. P. Woods beamed, pleased at what she thought would be Emily's agreement.

"Not today, Martin. Right after the holidays, though," Emily told him.

"Fine, fine. I want you to know I'm going to be naming J.P. to replace me today," Martin Stratford said quietly. "I'm going to be seventy next year, and it's time for me to enjoy a little of life while I still can. My wife and I are going to take that fantastic Cunard around-the-world cruise this winter. We won't be back until spring. We've booked a minisafari while the ship is visiting Africa."

"How wonderful!" Emily exclaimed. *Oh, shit!* She was going to have to be nice to J. P. Woods for the rest of her life. "J.P. deserves this promotion, Martin. As for the trip, I envy you. It's something I'd love to do myself one day."

"But not right away," J.P. chimed in cheerfully. "You have books to write for us, Emily." Her white teeth twinkled again. "Oh," she exclaimed. "There goes my beeper. Our special guests have arrived. You stay right here, Emily. I'll bring them to meet you. We've got ARCs bound with the cover for them. You'll sign them." She hurried off, her Jimmy Choo heels making indentations in the carpet.

"Is someone going to offer us a drink?" Aaron complained.

"Sorry," Martin Stratford said, signaling a waiter so they might give him their order. "You did good, Emily," he told her. "I know J.P. isn't your favorite person. You're a smart girl. She knows how to run a company, but believe it or not she's unsure of herself, which is what makes her so abrasive to deal with, I'm afraid."

The drinks came. Emily had ordered a shot of Glenfiddich Scotch for her cold. She sipped it slowly, her eyes sweeping the room. Where was Devlin? Where the hell was he? She was going to have to ask, if he didn't show up soon. Had anything happened to him? she wondered. No. J.P. would have certainly said so. The three distributors were brought over to meet her. She was charming. They were flattering. They chatted. She signed their ARCs for them, and they drifted off. Aaron was deep in conversation with a senior editor of his acquaintance. Martin Stratford had made his announcement, passed out bonus checks, and was now making his departure, wishing them all a happy holiday.

Emily saw him to the elevator and kissed his cheek. "You like the contract?" he asked her.

"Aaron and I will discuss it in detail this weekend. He'll be out in Egret Pointe for the holiday. Martin, I didn't see my editor. Where is Michael Devlin?"

"I believe he got stuck in London," Martin Stratford said. "J.P. spoke to him this morning. She'll know."

"Oh," Emily said.

Her companion stepped into the elevator. "Good-bye, my dear," he said as Bill closed the doors.

Emily stood alone for a moment or two. She had spoken to Devlin only last night, and he said he was coming home. He should have arrived early this afternoon. As much as she disliked it, Emily sought out J. P. Woods, who was mellowing with her fifth drink. "J.P. Where is my editor? I understood he would be here today. I did want to wish him a merry Christmas," Emily said, as if that were actually the case. Then she smiled at J.P.

"Oh, he called this morning. Something came up in London, and he said he couldn't make it back to the States in time for Christmas." She laughed knowingly. "Probably some pretty creature he met, knowing Devlin. He really is a wicked devil. He was all business with you, I hope."

"He was extremely professional," Emily replied, "but I can see what you mean, J.P. Devlin is a charming guy. But then, all Irishmen are—even your elevator man, Bill," she said with another smile.

J.P. laughed. "Yeah," she admitted. "Those Irish boys do have their charms, though I never before considered putting little Bill and Mick in the same category. But I suppose you're right, Emily. Well, as long as he edits you well, what do we care, right?"

Aaron joined them. "Emily has been a good sport long enough, J.P. I'm going to take her home now. I hope you'll have a good holiday."

"What's wrong?" J.P. was suddenly businesslike again.

"I just have a little cold," Emily said. "Aaron worries like an old woman, but I am a bit tired. Going home sounds really good to me."

"Well, I'm not surprised," J.P. said. "It was a big push, and you came through for all of us, Emily. I won't forget that. Yes, go on home and cosset yourself."

"Have a good holiday, J.P.," Emily told her.

"I will," J.P. said. Then she lowered her voice and said to Emily, "Have you ever heard of that women-only network? It's called the Channel. A friend suggested it."

"Yes," Emily murmured. "I suspect you'll like it, J.P. Everyone I know who gets it just adores it. But be careful. It can be addictive sometimes, I'm told."

The two women air-kissed, then parted. Emily and Aaron made their way out to the reception room and took their coats from the closet. Denise was nowhere in sight. Bill, the elevator man, was slightly tipsy, they both noted with amusement as he took them back down to the building's lobby. Outside it was already dark, but Frankie was waiting patiently, and to their surprise Kirkland Browne was already in the car.

"I walked over," he said. "This way we can just get out of town. A messenger came, picked up the hamper, and delivered another. I didn't want to open it until you got here, as it's Emily's ride. I'll sit up front."

Frankie helped them in, and Emily realized as she sat down that she was absolutely exhausted. Despite the Scotch her cold was back full bore. She coughed as she fell into her seat. "I'll see what's in the new hamper," she said. "They sent me soup and little sandwiches for my ride into town." She lifted the wicker lid. Tea sandwiches, miniature tarts with lemon curd, raspberry, and mincemeat met her eye. There would be tea in the large thermos. "Frankie, you want some tea and goodies?" she asked the chauffeur.

"Nah, when Mr. Browne came I took the opportunity to run to the deli in the side street and get lunch. I got a couple of packages of Twinkies and some seltzer with me now. I'll be fine. Thanks, Miss Shann."

Emily poured tea in the cups provided and handed them around to Aaron and Kirk. Frankie began the trip from the city out to Egret Pointe. The two men demolished the little sandwiches and tartlets. Emily fell asleep again, awakening only when Aaron shook her shoulder gently.

"Em, you're home," he said. "I'm going to take you in." He helped her from the car and walked her into the house. The Christmas lights had gone on automatically at five that afternoon. "I'm going to have Sam stop by tomorrow. You've got bronchitis, if I'm not mistaken. I can hear it."

"Okay," Emily said weakly. "Thanks, Aaron."

When he had left Emily put on her electric kettle and climbed upstairs to get out of her author clothes. She hung everything neatly, pulled on a violet-sprigged flannel nightgown, and wrapped herself in her fleece robe. Padding downstairs to the kitchen, she made herself a cup of chicken bouillon, and sat down to drink it. A knock sounded at her back door. Emily got up and answered it.

"Aaron says you're sick." Dr. Sam came in, reaching for Emily's wrist. "Sit."

She obeyed. "It's the first night of Hanukkah," she said to him.

"So? I've got a sick patient. I'm a doctor. The grandchildren have already lit the first candle in the menorah and ripped open their presents. Rina is in her glory feeding everyone. Aaron and Kirk are both concerned." He took out his stethoscope and listened to her chest. "Yep, bronchitis, but not too bad yet." Pulling out a digital thermometer he said, "Open," and stuck it in her mouth. When the thermometer beeped Dr. Sam pulled it from her mouth, looked at it, and said, "Emily, you have a temperature of one hundred and two. You are sick. You have to go to bed and stay there." He put the stethoscope back in his bag and pulled out a small bottle. "There are eight antibiotics here. Take two now, and then tomorrow morning start taking one every six hours until they are gone. Are you all right alone? Rina will come check on you tomorrow, okay?"

"Devlin was supposed to come," Emily said. "He got stuck in London. I'll be fine; Rina doesn't have to bother. You've got the family here, for heaven's sake, Dr. Sam."

"You're family too, sweetheart," he told her. "I couldn't keep Rina away, and you know it. Even her brother won't have to nag her to come." Dr. Sam chuckled, getting up. "Now I'm going home, and you go to bed," he ordered her.

"Okay," Emily agreed, seeing him out and then locking the kitchen door behind him. She went to the sink, rinsed her soup cup, refilled it with water, and took two pills. She really was beginning to feel lousy. She was clammy and hot, and the skin across her chest itched. Vicks! She had some in the upstairs hall closet where she kept medical supplies. She climbed the stairs slowly, got the Vicks, rubbed her chest with it, and after taking her robe off climbed into bed.

Emily did not sleep well, however. She awoke several times in the night, coughing a deep, racking cough and spitting up amounts of thick green gunk. She thought her fever might be higher, but she couldn't remember where she had put her thermometer. And finally, when she had awakened for the fourth time, and the clock in the hall struck six a.m., she got up. She didn't feel any better lying in bed. She was sweaty and chilly by turns. Wrapping herself in her robe, she went downstairs and made herself a bowl of oatmeal and a cup of tea. She took another of Dr. Sam's pills, then fell asleep in her comfortable recliner in the den, only to be awakened by the ringing telephone. Devlin! It had to be Devlin. She grabbed for the receiver.

"Emily, it's Rina. How do you feel?"

"Terrible," she admitted.

"I'll come over," Rina said.

"Rina, please don't. I have everything. I'm not up to company. I love you, but I feel like crap right now. I just want to be left alone to die quietly."

Rina chuckled. "Okay," she said. "I'll call you this afternoon to see if there's any improvement. You have to let me do that."

" 'Kay. Bye." Emily hung up. And then she began to cry. She was alone, and she was sick, and it was Christmas Eve. Where was Devlin, and why the hell hadn't he called her? He had said he would be home, but instead he was cavorting in London with some young thing, J.P. had said. Well, she hadn't quite said it.

She had just suggested it, but J.P. had known Devlin longer than Emily Shanski. Emily sobbed and sobbed, until her nose was so stuffed up she could hardly breathe. Then she began to cough the green glop up again. Gradually her sobs died away. She felt empty. Putting her head down she fell asleep again.

It was almost four in the afternoon when she was awakened by the sound of pounding on her front door. Stumbling to her feet, she made her way into the hall and opened the door. Michael Devlin was standing there, a worried look on his face.

"Jaysus! You look like merry hell," he said to her as he came inside.

"Thank you." Emily sniffed as she closed the front door. "What are you doing here? J.P. said you were staying in London. That you couldn't get back. There's no food in the house. I couldn't shop." She began to cry.

Michael Devlin shook his head and took her into his arms. "I couldn't get back in time for the Stratford party, angel face, that's all. I didn't say anything about not being back in time for Christmas."

"She said you had probably met some young thing," Emily sobbed.

Michael Devlin sighed. "A lot J. P. Woods knows about me," he said. "How late are the markets around here open tonight? I'd better make a run for some food."

"The IGA is open until five thirty," Emily told him, beginning to pull herself back together. He was home! Devlin was home, and it was Christmas Eve! "The butcher will have the beef for tomorrow. I ordered it," she told him. "At least get the roast beef. We need other stuff, but I can't think right now."

"I'll take care of it, Emily. You just go back to wherever you were and get some rest. Has Dr. Sam seen you?"

"He brought me pills. Oh, Lord! I'd better take another one. I'll leave the kitchen door open for you. Don't lose my beef. And Devlin, I want an ice cream sundae. Stop at Walt's. Forbidden Chocolate with marshmallow and butterscotch. He's open until seven, even tonight. The early churchgoers usually stop in on the way home."

With a grin he hurried from the house. He gunned his Healy into the village, noting that the parking lot at the IGA was still full. Going inside, he grabbed a cart and headed directly for the butcher's counter. "I'm picking up Miss Shanski's roast beef," he said to the man behind the counter.

"You the boyfriend I've been hearing about?" the butcher asked with a friendly grin. "I got her meat all ready and wrapped. You pay at the checkout."

"Yeah, I'm the boyfriend," Michael Devlin said, grinning back. "Gimme that roasted turkey breast too. It'll do for sandwiches tonight."

The butcher took the turkey breast from beneath the heat lamp and put it into a clear plastic container. "Just came off the rotisserie an hour ago," he said.

"Thanks, and happy Christmas to you," Devlin said, putting both items into his cart. Then he began to make his way around the grocery store, choosing items he thought they would need for a few days. Rye bread for the sandwiches, Country Crock mashed potatoes, frozen Southland turnip, a small jar of onions, frozen French-cut green beans, heavy cream, and milk. He spotted a small bottle of horseradish sauce among some gourmet items, and took it. A carton of orange juice, and another of pineapple juice. Emily had a weakness for pineapple juice. He took a wooden carton of Clementines, and bagged some green grapes. Butter! You could never have enough butter. And very fine sugar, if she was making hard sauce for the Christmas pudding in his luggage. Passing the vegetables he grabbed a bag of mixed field greens. Then, glancing at his watch, he headed for the checkout.

"You just made it," the girl at the register said, eyeing him and smiling.

"I did, didn't I?" he agreed, smiling at her.

Putting his groceries in what passed for a backseat in the Healy, he headed for Walt's and got two sundaes.

"Only one person in town does Forbidden Chocolate with marshmallow and butterscotch," Walt said, "and that's Emily Shanski. You must be the boyfriend I've been hearing about."

"Guilty as charged," Michael Devlin admitted with a smile. "I'll take coffee ice cream with chocolate and marshmallow."

"You got it," Walt replied, making up the two sundaes to go and bagging them.

"What do I owe you?"

"It's on the house," Walt said. "Tell Emily I said 'Merry Christmas.' I've known her since she was born, you know."

"I'll tell her, and happy Christmas to you," Michael Devlin said as he departed the little ice cream shop with the two desserts. Driving back to the house, he remembered how nice it was to grow up in a small town—the warm feeling you got in the shops knowing people's names and families. And it was obvious that, as quietly as Emily Shanski lived, she was well-known and well liked by the people of her hometown of Egret Pointe. He hadn't felt a twinge of embarrassment at all when people had identified him verbally as "the boyfriend." It had tickled him. Emily had been so discreet, and yet it would appear that everyone in Egret Pointe knew all about them, and it didn't bother Michael Devlin one bit.

Getting back to the house, he brought the groceries inside and checked on Emily. She had fallen asleep in the den again. He put everything away, setting the sundaes carefully in the freezer. Then he made them turkey sandwiches on rye bread with mayo. He fixed individual bowls of salad and dressed them with a raspberry vinaigrette he found in the fridge. Lastly he brewed a large pot of tea in the big brown teapot that had belonged to Emily's grandmother, Emily O. Setting everything on a tray, he brought it into the den and put it down on the table.

"Wake up, sleepyhead," he said, shaking her gently and kissing her brow. She was very hot. Dry and hot. Not good, he thought.

Emily opened her eyes. "You really are here," she said. "I didn't dream it, did I? Get the meat? And my sundae?"

"Got everything. Walt says, 'Merry Christmas.' The sundaes were on the house," he told her.

"He always did that when I was a little girl," Emily said. "What did you do, Devlin? I didn't know you could cook."

"I can't, really. And this is nothing fancy. I just made us turkey sandwiches and salad, angel face. The turkey breast was already cooked." He handed her a plate.

She still wasn't really that hungry, but she nibbled at half of the sandwich and a few mouthfuls of salad to please him. When he returned from the kitchen after taking their supper things back, she had fallen asleep again. The telephone rang, and he grabbed it before it could awaken her.

"Devlin?" It was Rina Seligmann. "You got here."

"Traveling at Christmas is not advised, Rina," he told her. "I got on the red-eye. Since I had left the car at the airport I just drove straight out. I've done her shopping and fed her—she didn't eat much, and she's asleep again."

"You're a good man, Mick," Rina said quietly. "Is she taking the pills Sam left her last night?"

"Yeah, but she's still got a temperature, I believe. She's hot and dry," he said.

"Keep her warm," Rina advised. "With luck the fever will break tonight or tomorrow. Still coughing?"

"Yep. And she smells of Vicks." He chuckled. "Reminded me of me grannie."

Rina laughed. "I doubt Emily has ever remotely reminded you of your gran, Vicks or no Vicks. I'm glad she had the sense to use it. It's old-fashioned, but it will help break up that congestion in her chest. Sam will come over tomorrow in the afternoon," Rina said. "If you need him before, just call. Good night, Mick."

"Good night, Rina." He hung up the phone.

"Who was that?" Emily asked sleepily.

"Rina, checking up. Are you awake enough to go up to bed?"

"Uh-huh," she said, struggling to her feet. "Where's my sundae?"

"In the freezer. You can have it later. Now you have to go to bed," Michael Devlin said, helping her upstairs and into her bed. "I'll be back. I want to clean up first."

"You're a great editor, a great lover, and it would seem a great houseman too," Emily half whispered.

He went back downstairs again to clean up, and when he had finished he sat down in the den, with its little Christmas tree on the table in the bay window and the crackling fire in the hearth. He was home. And the woman he loved above all else was asleep upstairs in her bed. He had been delayed in London for two reasons, one of which was to purchase Emily's Christmas present. He knew what he wanted, and it had taken the jeweler some extra time to find it, but he had. Michael was through with indecision.

He sat for some time until finally the fire had burned down to glowing red-orange embers. It was Christmas Eve, and everything around him felt magical. The clock from St. Luke's struck ten. Santa would be on his way, Michael Devlin thought with a small smile. *Give me just a little time, Santa,* he said silently. Then, standing up, he went upstairs, washed, got into his pajamas, and climbed into bed with Emily. She murmured softly and burrowed into him. Wrapping his arms about her, he knew that he had been given the greatest Christmas gift he had ever received.

Emily awoke to a bright, sunny day. She could hear Devlin in the shower and rolled over, smiling. She ran the tips of her fingers over the indentation his head had made in the pillow. She was sweaty, but she knew her fever was finally breaking.

"Happy Christmas, angel face," he said, coming into the bedroom, a towel about his loins.

"Damn, you look all fresh and clean, and I am so scuzzy. I think my fever's breaking, Devlin. I'm suddenly hungry, and I want a cuppa."

"Let me get my clothes on, and I'll go down and bring you one," he said.

"And my sundae too," she said.

He laughed as he dressed, pulling on his jeans, and a soft crewneck sweater. "Ice cream for breakfast, angel face?"

"Why not?" she asked. "It's Christmas. I'll come downstairs, but first I need a shower too."

"Is that wise if the fever hasn't broken yet?" he asked.

"Go make tea, Devlin. You're starting to sound like Rina," Emily chided him.

He left her, and Emily jumped out of bed and hurried to shower, tucking her hair in a cap to keep it dry. Drying herself thoroughly, Emily pulled on a pair of peach-colored fleece sweatpants, a matching tee, and over it a peach fleece sweatshirt. She ran a brush through her hair. It didn't look too bad, considering. Sliding her feet into her sheepskin slippers, she padded down the stairs. She felt suddenly normal. The fever had obviously broken while she was in the shower.

"In the den, angel face," he called to her, and Emily joined him.

"Two sundaes?" she said, surprised.

"One for you and one for me," he told her. "Tea?"

"No, ice cream first. My fever is gone, Devlin."

He popped the lid from a sundae container and handed the dessert to her with a spoon.

Emily accepted it, digging her spoon into the ice cream, and then suddenly she stopped and stared. Sticking out of the whipped cream atop the sundae was a diamond ring. Carefully she set the sundae down on the table and pulled the ring away from the cream. The diamond was a square-cut, with two rectangular baguettes on either side. The stones were set in platinum. Emily licked the cream from the band, rubbed it against her shirt, and put it on her finger. Holding out her hand she admired it, and then she said, "Well, this sure beats a cherry, Devlin. Yes."

"I haven't asked you yet," he said.

"Just take the yes," she told him.

"No," he said. "I am going to ask you, Emily Katherine Shanski, if you will do me the honor—the great honor—of becoming my wife. Now you may answer."

"Yes," she said, and, throwing herself into his arms, she added, "I don't think I'm contagious anymore." And then they kissed. When he was finally able to release her from his embrace several minutes later, Emily said, "I have to call Rina. She will never forgive us if I don't." Picking up the phone, she punched in the Seligmanns' number.

"Hello?" Rina answered.

"Rina, it's me. The fever has broken. Who's there with you?"

"Sam, my brother, and Kirk. The boys came for breakfast," Rina answered.

"Put me on speakerphone," Emily said excitedly.

"Okay, you're on," Rina said, suspecting what was coming, and unable to contain her smile. "What's up?"

"Devlin and I are getting married," Emily said happily.

Rina looked to her husband, her brother, and Kirkland Browne, nodding. "Emily, that is wonderful! We'll come over later, all right?"

"Okay," Emily said, and hung up.

"What did I tell you three doubting Thomases?" Rina Seligmann said triumphantly, looking at the three men sitting around her breakfast table. "Did I call it or not?"

Kirkland Browne and Dr. Sam nodded silently in acceptance of her wisdom, but Aaron Fischer, smiling, looked up and said only two words: "Thank heaven!"

"Thank heaven?" his sister asked. "For what?"

"For the miracle I asked for, Rina. My Hanukkah miracle," Aaron replied.

"For my Christmas miracle," Kirkland Browne added.

And then the four broke out in happy laughter, clinking their coffee mugs together as they toasted the wedding to come.

EPILOGUE

꒰ꕥ

They were married the last Saturday in April in a small wedding attended by family and friends. The bride wore the antique ivory satin-and-lace wedding gown that had been worn by her great-great-great grandmother in 1860. The tiered gown and its hoop, along with its exquisite handmade lace veil, had been loaned to Emily by the Egret Pointe Historical Society, which now possessed it. The starchy longtime president of the society, Mrs. Hallock Dunham, a very distant relation of Emily's, deemed it only appropriate, and Emily was delighted to accept. The groom wore an Irish kilt, a ruffled white shirt, and a black velvet jacket.

Each had only one attendant. Martin Stratford, tanned and just returned from his round-the-world cruise, was best man. Savannah Banning had flown in from England to serve as her best friend's matron of honor. Emily's mother and her stepfather Senator Phelps, were in attendance, along with her Phelps half siblings, Phoebe and Carter V. Emily's father, Dr. Joe Shanski, his wife, and their three sons were there, but Emily had not asked Joe to escort her down the aisle.

"You helped create me, Joe," Emily had told him when she'd

called to say she was getting married, "but you've never really been my father. You never had the time, and I understand. I want my agent, Aaron Fischer, to take me down the aisle. No hard feelings, huh?"

Joe Shanski realized in that moment just what he had lost, but he swallowed hard and said, "Nah, kiddo, no hard feelings. Mary Shannon, the boys, and I will be there with bells on. I'm glad you've found happiness. I still want to meet this guy before you do it."

"I'll have him call you, Joe, and you two can do lunch one day," Emily said.

Her mother had been a different cup of tea, but then, Katy always had been her own woman. "I'll have to check my schedule," she said. "The spring hunt is just around then, Emily. Can I call you back?"

"No," Emily said, "you cannot call me back. I'm getting married at St. Anne's in Egret Pointe at one thirty in the afternoon on the last Saturday in April. I expect you, your husband, and my half sister and brother to be there, Katy. This is not a negotiation, and for once you will do the right thing by me. Carter's up for reelection this year, isn't he?"

There was a long silence, and then Katy O'Malley Phelps laughed. "When did you get so tough?" she asked Emily.

"You don't know me at all, do you?" Emily said quietly. "Well, no matter. Just consider what a marvelous photo op it will make for Carter's reelection campaign, Katy." And Emily chuckled, imagining her mother's face at that moment.

"You really are a little bitch," Katy remarked.

"But you'll come *en famille*, won't you?" Emily responded.

"We'll be there," her mother replied.

"Do you want me to make a reservation anywhere for you?" Emily asked politely.

"God, no! We'll fly in and out in the same day," Katy exclaimed. "I suppose Joe and his wife and children will be there too. He has to escort you down the aisle."

"They'll be there," Emily said, not bothering to explain, and thus avoiding a lecture from Katy on manners and tradition. Joe understood her position, and that was all that was necessary, as far as Emily was concerned.

Their wedding day had dawned sunny, with a hint of real warmth in the air. The church was banked in lilacs brought in from the South. Aaron could not have been prouder if Emily were his own offspring. While old Father Mulligan looked a bit askance that the Jewish gentleman, as he referred to Aaron, was escorting the bride, he knew the full history of Emily Katherine Shanski, and understood her position. There were some things the bishop didn't have to know.

And afterward they adjourned back to Emily's house for canapés, wedding cake, and champagne. Most of Egret Pointe had crowded into St. Anne's, or stood outside of it, but only invited guests came back to the house. J. P. Woods had poked Emily playfully, and said she now understood how Emily had managed to write such a deliciously sensual book. Ever since the new year J.P. had been a changed woman, and no one understood why, except perhaps Emily, who grinned at J.P.'s remark and winked.

Joe Shanski and Michael Devlin had easily become friends over the several months before the wedding. Both discovered they had a taste for a certain malted Irish whiskey. And Katy was bowled over by Devlin's charm which her daughter found amusing. Few people got past Katy's armor. Her half sister, Phoebe, sighed and said she hoped she married someone that hot one day, and then lamented to Emily that the only men she met were a lot like her father and brother—booooring!

Rina was in her glory, directing the girls hired by Essie to serve the guests. And then it was time for them to cut their wedding cake. The champagne flowed freely, and Emily caught her three young Shanski half brothers each with a glass. She shook a finger at them, but they just grinned. While the guests were devouring the cake, she and Devlin slipped upstairs to change. Savannah was waiting with two ladies from the Historical Society to help Emily out of the precious antique gown, while Devlin changed in another room.

"Please tell Mrs. Hallock Dunham how very honored I was that she allowed me to wear Great-great-great-grandmother Mary Anne's wedding dress," Emily told the two ladies. "I hope one day my daughter will wear it."

"You looked absolutely beautiful in it, dear," one of the ladies said. "I hope you will allow us to put a picture of you in it with the exhibit."

"Of course," Emily agreed. "It's the least I can do."

The gown was carried off, and Emily quickly got into a little lavender silk suit.

"Has Mick told you yet where you're going?" Savannah wanted to know.

"Nope. He says he won't tell me until we get on the plane," Emily replied. "It's all very mysterious, and frankly I can't wait. He wouldn't even let me pack. Said he would do it. I was only to do my cosmetic case."

"I can't wait to hear all about it when you get back," Savannah said. "Send us postcards, Emily." Then she hurried off.

"Are you ready, Mrs. Devlin?" he asked her, coming into their bedroom.

"I'm ready, Mr. Devlin," she answered him with a smile.

Together they descended the staircase to the waiting guests, who had been alerted by Savannah. Emily stopped a quarter of the way from the bottom and threw her small bouquet of white rosebuds, freesia, and white lilacs to the assembled squealing women. Her husband's assistant, Sally, caught it, and then blushed. Calling their good-byes, Emily and Devlin ran from the house and into the waiting town car, the good wishes of their guests ringing in their ears. To Emily's surprise they did not go to Kennedy. Instead they went to the local airport, where they boarded a small corporate jet.

"A perk of working for Stratford," Michael Devlin told his wife.

"But where are we going?" Emily asked him.

"Lovers Cay," he told her.

"Where is that?" She accepted the champagne the steward brought her.

"It's a small private island in the Bahamas. I've let it for ten days with its staff. Just you and me. A beach. A warm sea. Discreet servants—and a very large bed," he said.

"Sounds heavenly." Emily was intrigued.

They landed several hours later on a small airstrip, and were driven immediately to the great house where they would be staying. The first thing Emily noticed was that the servants were virtually naked but for small loincloths. She looked to Devlin as a maid brought in her cosmetic case and set it on the dressing table before hurrying out.

"Where are the suitcases?" she said.

"Aren't any. We're not going to be wearing clothing for the next ten days, angel face," he told her, a wicked smile lighting his face. "Just you and me."

"Oh, Devlin!" Emily began to laugh.

"Let's hang our clothes up now so they'll be ready for our return home," he suggested, and he went to the closet and opened it.

Emily looked about her as she began to unbutton her jacket. It was perfect. Just perfect. The floor was plush with its thick carpet. An entire wall of glass with sheer curtains blowing in the trade winds opened onto the palm-lined beach, and the blue sea beyond. The silk-sheeted bed was the biggest one she had ever seen. Then her eye lit on the beautiful basket by the bed. It was filled to the brim with sex toys and lotions. And on the other side of the bed there was a footed silver champagne bucket with a bottle of outrageously expensive champagne sitting amid a hill of ice. Emily looked across the room at her husband, who was now totally naked, and utterly gorgeous. She shrugged off her jacket and, unzipping her skirt, stepped out of it as it dropped to the floor. Then she walked across the carpet to him and slipped her arms about his neck. Her nipples were just touching his smooth chest.

"I love you," she said, "and this is so perfect, I don't think I'll ever want to go home."

"Wherever we are together, angel face, it will always be perfect. Always paradise," Michael Devlin said. And then he kissed her, and Emily knew that what had begun as something forbidden had become something wonderful. She had gotten her happily-ever-after, and wasn't that the way every love story was supposed to end?

About the Author

Bertrice Small is a *New York Times* bestselling author and the recipient of numerous awards. In keeping with her profession, Bertrice Small lives in the oldest English-speaking town in the state of New York, founded in 1640. Her light-filled studio includes the paintings of her favorite cover artist, Elaine Duillo, and a large library. Because she believes in happy endings, Bertrice Small has been married to the same man, her hero, George, for forty-three years. They have a son, Thomas; a daughter-in-law, Megan; and four wonderful grandchildren. Longtime readers will be happy to know that Nicki the Cockatiel flourishes along with his fellow housemates: Pookie, the long-haired greige-and-white cat; Finnegan, the long-haired bad black kitty; and Sylvester, the black-and-white tuxedo cat who has recently joined the family.